Magic Moment

Angela Adams

CRIMSON ROMANCE

Avon, Massachusetts

This edition published by
Crimson Romance
an imprint of F+W Media, Inc.
10151 Carver Road, Suite 200
Blue Ash, Ohio 45242

www.crimsonromance.com

ISBN 10: 1-4405-5494-3
ISBN 13: 978-1-4405-5494-0
eISBN 10: 1-4405-5495-1
eISBN 13: 978-1-4405-5495-7

Chapter One

"Laura. Laura Roberts." The deep, detached voice came from behind her.

Laura swiveled on the round, brown vinyl-covered stool, meeting the hard eyes and two dour faces. Her last name was Roberts, but she didn't reply, didn't even nod. Neither man looked familiar. Who were they?

"Special Agent Ross Saunders, FBI," the grimmer of the two said, waving a badge and I.D. before her eyes.

She stared at the men. FBI?

Sanders tucked the folder inside his jacket pocket. "This is Special Agent Ed Phillips," he said with a quick nod to the man standing to his left. "We'd like to ask you some questions. Come with us please."

Laura had seen the two men enter the diner. Identical navy suits, both appeared to be in their forties, graying crew cuts, and equally sour expressions. Although not the customary Rita's Diner patrons, or Food Mall clientele for that matter, Laura had turned her attention back to her iced tea without giving them a second thought. Now they stood in front of her, flashing badges and identification cards too quickly to read, let alone give her time to note if the picture matched the face.

"FBI? There must be some mistake." She offered with a polite smile. "I'm Laura Roberts, but I doubt you're looking for me."

Saunders' brow crinkled. "Laura Ann Roberts?"

Ann had been her mother's name. Laura's cordial manner disappeared and anxiety crawled through her. "Yes."

Saunders pushed the glass out of her reach.

"What—"

He grasped her fingers. "You're the one. Come with us."

Laura yanked from his grip. The other agent cupped her elbow, sliding her off the stool.

"Miss Roberts, don't make a scene," Saunders whispered. "Come with us. It will only take a few minutes."

Laura glanced around the nearly filled-to-capacity diner. The customers, although employed by different proprietors, worked in the Food Mall. Those who hadn't been gawking, suddenly stopped their conversations and meals to take notice. This was a popular lunch hour, and she was now the afternoon's gossip.

"Laura, everything okay?"

She recognized the male voice and managed to stifle her plaintive groan. Could this calamity get any worse?

Chase Donovan had joined the fracas. Dressed in jeans and a black leather jacket, he was tall and athletic, in his mid-thirties, with a wavy mixture of light, nearly blond, and medium brown hair.

He was also her boss's son.

A bewildered expression covered Chase's handsome, chiseled features. He stood so close that as Laura jerked from Phillips's hold, her elbow nearly whacked Chase in the stomach.

Saunders identified himself to Chase. "We need Miss Roberts at headquarters to answer a few questions."

"I'd like to see some I.D," Chase said firmly.

Saunders arched a dark, hairy eyebrow. "And you are?"

"Chase Donovan." He rested a hand lightly on her shoulder. Laura stiffened at his touch, unaccustomed to Chase putting a hand on her, even if in a protective manner.

"Laura works for my father," Chase said. "If I don't see some identification, she's not going anywhere with you." To prove his point, his hand moved downward and his fingers wrapped gently around her forearm.

Chase also worked for his father, although what his role was within the business was generally debatable among the clientele.

This was so embarrassing. In the three years Laura had worked as Dick Donovan's bookkeeper, her conversations with his son had been work-related or cordial exchanges about the weather. If there was any chance of the floor opening up and swallowing her, she considered now the perfect time.

She turned to Chase. "Thank you for your concern. I've seen their identification." She didn't mention the hasty badge flip. "They have me confused with someone else. I'll take care of the error, and get back to the office as soon as I can."

"Let me go with you." Chase tossed the men a wary glance. He still held her arm. "You should have an attorney."

Laura winced, truly mortified. There was no need for an attorney or involving Chase Donovan in calling one. She had done nothing illegal. "I'm fine."

Saunders grew impatient. "Miss Roberts."

She eased from Chase's hold. "Yes, I'm coming."

She grabbed her purse from the counter and noticed the plate with her turkey on rye sandwich had arrived.

"I need to pay for my lunch." She looked down the counter for the waitress. "Dinah, I need my check."

"Miss Roberts, *today*," Saunders snapped.

Laura whirled, glaring. "You can't expect me to leave without paying for my lunch."

"Laura, go ahead," Chase said. "I'll take care of the bill, and the office. Don't worry about anything."

Already a bit unnerved by the two intimidating agents, she turned and stared into Chase's mesmerizing blue eyes, adding to her lopsided equilibrium.

"Thank you," she said softly.

Following the agents through the diner, she stopped and pulled her coat from the wall hook. Sandwiched between the two men, she walked to a brown sedan parked outside the Food Mall's chain-link gated area. A white cardboard "FBI OFFICIAL BUSINESS" sign rested on the front dash. Saunders opened the vehicle's back door and waved Laura in before sliding next to her on the ivory-colored cushioned seat. Phillips adjusted himself behind the steering wheel.

"That couldn't have gone better," Phillips said and shoved the key into the ignition.

"Yeah. That guy was the kid." Saunders frowned at Laura. "We'll take you to headquarters for a few questions, and then you can go. This is no big deal for you."

Laura smirked at the man. *No big deal?* Maybe not to him, but try to convince her wounded pride and tainted reputation.

*

The Food Brokers Association Market Mall was one long Philadelphia city block. Known as simply the "Food Mall" to the locals, the conglomerate was a smorgasbord of warehouses. Proprietors supplied produce, fish, meats, poultry, dairy, cheeses, and fresh fruit to restaurants, supermarkets, street hucksters, or even the average consumer who purchased bulk merchandise wholesale.

Chase strode along the cement walkway. He took the steps to Warehouse 106, The Produce Market, and maneuvered his way through stacks of apple boxes and lettuce crates. Several of the men stopped counting boxes when they saw him and shouted greetings. But instead of stopping for his usual postmortem on last night's basketball game, Chase simply waved and continued toward the office area.

He pushed through the double glass doors and stepped into the suite's reception area. Two black six-foot metal double-door cabinets. A photocopier. A square table with a fax machine. Three desks with computers. A small refrigerator, and a stand with a microwave, toaster oven and coffee maker. Chase's glance strayed to an unoccupied desk, Laura's desk. An opened manila folder held a stack of papers. Green numbers glared from the computer monitor.

Rachel, his father's twenty-something secretary with bleached blonde spiked hair, sat at her desk, telephone receiver pressed against an ear. Chase recognized a conversation with her sister, embellishing last night's date.

He didn't wait for a response to his hurried rap on the varnished wood door, and pushed into his father's private office. Even with the accepted dress code of jeans or business casual, Dick Donovan had dressed as a professional from the day he stopped being warehouse foreman. Today, wearing a richly designed charcoal suit, he resembled more of a trial attorney than a produce salesman.

In his sixties, and tall like his son, Dick's eyes were overcast gray rather than his son's vivid blue. The only signs that Dick soon qualified for withdrawals from the company pension plan were the intensely receding hairline, the silver gray hair that remained, and telltale lines of good living forming around his eyes and lips.

"I went to the diner for a sandwich, and the strangest thing happened." Despite his father's lack of acknowledgment, Chase continued. "The FBI came in and took your bookkeeper away."

This time Dick's head popped up from his green and white lined computer sheet. "My bookkeeper? Laura?"

"You got another?" Chase replied with a touch of sarcasm.

Dick arched an eyebrow. "What does the FBI want with Laura?"

"They want to ask her a few questions." Chase paused. "She said it's mistaken identity."

"Laura and the FBI," Dick mused aloud, more bewildered than concerned. "It's hard to believe she's involved in anything illegal. I can't imagine Laura even jaywalking."

Chase suppressed a cringe. The sound of his father's voice had always grated on his nerves, like the sound of fingernails scratching on a blackboard. Dick Donovan forced his vocal timbre to sound like that of an English aristocrat rather than a member of the South Philly working-class neighborhood he was born into.

Dick paused. "But we don't know what Laura does, or who she

sees, in her private life." He shrugged. "Who knows what goes on outside this office? Or in her home?"

"I offered my services as an attorney, but she refused."

"You?" Dick laughed. "With the FBI sniffing around her, the woman already has problems."

Chase flinched. "Okay, I can't find my way around a courtroom," he admitted soberly. The politics of being a practicing attorney had disillusioned him years ago. "I still keep up my license. Those guys just walked in and grabbed her like she was a modern-day Bonnie Parker." He stopped, recalling how Laura's forlorn expression had torn at his heart. "I wish she had accepted my offer. She wouldn't be alone. She'd have someone advising her."

Dick exhaled a deep breath. "Chase, don't get involved. Sometimes you have your mother's overly kind heart."

"As opposed to your screw 'em attitude." Chase never appreciated his father's remarks toward the late Michelle Donovan. As if his mother's kindness toward others had been a bad attribute.

Dick ignored his son's comment. "Laura is an employee. Granted, a good one, but still an employee. If the FBI made a mistake, and I'm sure they have, she'll return to work. And this will all be forgotten. I repeat—let's stay out of it."

Chase silently conceded his father's point. He, too, found it difficult to believe Laura was involved in any illegalities, but he really didn't know much of her personal business and liked it that way. Chase tended to keep his distance from the female staff. On the other hand, being forced to admit his father was right galled him.

"I doubt if she'll be back today," Chase said. "Have Rachel shut down her computer."

"I'll tell Rachel there was a family emergency, and Laura had to go home." Dick paused. "Although Laura doesn't have any family. I remember her once saying her father was killed in a car accident when she was a little girl. Her mother died a few months ago. Stroke, I think."

Laura's mother had passed away on Thanksgiving Eve. Chase remembered Rachel asking him to sign a check to a charity in the woman's name. Years earlier, Chase's own mother had passed away a few days before his birthday and as he had signed the check in memory of Ann Roberts, he recalled feeling badly that Laura's mother had died near a holiday. He knew well that in the following years, an occasion that should be happy would have a dismal overcast.

"I don't care what you tell Rachel as long as it's not the truth." Chase frowned. "Gossip is Rachel's national obsession."

Dick relaxed back in his brown leather chair and picked up his computer printouts. For Chase, it was a familiar signal that their conversation was finished and he was dismissed.

"I'm heading down to Atlantic City." Chase walked toward the door. "If you hear anything on Laura, call my cell phone."

*

The Food Mall residents considered 8:00 a.m. mid-day. Workers, dressed in overalls and wearing thick padded gloves, loaded crates of apples, spinach, blocks of cheeses, and other edibles from the various warehouses onto the customers' vans and massive freight trucks. The atmosphere was loud, full of activity and rambunctious.

Beneath her beige wool coat, Laura was dressed in a simple black long-sleeved knit dress with red trimming around the crew neck collar and cuffs. As she took the stairs with tentative steps, she did her best to quash the butterflies in her stomach. The previous day's mortifying meeting with Special Agent Ross Saunders, still etched in her mind, had kept her tossing, turning, and staring at the ceiling all night.

Inside the office, she didn't take off her coat and go straight to the coffeemaker as she generally did. When she switched on her computer, she didn't immediately click into her email. She called up a blank screen, sat down, and typed.

Through the closed door, she heard Dick Donovan's hushed

voice. He was on the telephone. Dick Donovan, if he didn't have someone in his office, was *always* on the telephone. Laura printed and signed the letter, and waited until she was certain he had finished his call. She took a deep breath, straightened her posture, and knocked on the wooden door. This had to be done quickly.

"Come in," he called.

Her boss pored over the spreadsheets that indicated how his business was profiting. Seeing Laura, Dick looked up and broke into what she thought might be a relieved smile. As always, he wore an impeccable Italian designer suit, this one a deep blue.

"Laura." He stood, and walked around to the front of the desk covered with financial spreadsheets. "Sit down. I'm glad to see you." He pulled out the straight-backed chair. "Chase told me what happened yesterday."

"There's no need for me to sit down," she said with as much grace as she could muster. "Before I forget, Chase was very considerate yesterday. Please thank him for me."

"We were both worried." Dick sat on the desk's corner edge. "What's going on? Is it something you can discuss? Something I can help with?"

Laura gave a brief smile and shook her head. "It was all a mistake." She sort of lied. It was a mistake if anyone assumed her involvement in criminal activities. "Something has come up, and I need to resign." She handed him the folded paper.

Dick's gray eyes widened. "Resign?" His words rushed out. "Laura? Why? Are the hours too long? Salary and benefits not competitive?"

Laura shoved each hand in a coat pocket. "No, that's not it," she said, shaking her head. Instinct told her to say something positive. "I've enjoyed working here. It's a pleasant atmosphere, the salary and benefits are more than fair." Rattled nerves threatened her poise. "It's in the letter."

"If this has anything to do with yesterday," Dick said. "I understand a lot of Food Mall people were in the diner. I'm sure you feel awkward. Let's talk—"

"Read the letter," she said with more snap than she had intended.

He unfolded the paper and read aloud. "Dear Mr. Donovan. Due to an unforeseen personal situation, I must resign from my position as bookkeeper, effective immediately. Thank you for the opportunity to work for The Produce Market. Sincerely, Laura Roberts." He refolded the paper, breathed deeply, and looked up. "I don't understand, and definitely don't know what to say."

Her heart beat rapidly. She just wanted to leave and blurted out whatever words popped into her head. "I have this—issue." Her thoughts came in a rush. "I'll need so much time off, and it's not fair to your business."

"We can talk about a leave of absence."

A cold sweat formed on her brow. "A leave won't do. Resigning is best."

Dick's forehead furrowed. "If leaving is what you want, I can't change your mind. You've always kept your private life out of the office, which I appreciated. All I can do is respect your decision and wish you luck." He sighed. "But I'm not happy. Your work is perfect. You don't spend time on the phone with personal business. I hate losing you."

"That's kind of you to say."

"Along with your accrued vacation, I'll add two weeks' severance."

Laura was taken aback. "That's not necessary. I don't deserve it. I'm not giving the proper notice."

"I insist." He slid off the desk. "Consider it my appreciation for the excellent job you've done. It goes without saying you're welcome to a recommendation."

She smiled. "That's more than generous. Thank you." Laura didn't want the money, didn't need the money, and didn't care about a recommendation, but if she refused, a new discussion would develop, delaying her departure.

"I do have one favor to ask," Dick said.

It figured strings were attached to the severance. "Yes?"

"That you not pack your desk right now." He nodded his head toward the door. "Rachel will be in at any minute. If she sees you packing, she'll start with her questions. I have a report she needs to start on immediately."

For Rachel, badgering Laura for details took priority over work. She saw the point to Mr. Donovan's request. As much as she hated returning to this office, avoiding the secretary was appealing.

"Sounds fair." Rachel left at five p.m. like the proverbial bat out of hell. "I'll come back at 5:30." There would be no one around asking questions.

*

In a large, luxurious Atlantic City hotel room, Chase awoke in a king-size bed wearing only his white boxers and nagged by the worst hangover of his life. With a slight groan and a considerable wince, he pictured two munchkins from Oz standing on his brain, smacking his skull with a hammer. Normally he held his liquor with no problem, but when he did overdo, his hangovers sucked big-time.

Rolling on his back, he pressed his throbbing head into the pillow. The two munchkins banged out a classic Rolling Stones tune. Agonizing temples could be only the beginning.

Chase nestled his head into the pillow. He enjoyed his own space in bed. Even when sharing one, he had a tendency to settle himself as far away as possible from his bedmate. Once the sex act was over, he wanted his breathing room.

He closed his eyes, put each index finger to a temple, and massaged until the immense pain turned into more of a dull ache. Tossing his bare legs over the side of the bed, he decided a shower would take care of any remaining kinks.

Standing under the running water, the warmth soothed his tired muscles and settled the thumping in his temples. His body relaxed and he started to feel like a coherent person again. He stepped out of the shower, dried himself off, and pulled the complimentary white robe from the back of the door.

Perched on the edge of the bed, Chase called downstairs for room service. He needed coffee, hot and black. He glanced at his watch laying on the nightstand. Ten-thirty. By now, he had generally been at his warehouse desk for three hours, reading his third news-related website and drinking his fourth cup of Laura's special-blended brew. *Heavenly Hazelnut*, she called it. He sniffed, almost smelling the sweet aroma, and smiled.

There was seldom anything pressing for him at the warehouse, which was why he spent most of his day tuned into world events or sports updates via the Internet. Nevertheless, while he waited for room service, he made the dutiful phone call.

"There's nothing on your calendar." Rachel paused. "Oh, I do have a note from your father. He wants you to meet his new lady friend. He's planned a dinner tonight." She rattled off the specifics.

Chase listened with a frown. His father had a different lady friend every evening. Most were not ladies, and none were friends. Whatever made this particular one so special that Chase had to meet her, he had no idea, and he didn't want to go.

As the knock on the door announced the arrival of breakfast, he thanked Rachel and disconnected. After signing the receipt including a generous tip, Chase left a message on his father's voicemail. He was stuck in Atlantic City with a stomach bug, he lied. And he was sorry he had to miss the dinner. Another lie.

He poured from the coffee pot. The aroma of dark, roasted coffee caressed his senses, and he salivated at the prospect of his first sip. Gulping half of the strong brew, he regretted not asking for Laura when talking to Rachel. If the busybody secretary had thought the request suspicious, Chase could have claimed he needed a vendor check processed.

He had always liked Laura. She was a pleasant, quiet woman.

Pretty, too. He often admired her shoulder-length blonde hair. It wasn't a cool or brassy blonde, but a warm golden color with a copper twinge. She wore dresses often, and Chase enjoyed looking at her long, slender legs. He munched on a bacon strip. She had looked so damn scared yesterday, her expression wringing his heart. He hoped she was all right.

Chase downed the rest of the coffee. He'd come to Atlantic City for a night of casino gambling, drinking, reminiscing, and debating sports and politics with two of his college fraternity brothers. One, Tom Paulson, lived in Atlantic City and worked for the county. The other, Ned Stahl, was an attorney and lived in a central New Jersey yuppie development complex. Both were married. Both had kids. Both always welcomed the opportunity for a night out with Chase to see how the single half lived.

While Chase overstated most of his colorful bachelor stories for their amusement, there was one convenience being single afforded him. Like Cinderella, his two buddies had to be home by midnight, or there would be hell to pay with their wives. Chase, on the other hand, reserved a hotel suite. Midnight was much too early for a healthy, wealthy unattached male to call it a night. Prowling around in search of other mischief-making activities, Chase had ended up in the casino at the blackjack table, requesting that the cards and drinks keep coming.

But the remaining hours hadn't brought Chase the enthusiasm he'd anticipated. He felt drained, and not from the hard night of being a carefree bachelor, but from his life. On the books, he had the freedom to make his own choices and be with anyone he wanted. Women were lining up, even knocking each other over for a roll with him. He stayed out until all hours. Being on his father's payroll, no one cared if Chase showed up for work on time, or if he even showed up at all. He had the life, his buddies had insisted. Chase chuckled at their envy.

So why was he miserable?

Drinking, gambling, plenty of money, and picking from a buffet of delicious women, Chase mused over his life's options. Oddly, none held the same magnetic appeal he had grown accustomed to. Last night, while sitting at the blackjack table, he had ignored the flirtations of a buxom, bouncy redhead in a too-tight scarlet dress. He had only stopped drinking when the dealer's cards no longer made sense.

Chase was in the mother of all funks and was stymied on how to shake it off.

He eased back on the bed.

Magic Lake Island.

The ocean, tranquility, solitude . . . the most peaceful place on earth . . .

Magic Lake Island, where nothing out of the ordinary ever happened . . .

. . . and exactly what Chase needed.

Chapter Two

"How much of that shit you give her?" the male voice drawled.

Terror gripped Laura's very soul. Her head ached, and her throat was dry. Breathing weighed down her lungs. She had to stay still. She couldn't let on that she was awake.

Visions blurred in her head.

Earlier events all rushed back. Returning to the warehouse precisely at 5:30. No one there but Dick Donovan. Leisure Limo, the car service the Donovans used, both professionally and personally, arrived. Dick's insistence that he wasn't ready to leave, more paperwork to be done, and his offer of the car and driver to take her home. The avenue's dark, deserted stretch. The misplaced cell phone. A rank smell, then darkness.

"Damn, man," the man said. "You gave her too much."

She recognized the male voice, a soft, southern drawl. It belonged to Ron Caldwell, the Leisure Limo driver. The Donovans always requested the same driver.

Laura lay motionless, unmoving, barely breathing. Her heart thumped so loudly she was certain the entire universe heard the rapid beat. She willed it to be silent, but her nervous nucleus refused. Her eyes were closed, her body numb, the foul odor still clogged her nose.

"I hardly gave her any," another man said. "Should'a been out two, three hours at the most. I can't believe she ain't comin' around."

This voice, its tone hard, belonged to the second man. The one who had jumped into the car when Ron had pulled over to the side, insisting he needed to search the trunk for his cell phone.

"We're lucky these boats are only used in the summer." Ron's voice was jittery. "The order said quick. Let's forget doin' her, and get rid of her."

The other man grunted. "I ain't leavin' until I get my shot between her legs."

"What if she doesn't wake up 'til morning?" Ron asked. "We can't toss her in the daytime. People work in the office. They'll see."

"She can't be out much longer," the second man said.

"Let's do her now, and get it over with."

"I don't like bangin' a comatose broad. No fun. I like some fight." The second man laughed, a sinister, echoing sound. "You know, all that twistin' and wrigglin' as they try and throw you off. Then they realize they ain't gonna win, and give up, whimperin' while you do 'em."

Laura maintained her sedate position, eyes closed, her body not moving a muscle, not even a twitch. She grew faint, fear mixed with the lingering effects of the drug they had used. She prayed to remain aware. They were bastards, sick, perverted bastards.

Her stomach churned, her head pounded, but she managed her struggle with consciousness. She was on her side, feeling the softness beneath her. They had her on a bed. Her arms were in front, tied at the wrist with what felt like string or yarn. Her feet were bound together at the ankles. She wasn't wearing her pumps. Since they had rendered her unconscious, she wasn't gagged. Their oversight could be her advantage.

Her right side, the side they had dropped her on, was sore as if she'd been poked with pins and needles. She wanted badly to roll over on her back, but that comfort wasn't feasible. Her parched throat burned. How long could she pretend to be sedated?

A hand grasped her shoulder and shook her roughly. She concentrated on keeping her eyes closed, her breathing even.

"She's still out," Ron said.

Dear God, she was so scared. Laura didn't know what she expected to accomplish by imaginary lifelessness, except to buy time before the inevitable. They had kidnapped her, planned to rape her, and had no intention of letting her live to tell the tale.

Thoughts of her mother, how much she loved her and missed her passed through her mind. In death, she would be with her mother.

But she wasn't ready. Laura wasn't ready to die, and not like this, not after being brutalized.

Where was the FBI now? When she needed them? When there was a real crime in progress?

"I'm getting damn tired of waitin'," the nameless brute snapped. "She can't be out all this time. She's fakin'."

Laura's heart pounded so fiercely she heard the hammering in her ears. Cold, sharp metal pressed against her cheek. Her stomach tangled with fright, and it took every ounce of willpower she possessed to remain passive. This creature didn't enjoy violating an unconscious woman, and his enjoyment was his priority. As long as she convinced him she was still unconscious, perhaps she could seize an opportunity.

The brute laughed, a crude taunt shading his voice. "Maybe if I cut her a little, that'll bring the bitch around."

The mattress dipped and he cupped her chin with one hand. She remained frozen. His other hand stroked her neck. Fear latched onto Laura like a shark's jaw.

A sudden twitch, and the thorny, prickly point slashed along her jaw line. Her heart's panicked beating increased. A light, sticky stream trickled down her neck. Blood, her blood.

With a curdling scream, Laura's eyes flew open and her bound fists came up, smacking her attacker square in the mouth. The unexpected and swift move threw him off her, and he fell to the floor with a hard thud.

She scanned her surroundings. She was in a cramped, tiny, knotty-pine paneled room. The mattress was on some kind of contraption—a bed—secured to the wall. Fluorescent light beamed from the nightstand lamp. She focused on three small, round windows; none were opened. She heard water sloshing from outside. Ron stood by the bottom of the bed.

Laura tried scampering off the bed, but was yanked back by her hair. A knee slammed between her shoulder blades, whacking the air from her lungs. A sharp pain tore through her body.

Flipping her over on her back, Ron straddled her waist. She saw wickedness in his dark, cold eyes. He pulled her arms up over her head and tied them to a knob in the middle of the headboard. The throbbing in her back and chest ran full force. She squirmed and twisted, fighting to throw Ron off her body.

"Stop it. You can't win," he said.

Laura halted her struggles. Her breathing came in heavy spurts.

"That's better." In his white shirt and black pants, typical driver's uniform, dark hair, average built, regular height and weight, Ron looked like a standard average guy.

Solidarity wasn't her intention. Staring hard into his murky eyes, she spat in his face.

Ron flinched. "Bitch."

Brief satisfaction passed through Laura, watching the wet spittle drip from the tip of his nose. She wriggled, trying to slide from beneath him.

Laughing, the other man moved and stood alongside the bed. He was short and lanky, his eyes sunken and hollow. His black turtleneck and pants hung on his skeleton frame like an oversized suit on a hanger. He was all skin, black wool, and bones.

"She's a wild one," Bones said. His tone was jolly, despite the blood pooling in the corner of his mouth. "I'm gonna like hurtin' her."

"Me, too. What I'll like even more is her begging me to stop." Ron's black eyes hardened, and his lips twisted.

Panic overwhelmed Laura. She opened her mouth to scream, but Ron's fist smashed brutally into her cheek, cutting off the sound. Paralyzing pain shot along the side of her face, traveling up through her eye, and settling in her head.

He balled a washcloth and stuffed the rag in her mouth. "That ought'a hold you."

"Get her legs," Bones grunted.

The knife sliced through the restraints wrapped around her ankles. Each man grabbed a foot, yanking her legs apart. Her ankles were quickly re-tied separately, secured to the bed's bottom posts.

Running his skinny, calloused hand along the inside of her left thigh, Bones grabbed her soft flesh, pinching hard. The gag muted Laura's agonizing scream.

"Oh, you like that?" Aiming higher, Bones squeezed harder.

Her eyes shimmered with tears, and she bit down on the washrag, curbing her scream. Bones's hard, cruel features twisted, enjoying her anguish.

"Oh, yeah. She'll be fun." He laughed, the sound a revolting grunt.

Bones sliced the dress, leaving her in a thin beige slip. The room's cold dankness added to her quivering fear, and for a crazy instant, she wondered what the two men had done with her coat.

Bones's skeletal hands moved up her body, stopping at her slip-covered breasts. He squeezed them hard. Laura cringed and clamped her eyes shut against the hands kneading her flesh. Her head pounded. Breathing was difficult. The cloth fixed firmly in her mouth choked her. The soft sobs she failed to contain didn't help.

They were going to rape her. They were going to kill her. Ready or not, she was going to die.

*

The silver BMW's headlights illuminated the Garden State Parkway. Chase turned off at the exit and slowed for the upcoming traffic light. Magic Lake Island was the New Jersey shore's greatest secret. Located north of the more popular Atlantic City and south of the more exclusive Long Beach Island, the tiny seaside resort had a total population of less than five thousand people, perhaps twelve thousand at the height of the summer season. Most tourists were discouraged from choosing Magic as a vacation spot because the town had an extremely high insect-to-people ratio. Those damn green-headed flies virtually ate grown men alive.

The community did have a charming, laid back appeal and its lack of popularity attracted Chase. If being a sociable party animal was his mood, he drove to Atlantic City where raunchy bars, casinos, and women were plentiful. When he wanted calm solitude, he drove to Magic Lake and, *Madre*, the boat he docked at the marina.

Chase was the only tenant who visited his boat during the "off season," the months of October through May. With the exception of Mac, the night security guard who made rounds only if inclined, the area was pretty much deserted. A retired Magic Lake Island police officer, Mac stayed in the office, watched television, drank coffee, ate cookies and collected his pay. Nothing out of the ordinary ever happened in Magic.

The traffic light flashed green, and Chase turned the BMW right. He rolled down the window, inhaling the seashore's stale, salty scent. All was quiet. The air was cool, the breeze blowing a mist against his unshaven face. He loved being in Magic.

The parking lot's gate was open. The overhead lights changed to a lesser wattage after Labor Day. Chase pulled the BMW into his assigned parking space. The only other parked vehicles were the pea green van he knew was Mac's, and a dark Lincoln limo parked in the spot assigned to Ben and Lily Rollins, nice senior citizens who headed to Florida around October first and didn't return North until Memorial Day weekend. Chase was surprised the Rollins were in Magic Lake on a dreary night in March.

He stepped out of the car, eager to take his boat out on the open sea. There was nothing more peaceful than the lull of waves beneath you. He had christened his boat, *Madre*, not only for his late mother, who, like Chase, had been comforted by the ocean, but also for his four years of Spanish, a beautiful language, and the only college course he had enjoyed. *Madre* wasn't a big vessel, but she was comfortable. Seating accommodations for up to eight passengers, a heated cabin and wheelhouse, and cooking and bath facilities.

He locked the BMW's door and glanced at the Rollins's boat docked three spaces from his. The cruiser was dark and appeared unoccupied. He blinked, shook his head as if to clear a few whiskey-laced cobwebs, and blinked again. A faint light gleamed from a boat . . .

Chase's eyes widened. Damn, the light came from *his* boat. Someone had broken into his boat! *Damn!* His lips tightening, he considered storming the office and rousing Mac. Little good that would do. It was unlikely the old man would investigate, his only assistance a telephone call to the cops. Another seven to ten minutes before they arrived. The intruders would be gone—likely with Chase's boat.

He reopened the driver's door and leaned inside. Not knowing what or who he'd find on the boat, Chase reached into the glove compartment. He groped until his fingers gripped the butt of a handgun. Although he had a permit to carry the weapon, he had never needed to use it. He barely remembered the last time he took target practice.

His fingers wrapped tightly around the gun. Since when did people break into boats on Magic Lake Island? Crime on Magic Lake was a driver ignoring a stop sign or a couple of underage kids trying to steal a six-pack. Anger seeped in Chase's veins. And why the hell did these assholes have to pick his boat? The star-studded sky guided Chase toward *Madre*. He moved panther-like on the wooden dock, throwing first one leg, then the other over *Madre's* side.

He stalked the deck, finding the eerie silence disturbing. A faint light streamed from the bottom of the cabin door, and he followed it. Holding his breath, he pressed his ear against the closed door. Voices were muffled. He raised the gun. With his free hand, he cracked opened the door enough to scope the cabin.

It wasn't what he saw that pulled at his gut, but what he heard. A woman sobbing. Chase winced. He had heard that familiar whimper too many times while growing up. From his mother. These particular muted cries ripped his heart.

He nudged open the door a splinter more. A man wearing dark pants and a white shirt stood with his back to the door. Chase looked beyond him. Another man, dressed in black pants and a black turtleneck sweater, sat at the bed's bottom edge. Chase couldn't distinguish what the man held in his hand.

Both men laughed, a callous, malicious sound that made Chase grimace. Even above their merriment, he still heard the woman weeping.

He saw the bare, shapely legs from the knees on down and realized what the man held. In one hand was a dagger-type knife; in the other, beige lace panties he had cut off the woman.

Damn the bastards! Chase swallowed hard. His insides twisted and he battled to control his anger. He needed to keep a level head. No way was he allowing a woman's assault.

She was on her back, legs tied spread-eagle. Chase concentrated on the two degenerates. They happily recited the cruel acts they had in store. Nausea cramped his stomach. He heard her stifled pleas. She ignored her restraints, twisting in useless efforts to jerk away. Her fruitless attempts only made her captors laugh harder and probably turned them on even more.

Gun cocked, he slithered into the room. He saw the woman's body to her waist. She wore a flimsy slip. The man on the bed slid the knife beneath the garment, and a sharp but barely audible scream stopped Chase in his tracks. A hearty cackle echoed the man's laugh as he stood and unzipped his baggy black pants. They fell around his ankles.

Chase gritted his teeth. He feared how the creep had used the knife on the woman. His best chance was to grab the one by the door. His back to Chase, the man was totally engrossed in the woman's struggles. Chase snuck up, and pressed the gun's tip against the back of the man's head.

"Enjoying the show?" he asked, his tone as casual as if asking for the correct time.

The man stiffened. His companion, too, froze, his thumbs tucked in the waistband of his white boxers.

Chase fixed on the two scumbags. While his conscience demanded he help the woman, he had no idea how to handle these two buffoons.

"Well, I know you're not going anywhere. But just so your friend knows." He patted the man down. "If either one of you makes a move, it's *your* head I'll blow off." Satisfied there was no weapon, Chase turned his attention toward the bed.

"Okay, you, in the boxers. Toss the knife over to the corner."

The man didn't move.

Chase pressed the gun. "He's not a very good friend of yours, is he?"

With a gun nuzzled behind his ear, the man shuddered. "Hey, d-do what h-he said," he stammered. "This is Chase Donovan."

Chase stiffened, startled by hearing his name, but maintained control. This creep knew him? Just by his voice? Who were these guys? The cabin's lock hadn't been broken or picked. So they had a key? Only his father had a spare key. How had these two stolen *Madre's* key?

The pantless man disregarded Chase's directive, and clutched the knife.

Chase's stomach tightened. Did he have to shoot one of them? His pulse quickened, but he managed a confident calmness.

What a time to realize he hadn't checked to see if the gun was loaded. "Okay, don't drop the knife. That's fine with me. On the count of three, I blow his brains out. One . . . two . . . "

His hostage quivered. "Shit! Do what he says and get rid of the damn knife!"

Pantless, his expression a defeated smirk, tossed the knife. It landed on the floor by Chase's feet. He kicked it to the corner. The man reached for his pants.

"Stay where you are!" Chase shouted. The idiot might very well have another weapon in his pocket.

Pantless jerked to abrupt attention. His pants remained bunched at his ankles.

"Come on, Chase," his detainee groaned. "She may come off like a cool bitch. You gotta admit they're the hot ones. You're father said it was okay as long as we got the job done."

Chase tensed where he stood. His father? What did his father have to do with a woman being assaulted?

He studied the individual who stood before him and relished a brief twinge of satisfaction. The bastard was scared. Good. After terrifying this woman, Chase hoped the bastard crapped his pants.

His breathing nearly stopped. Chase recognized the man he held at gunpoint. Ron Caldwell, his father's dependable Leisure Limo driver. What the hell?

He took a moment to regain his wits. "My father picked you."

"H-he said a-as long as the job g-got done," Ron stammered.

Job? What job? Chase shook off the question as rambled thoughts gave way to a strategy.

He took a deep breath. "Well, Caldwell, he didn't realize you're an ass." Chase took a gamble, easing the gun, and stepping back. "It's lucky I came to check. Your car's recognizable in the parking lot. The cabin light is blazing, and the guard makes rounds in fifteen minutes." That particular lie sounded believable. "This job should be finished. What's the matter? Can't get it up?"

Ron's features hardened. "I got no problem in that department."

Chase let his arm relax, but gripped the gun, ready if necessary. "So what's the problem?"

"We chloroformed her," Ron said. "It took forever for her to come around. The bitch was faking it."

Thank God, Chase thought. The extra time saved this woman.

"Oh, in other words, you're not impotent, merely stupid," Chase chuckled. His demeanor toughened. "I expected to find you assholes cleaning up." He paused. "I hate a messy boat."

He had to get these two off the boat. That was the priority. Get them off the boat. Get this woman to safety.

"I'll take over," Chase said. "Get lost, the both of you."

"Hey, you, wait a minute," Pantless said with a snort. "We went through a lot of trouble gettin' this bitch, and we ain't gettin' a piece of her?"

"Yeah, Chase." A muscle in Ron's cheek twitched. "We got no

problem sharing her."

The bile in Chase's throat wrangled with the words in his mouth. "You've known me a long time, Ron. Do I seem like a guy who shares?" He managed some amusement in his voice. "Since I was forced to make this trip, I get her to myself. Now beat it."

Pantless gaped at Chase. "What about our money? Your father said he'd take care of payin' us. You tellin' me we ain't gettin' paid?"

Payment? His father? Even the implication made Chase's blood run cold, but he retained his composure. "You want to get paid?"

"You bet." Fists clenched, Pantless took a step toward Chase. "Especially if I ain't gettin' between her legs. I was lookin' forward to a good piece. Of cash. And her."

With his eyes focused on Pantless, Chase pointed the gun back at Ron. "What did I say? You move, he gets the bullet."

Ron cringed. Pantless halted.

"There's a change in plans." Chase piloted on adrenaline. "You guys are too inept for me. Take a hike."

He wished the sick bastard saw how ridiculous he looked wearing a black turtleneck, his pants clustered around his ankles, his shapeless white shorts, and his knobby knees visible to the world.

"You want payment?" Chase had two one hundred dollar bills in his pants' side pocket. Money, hopefully, would get them off the boat a hell of a lot faster. He tossed the cash to the floor, and waved the gun at Ron. "Pick 'em up."

Ron hesitated, then stooped down and retrieved the money.

"One for each of you," Chase said. "Go!"

Pantless, attempting to appear dignified in his boxers, wasn't pleased. "A lousy hundred bucks. Sh-iitt."

Fingers firmly gripping the gun, Chase backhanded the right side of the man's face. The force sent him careening against the wall. His skinny body hit the panel with a dull thump, and he slid to the floor. Satisfaction filled Chase's soul.

"Problem?" Chase asked casually.

Pantless stared back. He sported a split lip and a new bruise to his mouth, matching one he previously had. With the back of his hand, he wiped the blood dribbling down his chin.

Chase studied the man's bruises and repressed a smile. The woman had obviously gotten in a shot of her own.

Pantless struggled to stand and reached for his pants.

"Leave them." Chase waved the gun toward the door. "Start up. I can't stand looking at either of you, and my finger's getting itchy."

Ron started out the cabin door, followed by the knobby-knee man whose movements were hindered by his bunched up pants. Halfway up the stairs, he tripped and slid down, adding a fresh bruise to his chin.

They paused while Pantless regained his stance. Chase caught a glimpse of the bed. The woman had stopped crying, but lay motionless. Chase prayed she hadn't gone into shock. He wanted to reassure her she was safe but couldn't without tipping off these idiots that he was clueless to their plan.

At the top of the stairs, Pantless tripped and slid down again. This time Chase rewarded him with a kick to the backside.

As the man struggled to his feet, Chase turned back to the woman. Her arms, bound at the wrists, had been pulled over her head. A white terry washcloth had been shoved into her mouth. Dried blood clotted on her chin and neck. One side of her face was a mixture of red, blue and purple bruises.

Chase started up the stairs. Acute awareness hit him, and he nearly missed a step.

The woman he had saved was Laura Roberts.

Chapter Three

Laura's heart raced wildly. Every inch of her body throbbed. The thin threads bit cruelly into her wrists and ankles. The pain lingered from fingers grabbing and twisting her flesh. This was no random act on Ron's behalf. Dick Donovan had planned her abduction.

After leaving the warehouse that morning, she had spent the day in her condo, alternating between staring blindly at the television and pacing the floor. She arrived back at the warehouse promptly at 5:30. All the dock and floor workers had gone, and as she had suspected, Rachel was long gone. Chase wasn't around either, but that wasn't unusual. He often didn't come into the office for days at a time. Not that he did much but sign vendor checks or schmooze the clients when he was there. Chase had a gregarious personality and people, whether staff or patrons, seemed to gravitate to him.

Her mind replayed her last few minutes spent in the office. She had quietly and quickly packed the few personal items from her bottom desk drawer into an empty copier paper box. As she was taping the lid, Dick exited his office with an envelope that he said contained her final wages. He was as cordial and as professional as he had always been with her.

Now, whimpering with a combination of fear and pain, she connected the dots. She knew it didn't simply happen that Dick wasn't finished with his work, and thoughtfully asked Ron to drive her home. She had been set up. After yesterday, and the questions the FBI had asked, she should have been suspicious. She was so naïve.

They knew about her FBI visit. Whatever criminal actions the Donovans were into, whatever had piqued the Bureau's interest, Laura had no knowledge. Whatever the Donovans thought she had told the agents, she was clueless. She would die anyway.

Her arms convulsed against her restraints. Chase, who had been so chivalrous in the diner, was a part of this debauchery. He had fumed, angry because the men hadn't completed the job.

Fear shook her, her head pounded, and pain crawled where that vicious man had sliced her. Chase was coming back . . . to finish the job.

*

Chase stayed in the shadows while the two men stood on *Madre's* deck in the dim light. He kept the gun in front of him, but out of sight.

"What's your name again, asshole?" Chase asked Pantless, as if the man was insignificant and the name had escaped him.

"Lou Kent." He shivered in the late evening chill, his crooked knees knocking together.

Chase kept his eyes fixed on him. "Well, Lou Kent, don't ever expect to do a job for us again. And pull up your pants," he added with a snicker.

Kent yanked up his pants and zipped.

"Now get lost." Chase waved the gun. "Both of you."

He watched as they climbed over the boat's side and ran up the dock. Returning the gun to the back of his pants, Chase took a long, deep breath. His eyes remained on the limo until it disappeared. Okay, he had gotten them off the boat. Laura, thank God, was safe.

Now what?

Common sense dictated that Chase call the police, but what did he tell them? He had a hard time grasping that this was real. He had been expecting a burglar and definitely wasn't prepared for what he had found. Or Laura as the victim. The situation with this woman got stranger by the minute. Even stranger was his father's name connected with these current events.

Sorting through the crap had to wait. He had a terrified woman to calm.

He backed down the steps and strode to the galley. A shiver ran up his spine from either fear or cold. After tinkering with the thermostat, warm air began circulating. He turned to the counter drawers, grateful he was conscientious about keeping the boat stocked with provisions. Rummaging through drawers and the tall wooden cabinet, he found what he needed and headed back to Laura.

She hadn't moved, not even a little shift in position. Not that she had much wiggle room, the way she had been tied. She had stopped crying. Wide, fearful green eyes stared back at him. After an initial glimpse, he looked away. Right now, he was ashamed to be a man, to be part of anything that inflicted such brutality on a woman.

He put the galley items on the small desk with the exception of a zip-closure plastic bag. Using his sweatshirt bottom, he stooped and picked up the knife, careful not to smudge prints or the blood he assumed was Laura's. He dropped the weapon into the bag, zipped it shut, and put the package in the desk drawer.

Taking a penknife from his pocket, he walked to the bed. Laura's face, battered, bruised, and sprayed with dried blood stayed fixed on him. Her eyes burned into his every move.

The two men had used string, the kind used on paper to wrap a couple pounds of beef. With a swift flick of the knife, Chase sliced through the cords that bound her wrists, freeing her. He examined the marks on her tender skin. The string had chafed, but not cut. Red and raw, the telltale signs would disappear. He massaged each wrist and flexed her fingers, rousing her circulation.

The string, along with the washcloth, he threw to the floor. Laura didn't utter a word; neither did Chase. What could he say? Apologize for having the boat used in her assault?

He moved down to the bed's bottom and had no choice but to glance up. The last thing he wanted was for her to feel her battered face disgusted him.

The knife ripped through one thread, and he rubbed her right ankle. The bruised flesh was raw. Blood, from several tiny cuts, dribbled along her foot. He pulled on her toes, and was grateful when she winced. There was no damage to her mobility. He cut through the string around the other ankle. He was about to repeat his examination of her freed limb when the foot shot up, the heel whacking him squarely in the eye.

"Damn!" Reeling backwards, Chase automatically clamped his hand over the eye she had hit.

She leapt from the bed, took off through the open door, and bolted up the stairs.

"Laura!" He sprang after her.

He had to catch her. To get off the dock, she would run past the office. With Chase's luck tonight, Mac had a sudden urge for rounds, and there was no plausible explanation for a half-naked woman running from *Madre*.

Chase caught her as she reached the top step. His arms clenched around her waist.

"Where do you think you're going?" he whispered. If Ron and his friend were nearby, Laura remained in danger.

"Please, no. No," she cried.

Her back pressed against his chest, Chase lifted her slight form. She was practically weightless. Her feet kicked at air. Sensing she was about to scream, his hand clamped over her mouth.

"Laura, damn it," he gritted through clenched teeth.

She wrestled and attempted to bite the palm covering her mouth. Chase held her tight, dragging her down the steps and back into the cabin. His right foot pushed the door closed. His arms grasped tightly around her, he let her struggle. Being the stronger of the two, he waited until she expelled all her energy and ceased thrashing. Moaning, she slumped against him.

"That's my girl." Now he could tend to her injuries and get some answers. All was calm. Chase sighed, ready to take his hand from her mouth.

"Ah, damn it!" he yelped, feeling her sharp, well-manicured nails dig into his bare wrist.

Laura wiggled and twisted. She screamed against his palm, squirming frantically while her nails dug into his exposed skin, piercing his flesh. Chase maintained his grip despite the pain. Laura's free hand jolted upwards punching him hard in the same eye she had attacked previously.

"Bitch!" The ache pulsing through his head, he dropped her to the floor.

She landed on her buttocks and rolled over. On hands and knees, she scurried forward. She was inches from the door. He reached out and grabbed a fistful of her golden hair.

"Ouch!" She cried out.

Clamping an arm around her waist, he lifted her lithe form. With a quick swing, he scooped her up and dropped her on the bed. Laura landed face down, arms and legs sprawled hap-hazardously. She turned her face, offering her uninjured cheek. Chase belly-flopped on top of her. His legs straddled her, and his hands pinned hers to the mattress. Her body shook again with sobs.

"Oh, damn it," he groaned.

Her cries crushed his insides. Not knowing what else to do, he pressed his coarse, unshaven cheek against her soft one. Her tears streamed down her face, dripping onto his, stinging his skin.

As a little boy, he had often found his mother weeping in her bedroom. Whenever he would ask what had made her sad, she replied that *sometimes a woman just needed to cry.*

So Chase let Laura cry.

He held her, cheeks pressed, fingers entwined.

"I-I c-can't fight anymore. Please be quick and get it over with," she muttered.

"Get what over with?"

"Whatever you plan to do before you kill me."

"What the hell—" Chase closed his eyes, easing his body from hers. His words, the ones he'd spoken to Ron and his partner rushed back, stinging Chase's ears. With a silent curse, he berated himself. He had aimed at avoiding any conflict or confrontation. He had wanted to be rid of them quickly. In doing so, he now realized, Laura assumed he was equally depraved. He had only succeeded in terrifying her more.

"Laura, listen to me. I swear. I'm not here to hurt you," he said softly. Their fingers still locked, he pulled her up. They sat on the bed. Pressing her back to his chest, his arms cradled her.

"I said what I did to get those men off the boat. I want to help you." He dug inside his pocket and pressed the knife into her soft palm. "You have a weapon. If you feel I'm about to hurt you, use it." He closed her fingers around the instrument, hoping she was reassured enough not to take him up on the offer.

"You have a gun," she said, her tone accusing.

An arm still draped around her, he reached behind him with the other and slid the gun from his waistband.

"Hold out your hand."

She opened her free hand. He pulled out the weapon's magazine and dropped it in her hand.

"You've been through hell," he said, his tone mirroring compassion. "You're frightened. If I intended to hurt you, would I give you a weapon? Bag Lou's knife for evidence?"

"You know his name."

"I never set eyes on the man before tonight. I asked his name and the jackass gave it to me. When we're ready, we can track him down and see him punished."

She remained pressed against his chest, nestled securely in his embrace. Neither said a word. Chase held her close, patiently waiting, prepared for her to make the first move.

"When they were finished, they were going to kill me," she whispered, breaking the silence.

Her pitiful voice broke his heart. "No one will hurt you. I promise."

"Your father."

"They tossed his name out to justify breaking into my boat. My father's a bragger, not a murderer." Chase kept his cheek pressed to hers, hoping the gesture offered comfort and assurance. Her body stiffened, but she didn't jerk from him.

"Laura, I'm in the dark. I was expecting a quiet night on my boat and walked into hell." He paused, and waited. "Tell me how I can help you."

There was a long silence. "I hurt all over."

"I'll get the first aid kit. Okay?" His tone sought her approval.

He remained quiet, not moving while Laura took a few minutes mulling his offer.

"Okay."

"Lie down. Hold the knife if you're scared," he added gently.

He eased off the bed, walked to the desk, and grabbed the metal box along with a water bottle. After walking back to the bed, he sat down, facing her. She was on her back, head deep into the pillows. Blood from the cut on her chin had dripped and pasted itself on her neck. Dry crimson dotted her blond hair. Her wary stare continued. He opened the kit and took out a brown jar and a stack of square white gauze pads. Her right fist tightly gripped the knife, her other the revolver's magazine.

He inspected the contusions. Her right eye was surrounded by a twinge of blue. A purplish yellow bruise marked her cheek.

"This will sting a little." With a light touch, he dabbed the saturated pad on the wounded area.

Laura flinched as the healing lotion touched its mark, but she didn't whimper or protest. He turned his attention to the cut, running about an inch, along her jaw. He patted away blood remnants from her chin and neck, until all that remained was a pink line where the knife had met her flesh.

"Will I have a scar?" she asked timidly.

He took a smaller clear jar from the kit. Twisting the cap off, a small brush, similar to a child's watercolor brush was inside. He dipped the brush in the liquid and stroked along the injured jaw area.

"No scar. This stuff will take care of that."

Next, he soothed the thin slices around her ankles and wiped away the caked blood. She was silent, her eyes fixed on his every gesture.

Chase's demeanor turned somber. "Laura, are those the only places where you're hurt? Do I need to take you to a hospital? I will." He didn't want to, unsure how to explain to personnel who would undoubtedly want information. They would want to call the police, which would put Chase in an uncomfortable position. He didn't know how to explain what had happened tonight without mentioning his father's name. Police, justifiably so, were suspicious people. They might not believe Chase had just happened to show up. Their natural instincts would suspect he knew more than he was telling.

But as he stared at Laura, nothing seemed more important than her welfare.

"No hospital. I don't want to go. I don't need to go," she repeated hurriedly.

"I saw Lou slide a knife under your slip."

She lowered her eyes, and his gaze followed. Several red stains smeared the garment's lap area.

Chase sucked in a breath. "Laura, how did he use that knife?" he asked calmly, although his heart pounded in his chest. Any sign of his boiling rage toward her attackers would alarm her more.

"Laura, what did Lou do with the knife?"

She remained silent.

"We can be at Atlantic City General in an hour," he said. Magic Lake was too small a resort town for its own hospital. "You need to see a doctor."

"No!" Laura shuddered. She pulled herself upright on the bed, shrinking back against the headboard.

"No, they'll call the police." Her words gushed. "I can't go through the story. I don't want anyone to know. No hospital. Please," she pleaded. "I just want the whole thing to go away."

"Were you cut anywhere else?" he asked softly, but firmly.

She hesitated before giving him an answer. "He cut my stomach."

"Laura, I need to see."

His eyes shifted to where her panties and hose had been thrown to the floor. She was bare beneath the slip.

She shook her head vigorously. "It's a little cut."

He understood her hesitation, her awkwardness. She might have still feared him, but her wound needed tending. "If you're frightened, keep the knife in your hand." He waited. "That cut may be deep, require stitches. If nothing else, it needs to be cleaned."

Fresh tears trickled down her cheeks. Chase waited patiently until her sobs stopped, and she slid back down.

"I need to lift your slip, to see. Okay?"

He waited for her permission, not wanting to move too quickly. Not only was she frightened, but embarrassed, too.

After a long silence, she nodded her consent.

With gentle ease, he lifted the material, tucking it around her midsection. He caught his breath sharply, eyeing the gash that started at her navel and ran about two inches downward. Blood streaked along her pelvis and down her thigh. Chase's eyes tried avoiding contact with that special part of her, the area those two monsters had planned to assault and abuse.

He dabbed some antiseptic on a gauze pad. "Laura, I'm going to clean the cut." He paused before receiving her muttered consent.

While he patted the wounded area, Chase was quiet, tending to the task with light, tender strokes. He couldn't help but stare at her flat stomach, admire the soft curve of her hips, feel the smoothness of her skin. He seethed. What they had intended wasn't about sex, or desire, but power, terror, and humiliation. Chase wished he had shot the sick bastards.

"Do I need stitches?" she asked shyly.

Her small voice brought him out of his musings.

"No. It's superficial, like the cut on your chin." He rearranged her slip. "Let me help you sit up."

He arranged the bed pillows against the headboard and assisted her into a sitting position.

"Thank you."

He smiled. Finished with his first aid, he arranged the supplies in the kit and shut the lid.

"What about you?" she asked, her voice timid. "Where I kicked you?"

Instinct brought his index finger to his inflicted left eye. It was sore and thumped a bit, but he saw fine out of it.

"I'll live." He made light of the damage, understanding the reason she had lashed out.

"How about where I dug my nails?"

He yanked his right sleeve up to his elbow. There were four red impressions on the inside of his wrist, two having drawn blood. He'd tend to them later.

"No big deal," he said.

"I'm sorry."

"Me, too. That I called you a bitch," he added quickly. "Reflex action when a woman beats me up."

"Do they beat you up often?"

He gave her a half grin. "You're the first." He twisted off the cap and handed her the plastic water bottle. "Drink."

"Thanks." She took a small sip, followed by a long swallow.

"Drink more," he ordered warmly. Her throat had to ache from crying and screaming.

Chase watched her take two small sips. Her green eyes, usually vibrant, were dull. Golden wisps of hair were matted with sweat and blood. Her face was bruised and swollen.

"Laura, did they rape you?"

"No," she whispered, shaking her head. "No. You got here . . . " Her voice drifted off as she choked back more tears.

His fingers itched to touch her. His arms ached to hold her, comfort her. No woman deserved this brutal abuse.

While she sipped from the water bottle, his thoughts raced through his head like a marathon runner pounding the track to the finish line. His decision came quick.

"Laura, we have to leave."

Chapter Four

"Leave? I don't even know where I'm at." Laura's eyes darted around. "I'm on a boat?"

He nodded his head. "My boat."

She was silent for a moment. "Where?"

"Magic Lake Island."

"The Jersey shore?"

"Yes."

"You'll drive me home?" she asked. "Back to Philly?"

He inhaled, then exhaled deeply. "We can't return to the city." Magic Lake Island was less than a two-hour drive to Philadelphia.

"Why not?"

He was silent for a moment. "Until we know why tonight happened, we shouldn't go back."

Ron and Lou might have gone for backup, more men who would return to silence her—and Chase, too. He needed more information, like how she got on his boat. And why? How his father's name had gotten tossed around. She needed time to heal.

"I want to go home." Her voice held an anxious edge. "I want to forget this happened. If you want to help me, you'll take me home."

Chase raked his fingers through his hair and let out another frustrated sigh. How could he make her understand? "Laura, Ron is still out there."

"No. I want to go home. Back to my condo. Please, take me home." She was insistent, her voice cracking. "Please."

"Laura, listen." He paused. She had been through a trauma. He had to remain calm, take his time with her. "They can find out where you live. They can hurt you again."

Her green eyes widened and her lips trembled. "Ron—Ron

knows where I live. I gave him my address when I got in the car," she whispered. "If I go home, Ron might be waiting for me. If I can't go back home, where will I go?"

Chase thought for a minute. His solution came quickly, like the decision to let Ron believe he knew what the hell was happening on his boat.

"Ever been to Chesapeake Bay?" he asked.

She shook her head. "Where on the Chesapeake? Why there?"

The person Chase trusted the most, the one person who never let him down, lived there. "Maryland. We can get there by boat. You'll be safe." He paused. "I need to think." If he couldn't think in Magic Lake, Sea Tower, Maryland was the next best place.

"I don't have any clothes." She lowered her eyes. "They cut off my underwear."

"We'll get you new clothes."

He kept some of his own clothes on the boat. He walked to the built-in wall closet, and opened the double doors. "For now, try this." He held up a green sweat suit.

She frowned. "Too big."

"Safety pins are in the kit." He nodded toward the first aid kit and handed her the garments.

She studied the suit. "Do you have some socks? My feet are cold."

The closet had three built-in drawers. He pulled out one drawer and dug until he found a pair of white tube socks.

"Thanks," she said, taking them. She started to tug one over her right foot, then stopped. "They said your father's involved." She stared at him. "Are you afraid I'll go to the police? I won't. I meant what I said. I don't want anyone to know."

Dick Donovan had many qualities, some of which didn't sit well with his son. Dick being involved in tonight's disaster was a combination of sick and laughable. But if Chase disputed her, he would only upset her further and she was starting to relax.

"Dick Donovan is my father, but if he's responsible for hurting you, he'll pay like anyone else," he said. "There's something screwy going on. I need to find out what it is, and keep you safely hidden in the process."

*

The minuscule, windowless room had a toilet, shower stall, and a sink. A mirror, no bigger than an 8" x 10" photograph frame, hung on the wall. Laura had a faint memory of Chase talking to the loading dock workers about a boat he kept at this small island. He enjoyed being here, he said, the serenity, the quiet. Magic Lake Island was his *get away from it all* place.

She closed her eyes, took a deep breath, slowly lifted her eyelids and gazed at her reflection. This horror had actually happened. Her blood, dried to the color of a vinegary Merlot, matted her golden hair. She inspected the thin, pink line along her jaw and cringed at the bruises spotting her face. She eyed the shower, desperately wanting the cleansing surge of warm water where lecherous, groping fingerprints lingered. Not a good idea, standing naked in a shower. A blush heated her face despite the shudder that ran through her. Should she fall on her wobbly legs, Chase had already seen more than she was comfortable with.

Filling up the sink with cold water, she took the liquid soap container from the wall-rack inside the shower stall. Pumping woodsy-smelling fluid generously into her hand, she washed every part of flesh, the chilly water nearly numbing her body, until she couldn't feel anything any longer. She finished by lightly finger-combing her damp hair.

Up until two days ago, life had been commonplace. She was simply Laura Roberts. An everyday bookkeeper for an ordinary produce warehouse. She got up every morning, went to work, performed her duties in a professional manner, and was affable in her dealings with vendors, staff, and customers. She lunched at the diner, sometimes joining another Food Mall employee, other times reading a book or magazine for company. At the end of the day, she returned to the simple condo she had recently purchased. Her first time living alone.

Living alone, being the only person at home, was new to Laura. After college and a dorm mate, she had moved back to the home she had grown up in, a step none of her friends understood. Life dictated a woman went to college, got a job and moved out on her own.

Laura enjoyed living with her mother. They had always been close. Always enjoyed doing things together, talking, shopping, baking cookies and bread for their neighbors at the Christmas holidays. Perhaps because her father had died when Laura had been so young, and growing up, mother and daughter had always had each other. Laura had always considered her mother her best friend. With her and Ann Roberts, there had never been any of the rebellious mother/daughter, tug-of-war, conflicts that Laura's friends had related about their own mothers.

Which was why her mother's death had hurt so much. Laura hadn't just lost the person who had given birth to her, but her pal, her confidante, her sounding board. While she was growing up, Laura's best memories were of Saturday flea market shopping with her mother, followed by lunch at The Food Court.

In college, Laura had gotten a business degree because she and her mother had been saving for Laura's dream, to open an antique shop on Philadelphia's Antique Row. When Ann Roberts died, Laura's ambition for the project went with her.

Laura had sold the family home, the dwelling just too lonely by herself. She'd walk in the front door, greeted by silence instead of Ann singing along with Beatles' CDs. She sat at the kitchen table with her coffee and rather than talk over the day with her mother, stared at an empty chair. So she sold the house to a couple awaiting the birth of their first child, and purchased the condo. Not really a home, just a place to live.

With all her good friends paired, Laura's college roommate,

Kate, insisted she needed to date more, have a man in her life. Jack Miller had been Kate's neighbor in her upscale apartment complex of six-figure-income professionals. Laura found Jack nice enough, their dinners out and movie dates had been pleasant, but no firecrackers splintered, not even an ember . . . perhaps she had read too many romance novels or heard too many stories from Ann Roberts about her courtship and love for Laura's father. Laura's sole remembrance of her parents together was how her mother had sparkled whenever her father had walked into a room. She thought love, relationship, marriage was supposed to be that way. Yet, no one she had met brought her that special glow.

After three months of dating, Jack's commercial real estate firm offered him a promotion to project manager. With the advancement came a transfer, overseeing a new commercial development in Oregon. He had relocated within ten days. A light email exchange for the first few weeks had followed, then nothing. If truth were told, the deal had turned into the perfect way out of a relationship that wasn't heading anywhere. With Jack's move, Laura was back to microwave dinners in her condo and movies on the television.

No, despite Kate's prodding, Jack hadn't been the one for Laura. She didn't just want a man to enjoy a movie with. She wanted a partner, someone to trust, someone to share life's burdens and joys, who made her cheeks twinge from smiling. Someone to laugh and cry with through life.

All of which seemed insignificant now as she stared at her swollen face in the mirror, finding herself in a living nightmare. She tried to make sense of what had happened, but her head hurt. She was thankful her mother wasn't alive to worry about her. *Dear God, two men had intended to kill her.* She couldn't even determine if she had made the right decision taking off with Chase Donovan. He had sworn his arrival had been by chance, his words a ploy to get those wretched men off the boat.

Chase had opportunity to hurt her if those were his intentions.

He seemed sincere in wanting to help her, or maybe she wanted him to be sincere, wanted somebody to help her. She wanted to not be afraid. Chase said he was in the dark about what was happening on the boat, maybe about the FBI, too.

She stepped into the green fleece. Besides, she wasn't defenseless; she had the pen knife in one pocket, and the gun's attachment in her other pocket. She decided to join Chase.

Inside the wheelhouse looked like one big ballpark scoreboard with buttons and lights. All it needed were bells and whistles. Chase sat on a stool, his hands clutching the wheel. The muted boat lights guided them. He concentrated on the vast body of water, dark and murky in the night shadows. Laura noticed the bright blue of his eyes. The intense expression on his handsome face as he concentrated on commanding the boat. A spark flickered inside her that she didn't quite understand.

"Chase," she called softly.

He hadn't heard her in her thick sock-covered feet come up behind him. "I hope you don't get seasick," he said, glancing over his shoulder.

"No. I like the ocean."

He slid from the stool and waved her to sit, all without losing his focus on the ocean before him.

"How are you feeling?" he asked.

She sat on the stool. "My head hurts."

"Can you describe the pain?"

"Like a dull toothache."

"But you're not dizzy, are you?"

"No."

"Nausea?"

She shook her head. "No."

He held his index and middle finger in front of her eyes. "How many do you see?"

"Two."

"Good."

"Why didn't you want me to stay below?"

"I want to keep an eye on you. Make sure you don't pass out or something." He flicked a switch on the control panel. "Plus, we need to talk. If you're up to it."

She nodded.

"What happened tonight?" he asked. "How did you meet up with Ron?"

She was quiet for a minute, sorting through thoughts, contemplating how much to relay.

"Were you in the office at all today?" she asked.

"No." His eyes stayed fixed on the sea before them. "I met my fraternity brothers in Atlantic City last night. They headed home. I stayed over."

"Then you probably don't know that I resigned."

"As bookkeeper?" Chase was flabbergasted. "Why?"

She told him of that morning's conversation with his father exactly the way it had happened, adding how she had returned to the office to pack her belongings. Chase listened quietly and intently. His only reaction was a low, exasperated breath when she had finished.

"Laura, your trip with the FBI agents wouldn't have anything to do with your resignation, would it?"

She wasn't sure how much she should reveal. "It feels like a hammer's hitting my brain when I try to remember this stuff," she said honestly.

He was quiet, as if trying to process her words. "Look, I understand you're confused. You don't know who to trust. But I want to help. What did those agents want?"

She wanted to trust someone, and he was the only one around. Besides, what she had told the agents wasn't as if she had given them information The Produce Market kept confidential. She hadn't told the two men anything that couldn't be found on a marketing brochure, including customers' quotes.

"Special Agent Saunders kept me waiting longer than we actually talked," she said finally.

"He wanted to make you nervous."

"You've had experience being questioned by the FBI?"

He shook his head. "I clerked in the public defender's office. Passed the bar exam the first try, too. Most people find it hard to believe. That's why I asked if you needed an attorney," he said. "What else do you remember about Saunders' questions?"

She had no idea that Chase had a law degree, let alone a license to practice law. Neither Chase nor his father had ever mentioned Chase being a licensed attorney. Usually fathers were proud of such an accomplishment in a son. She wondered why his father hadn't encouraged Chase to practice his profession, or at least rely on him for legal business advice.

"Laura?" Chase's voice interrupted her thoughts.

She hesitated. Being rescued by Chase was strange. Taking this boat ride was stranger. Confiding in him was the strangest.

"Saunders asked me questions about who your father did business with, his customers. He seemed curious about the imported fruit."

"Fruit?"

She nodded. "I mentioned what the warehouse imported, from where, but I didn't have all the customers and their orders committed to memory."

"How did Saunders react?"

"He seemed annoyed." Actually, Saunders had flung his notepad to the floor.

"You weren't giving him what he wanted."

"The name Farmer Dan came up several times," she said.

Chase arched an eyebrow. "They asked about Oliver Daniels?"

Farmer Dan was a white van, owned and operated by Oliver Daniels. Daniels was a steady customer, and Dick Donovan made no secret of their longtime personal friendship. Daniels parked his van in a variety of shopping center lots in the city's Boulevard section, selling his merchandise from the back of the vehicle.

"Saunders was interested in what Farmer Dan ordered. I remembered apples, lemons, but couldn't recall much else. Saunders got huffy and told me to go."

"Oliver Daniels," Chase muttered.

Pushing the disheveled mass of hair off her face, Laura continued. "Saunders made me uncomfortable. Looking at me with his beady eyes, staring at me accusingly."

Chase frowned. "That's part of the FBI graduation exam."

Laura ignored the quip. "Chase, I don't know what's going on at your father's warehouse. If the FBI is snooping around, I don't want to be involved," she said softly, her tone almost pleading. "I felt it best if I resigned."

"What the hell could intrigue the FBI about a produce warehouse?" Chase muttered, mostly to himself. He pressed on. "Okay, you give my father your resignation and he asks you to come back tonight to pack your things. What happened?"

A quick pain sliced through her head. "I took the bus back to the warehouse. I packed my desk. Put my stuff in an empty copier paper box." She closed her eyes, trying to remember, trying to force the image.

"Take your time, honey."

Her fingertips touched her temples and rubbed. The pain throbbed as if someone had wrung her brain so tight, she thought her head might burst. "I took the bus," she repeated. "From my condo to the warehouse. I took the bus. Your father said he still had work to do. Ron was downstairs. We went down and your father asked Ron to drive me home."

"You said you gave Ron your address, but you didn't make it home?"

She stopped massaging, the motion not easing the ache. "We were driving," she said softly. "Ron had put the box with my things in the trunk. He couldn't find his phone and thought he dropped

it in the trunk. He stopped the car. The door opened. The smell."
She shivered. The odor was back, clogging her nostrils. A vision
darted passed her eyes. The man in black, clasping the foul cloth
to her face. "I couldn't breathe."

Silent sobs shook her. "I couldn't breathe," she cried. Her head
pounded furiously, and her throat was raw. Her eyes, heavy like
lead, insisted on closing.

"It's okay, Laura. I get the picture," he whispered.

Violent memories flooded back. The big hand covering her
mouth, her desperation to breathe, and the pain, the horrific pain
each time one of them touched her.

"I need to go back to the other room," she muttered.

"Can you get back on your own?"

She nodded, sliding off the stool. Her legs were shaky and a
sharp twinge gripped her.

His strong right arm went around her waist, supporting her
slender frame. "I'll take you."

"You can't leave the wheel."

"For a bit, I can." His free hand pressed a button, engaging the
autopilot. The navigation device would regulate the boat for the
few minutes he was away from the controls.

"Put your arms around my neck," he said and clasped her hand.

She froze. Too many strange men had put their hands on her
this evening.

A gentle smile passed over his face. "I'll carry you."

Chase was tall with the strong, enduring body of a marathon
runner. She eyed him guardedly before sliding her arms around
his neck and clasping her hands together.

With extreme care, he lifted her and carried her down the stairs.
Her head dropped weakly against his shoulder. His arm squeezed
around her waist, holding her close. Being in his arms wasn't so
bad, and she relaxed. Shutting her eyes helped ease the throbbing
gnawing at her temples and his warm body soothed her.

When they reached the cabin, he lowered her feet to the floor. Her arms still clasped around his neck, Laura stared at the bed. She shook uncontrollably.

"What?" he asked.

Tangled, wrinkled white sheets glared at them, but Laura saw only the red spots. Blood, her blood, dried burgundy droplets that had dripped from her face onto the pillowcase; several smaller blotches covered the fitted sheet. A reminder of where the knife had sliced her stomach. She shuddered, burying her face against Chase's shoulder. His arm went around her waist, pulling her into him. Laura didn't shrink away.

"I can't get back in that bed," she whimpered.

His hand rubbed up and down her back until she ceased shaking. "I can change the sheets. There's another set in the closet."

His arm remained around her, and his free hand reached up, stroking her hair. Laura found an odd comfort in his touch.

"I'll change the sheets, and you'll feel better. Sit here." He eased her down onto the hardback chair nestled between the desk and the wall.

The anxious pace of Laura's heart returned to normal. After stripping the bed bare, Chase took a set of teal-colored sheets from the closet. He tossed the used bedding to the closet floor and remade the bed, adding a gray wool blanket and a navy quilt.

She stood. "Thank you."

"You're welcome." He smiled.

There was solace in his upturned lips, the way his blue eyes glimmered. Laura was being weak, and hated it. Feeling the shivers recur, she hugged herself. She needed to be brave and get into that bed.

As if running through a fire, she dove at the mattress. Chase drew up the covers, tucking them around her.

She looked up at him. "Where are you going?"

"Back to the controls. I want to get out of New Jersey. When we're in Delaware waters, I'll drop the anchor and catch a nap."

His smile echoed reassurance. "Everything will be okay, Laura. We'll figure this out. Relax, and go to sleep."

"Where will you sleep?" Her eyes drifted closed, exhaustion overwhelming her. She was asleep before hearing his answer.

Chapter Five

The blazing sun pierced her eyes. Blinking against the brightness, Laura struggled to sit up, only to collapse into the soft mattress. Her body ached as if she had been sandwiched between two SUVs.

She took shallow breaths as her head cleared. No curtains or shades covered the three small windows, and sunshine lit the small room. The ocean's ruffling waves and the birds' tweeting filled the air. The boat wasn't moving forward, but gently seesawing back and forth.

She pulled herself off the bed, kneading the kinks from her lower back and thighs. Her backside was sore from Chase having dropped her. She staggered, each hand massaging a buttock cheek. She opened the desk drawer, and saw the gun. Her eyes moved to the blood-covered knife, still in the plastic bag exactly where Chase had placed it. She slammed the drawer shut, and a jolt raced up her spine.

As she opened the cabin door, a pleasant, tangy sea breeze tickled her senses. Stiff limbs hindered her movements, but she climbed the stairs to the deck. The sun blazed in the clear blue sky. The boat teetered, alone, in a vast mass of water. A brisk chill nipped the air, and Laura hugged herself.

"Chase," she called. No answer. She called his name again, this time her voice having an edge.

He wasn't in the wheelhouse. She darted back down the stairs. If he had been moving around in the bathroom or "head" as he had called it, she would have heard him.

"Chase." Panic gripped her. "Chase."

Her heart pounding, she ran through the narrow corridor and stopped dead in the eating area. Propped up on the stool, he was asleep at the bar with a half-filled liquor bottle and an empty glass.

His head rested on folded arms, his breathing deep. A laptop was also on the bar. The monitor was dark, but the yellow light blinked. Laura hit the space bar and print appeared on the screen. Several windows had been minimized.

Clicking on one minimized window, she skimmed the on-screen print and gasped, amazed at the words she read. She clicked another window and saw a search engine page. Chase had been reading articles on women who had been assaulted. Her eyes scanned the list of titles. He had wanted to understand, wanted to know how he could help her. From what she had observed of Chase in the last three years, she never guessed he had this sensitive, compassionate side to his personality. Her perception of Chase had been that of a friendly, but overindulged, self-absorbed playboy.

Who would have guessed?

She blanked the screen and walked gingerly to the stateroom. A hand slid in each of the sweatpants' side pockets. Earlier Chase had given her the penknife and gun's magazine, thinking she might have been afraid of him.

After seeing the computer monitor, she wasn't afraid anymore, at least not of Chase. She returned the knife and gun's magazine to the drawer, she slid into bed, and went back to sleep.

*

"Hey, my sleepy first mate." Chase grinned as Laura entered the wheelhouse.

Dusk skimmed the sky. Having glided *Madre* into the marina, Chase aimed for an empty spot along the dock.

"You slept all day. I thought you planned on sleeping all the way to the Chesapeake." He focused on maneuvering *Madre* between two boats that were tied to the dock and secure.

"I did get up for a little while. You were asleep in the kitchen, so I went back to bed."

"Galley," he corrected.

"What galley?"

"On a boat, it's not a kitchen but a galley," he replied with an easy smile. "If you're gonna be a sailor, you have to know these things. Remember? A bedroom is a stateroom?"

"And the bathroom is a head. Gotcha." Her lips twitched and she returned his grin.

She looked cozy wearing his sweats. The swelling around her eye area had eased, but the heavy bruises showed more profoundly.

Physically, Chase had always thought Laura a knockout. She generally wore her blonde hair loose and flowing. Her green eyes kind of gleamed whenever she smiled. Their working environment was casual, yet Laura always wore a dress. Chase never seemed to mind. The woman had one fine set of legs and he had a helluva good time watching those limbs whenever she walked from her desk to the photocopier. They never talked much unless conversation was about the warehouse or the weather. Chase didn't encourage otherwise. If he did, and decided her personality matched her looks, he might forget his rule about not dating women who worked for his father.

His mood switched to concern. "I'm glad you were able to sleep. You needed it. Feeling better?"

She nodded. "Where are we?"

"The Delaware shore. We'll dock here for the night. I thought you might have cabin fever, and we could go out for dinner. When was the last time you ate?"

She hesitated, then shrugged her shoulders. "Maybe lunch . . . yesterday . . . "

"Well, you have to be hungry. We'll take care of that."

Last night, once assured that Laura was sleeping peacefully, Chase had spent hours searching the Internet for information on supporting an assault victim. Concern for Laura's well-being forced him put aside the accusation that his father was involved in what had happened to her.

His reservations weren't from doubting her words. Chase just found the idea of his father involved in a brutal crime difficult to believe. She had suffered a trauma. Her thoughts and feelings, Chase suspected, were a hodgepodge of confusion.

So while she had slept, Chase spent his time on the Internet . . . until he'd eventually had fallen asleep himself. He needed to know what she was dealing with emotionally. The articles he had read stated Laura might want to talk about being attacked. He disagreed. What good was rehashing? She had said she wanted to put the horror behind her, move on.

Still, he needed to try to make sense of last night. Chase decided in order to gain insight on what had happened, Laura needed to relax. What better way than a nice evening out?

She touched her bruised cheek. "Is going out a good idea? To be around others? We both look like we went two rounds with Rocky Balboa."

"I found some things beneath the bar belonging to you."

"What?"

"Your coat. Your desk items. Can anything in the box help?"

"My cosmetic case!" She paused, then frowned. "I don't have anything to wear."

Her dress and undergarments, sliced to shreds, were also spotted with blood. Although Laura hadn't mentioned or asked for them, Chase dropped them in a plastic trash bag and tucked them away in the back of the bedroom closet.

"I got you covered." He slid from the stool. "Let me get this baby docked and settle with the office."

When he returned from the marina office, Laura was in the galley, hunkered over the box. A pack of pantyhose lay on the bar, and she picked through her pink plastic cosmetic case like a child searching for all the red M&Ms.

"This is great! All my makeup. My comb. My toothbrush."

"Why do you keep all that stuff in your desk?" he asked, not hiding his amusement, knowing the habit was probably a "girl" thing.

She continued digging in the case. "I like to be prepared. Brush my teeth after lunch. Mayonnaise leaves an awful aftertaste." She wrinkled her nose.

He found the look captivating.

"And I like to fix my makeup before meeting my friends for drinks," she added, then stopped shuffling through the case. She looked up, perplexed. "Why do you think they're here? All my things?"

Chase's lightheartedness faded. "I don't know," he lied. The box was probably headed over the side of the boat with her dead body. "But I'm glad I found it."

"Me too." She stood, hugging the plastic case.

He slid a long, flat box across the bar.

"What's this?" she asked.

"Hopefully, everything will fit. It was a gift for a woman I dated a few years ago. Before I could give it to her, we stopped seeing each other. I was looking for my clothes in the closet and found it."

Laura removed the lid and peeled back the white tissue paper. Her green eyes, a mixture of awe and joy, stared at the contents. She ran a hand across a pair of black silk slacks and a red cashmere/silk blend boat-neck sweater.

"Chase, how lovely."

He was happy she liked the clothes. "Check the sizes."

She glanced at the tags. "The slacks will be a trifle big, but I can manage with safety pins. The sweater's perfect." She smiled, her green eyes twinkling. "You have excellent taste." Her expression turned pensive. "I'm sorry you and your girlfriend didn't work out."

Chase had met Rhonda in a bar. While spending a few days together, she had admired the outfit in a store window. An impulse purchase, he later decided against giving it, afraid that gifts gave the wrong impression of their relationship. She had been a woman he wanted to pass time with, and nothing more.

"She wasn't actually my girlfriend. And I'm glad you like the clothes."

An anxious joggle shook his stomach, a jolt not from hunger either. He couldn't wait to see Laura wearing the outfit.

They both showered, changed, and Laura masterfully applied the liquid concealer to her bruises. Her honey gold hair cascaded around her shoulders. The slacks and sweater complemented her slender frame, the silk clinging, outlining her curves perfectly. She wasn't wearing a bra. Even if she had one to wear, she didn't need it. He had noticed how firm her breasts were as she sat in her slip and he tended to her bruises.

Her perfect body had Chase fighting off some familiar stirrings. He focused on her face. With her golden hair, green eyes as dazzling as a precious emerald, and a rosy glow to her cheeks, Laura was one stunning woman.

He had dressed in navy trousers and a navy and white-striped sports shirt. He declined her dab of concealer around his black eye. Men should have battle bruises.

A light, misty breeze blew from the bay as they walked along the pier.

"Do you like seafood?" he asked.

"Love it."

"Me, too. I know just the right place."

Chase's restaurant choice, *ShipBottom*, was a good one. Crowded with patrons, *ShipBottom* was a small, homey family-type establishment, brightly lit with palm tree centerpieces on the white cloth-covered tables.

Chase ordered a bottle of white wine. They began their meal with seafood chowder, their conversation sprinkled with childhood reminiscences of summer vacations.

"I was so little when my father died." She crumbled crackers into her bowl. "My only clear memories of him are the amusement rides. We went round and round on the Ferris wheel for hours." Fondness nipped her tone.

"How old were you when he died?" He lifted the spoon to his lips.

"Seven."

Aware that Laura was in her late twenties, losing a father that early in her life was like not having had a father at all.

"After he died, my mother did her best to talk about him." She stirred the crackers in her bowl. "If we were baking cookies, she would say, 'Daddy loved chocolate chip.' I thought our conversations were so that I wouldn't forget him. As I got older, I realized our talks were so that she wouldn't."

"I'm sure she didn't. We don't forget the people we love who have left us."

As least, Chase didn't. Not a day went by that he didn't think of his mother, a woman Dick Donovan didn't care to discuss unless the barb was meant to criticize. After Michelle Donovan had passed away, Chase felt the need to talk about her in the same way, and for the same reasons, Laura's mother had chosen to reminisce about Laura's father. He missed his mother, the ache like a head-banging hangover, only the dull pain was in his heart.

Chase's father wanted no discussion of Michelle. The woman was dead and buried, Dick Donovan would say. She suffered. Her death was a blessing, his father would sigh.

Initially, Chase thought Dick's reluctance to remember his wife stemmed from despair that he had lost her. He even considered that his father's new lifestyle of whiskey, women, and casinos less than a month after Michelle's funeral was Dick's way of coping. Although Chase continued to mourn, he eventually figured out that Michelle being "dead and buried," was, for Dick Donovan, a blessing.

He put down his spoon and looked deep into Laura's green eyes. "I'm sorry you lost your mother," he said. "I don't think I ever offered my condolences." He had been away from the office at the time, a trip to the Poconos with a waitress he'd met at a casino in Atlantic City. His relationship with the woman lasted as long as the trip. Rachel had been waiting for him to return to sign the donation check.

"I lost my own mother my senior year of college." He paused. "A lot of years ago, but I still miss her."

Before Laura could comment or Chase could go on, the waitress rolled the entrée cart to the table. Chase was grateful for the opportunity to shift the conversation, afraid any more discussions on mothers would get him uncomfortably sentimental.

For the entrée, he had chosen the salmon, and Laura ordered rainbow trout. The delicious food and seafood restaurants in Philadelphia dominated their dinner talk. Given the provisions he stocked on the boat, he had munched on one too many granola bars throughout the day. He never wanted to see another. Since Laura hadn't eaten in over twenty-four hours, Chase coaxed her into a second slice of cheesecake. She insisted they share it.

"Why did you show up last night?" She sliced a wedge of the desert. "You said you were in Atlantic City."

He took a swig from his coffee mug. "Every couple of months, I meet two of my fraternity brothers. Tom lives in Atlantic City and works for the county. Ned's an attorney." He shrugged. "We have dinner. Talk sports. Debate politics."

She smiled. "Guy's night out."

Chase nodded. "Sometimes Atlantic City gets too noisy." He pushed the dish with the remaining cheesecake her way. "Once in a while, I need peace and quiet. The only place to find it is on my boat."

"I'm relieved Atlantic City was too noisy last night," she murmured, lowering her eyes.

"Me, too." He picked up her fork and dug into the cake. Smiling, he held out the chunk to her. "Now finish this."

It was nearly ten when they returned to *Madre*. He jumped inside the boat first, then held out his hand to her. She hesitated before smiling and slipping her hand in his. Chase gripped tightly, her fingers slim and delicate, as he helped her step onto the boat. He surprised himself by not being ready to let go. He liked her touch and entwined their fingers as they descended the stairs.

"Chase, thank you. You were right."

"Right?"

"I was hungry." She smiled again. "And I had a nice time."

With their hands still clasped, he led her into the galley. "I did too."
She had smiled a lot tonight, which made him happy.

"I didn't want to bring this up at the restaurant and ruin the evening," he said. "You and I need to talk some more about last night. Do you feel up to it?"

As she nodded her head, she sat down on a round brown-cushioned stool.

Chase let go of her hand, hating to do so. He walked behind the bar. The near-empty whiskey bottle was waiting with several glasses.

"I've been sorting in my mind what you told me." He poured the amber liquid into a glass. "Can I get you a drink?"

She shook her head. "I don't like whiskey."

"Some water?"

She smiled, shaking her head again.

"I've been thinking about Oliver Daniels." He raised the glass as if toasting. "He isn't a very nice man." That was an understatement if ever there was one.

"I don't know him. I've seen him walking through the Food Mall, but we've never spoken."

Having gone through elementary, high school, and college together, Dick Donovan and Oliver Daniels had remained tight friends, although they were as different as a polar bear and a cheetah. Dick with his expensive one-of-a-kind suits and silk ties, Daniels always dressed in food-stained overalls that looked as if he had slept in them. Dick was earnest where his longtime friend was concerned, but Chase was certain his father had better sense than to protect anyone from anything criminal.

"My father doesn't see the man's faults because they're friends," Chase said. "I can't stomach the bastard. He's had two sexual harassment suits filed against him by ex-secretaries."

"He doesn't think much of women, does he?"

"Human or otherwise." Chase took a mouthful from his glass. "I once saw him beat a thoroughbred that had lost a race. Nice little filly. She had to be put down."

"Oh, my."

"Some days the ponies got it. Some, they don't. Daniels had lost a bundle and was drunk and pissed." Chase gulped the remaining liquid. "His story was she reared up in the stall."

"Don't they investigate? For insurance purposes at least?"

"Only if a claim is filed," he said. "Daniels knew better. Said he could use the tax loss. I wrestled with my conscience. Wanting to go to the authorities. Slimy folks don't see animal abuse as a crime." His tone was wistful. "Only, it was my word against the two other people in the barn."

"Neither would go against Daniels."

Chase had been in high school. Even after so many years, guilt still plagued him for having pushed aside the abuse. "It was a long time ago. I dreaded a confrontation with my father," he smirked. It was a pitiful excuse. "Dad and I were having a lot of those back then. He gets on me for being too sensitive. Complains I take after my mother." He poured another drink.

Laura was silent for a minute. "Chase, what you're telling me is terrible, but I can't see where Daniels' shenanigans with a horse would interest the FBI. Or has anything to do with what happened to me."

"Daniels owns Leisure Limo."

Her eyes widened. "I didn't know. I pay those invoices. The address isn't the same address as his produce business." She paused. "Come to think of it, both businesses are post office boxes. Different post office box numbers."

"Daniels owns several businesses. Ron works for Daniels. I think the FBI, what happened to you last night, is all about Oliver Daniels."

"Chase, have you called your father today?"

"No. Why?" He drained his glass.

"You told your father about the FBI," she pointed out. "He told Oliver Daniels. How else would Daniels have found out?"

"I'll admit that this boat, Magic Lake, the marina was the perfect setting for what they had planned. That doesn't mean my father's involved in your attack."

"Chase, they are worried about what I might have said. Either knowingly or otherwise." Her lips thinned. "Your father conspired to get rid of me."

His frown waved away her theory. His father couldn't be capable of putting together such a plot. For one thing, he wasn't savvy enough. "My father has the boat's spare keys. Ron copped them. The keys are supposed to be in a safe place, but Dad can be pretty careless."

Laura's brow wrinkled. "I told you. Ron didn't come into the office. Your father carried the box with my things to the car. We met Ron at the gate. The only way Ron got these keys was if your father gave them to him."

"Did you see my father give Ron the keys?"

She shook her head. "No. But your father could have slipped them to him when I wasn't looking."

"You're being silly," he said, shrugging his shoulders. "Dad can be—"

"I'm being silly?" Her fiery eyes could almost burn craters into him. "Silly? I guess being kidnapped, beaten, and nearly raped does that to a person."

Chase realized too late his poor word choice. "I meant—"

"You're the one being silly. And naïve. Everything was too convenient, Chase." She jerked to her feet. "Asking me to come back and pack my things when no one was around. Having Ron available to drive me home."

"Dad didn't know you wouldn't have a cab waiting to take you home."

Her eyes were like scalpels cutting into him. "Cabs can conveniently be sent away."

There was a hush while Laura glared and Chase frowned, each waiting for the other to speak.

Laura broke the silence. "If you want to prove me wrong, all you need to do is call your father." Her chin tilted in a dare. "See what Dick Donovan has to say for himself."

"I don't want to," he said plainly. His father was gullible enough to give Daniels *Madre's* keys. Most likely Dick thought the schmuck wanted to entertain some bimbo. But Daniels had given them to Ron. Chase was convinced of that, and he intended to read Dick the riot act, but not right now. He always needed time to psych himself for any altercation with his father.

Laura's lips twisted downwards and she glowered. "I'm going to bed. If you want to keep your head in the clouds, there's no sense in talking." She whirled and strode to the door.

"Laura." Seeing her wounded and angry sliced at his heart.

A long silence passed before she slowly turned. "What?" Her features remained hard.

"My father is an arrogant, pretentious snob," Chase said. "I'm not blind to that. Lots of people were in the diner. They could have relayed what happened to Daniels." His gut tightened. "My father doesn't have the cojones to set up what happened on this boat last night. Since the FBI asked about Daniels, I suspect this is all about him."

She stared defiantly. "Your father slipped the keys to Ron while I got into the car."

"Keep thinking about your conversation with Saunders," he implored, still not persuaded to see the situation her way. "You know something. Something you may not be aware of."

"What could I possibly know? Invoices, packing slips. That's all I know."

Invoices . . . packing slips, the words raced through Chase's mind. And Saunders had inquired about the merchandise Oliver Daniels ordered and from what Laura had said, Chase concluded the agent seemed to be looking for a pattern. "I want a look at Daniels' warehouse invoices. I think Saunders is after Oliver Daniels," he reiterated.

"Chase, think whatever you want." Her sigh was a low, disgusted echo. "Goodnight."

He stared at the empty doorway, his teeth clenched so hard his jaw ached. Laura was wrong—confused, distraught, frightened, and wrong.

She did have a point. All could be settled with one phone call. His father's outrage over Laura's horrific ordeal would be clear. Dick was fond of her.

Chase had turned off the phone while driving from Atlantic City, and in the chaos of finding Laura, had forgotten to turn it back on. Flicking the top up with his thumb, he saw the blinking red light. He had two messages. His thumb quickly punched in his four-digit password.

Both messages were from his father.

Dick's first message, logged in shortly before 6:00 p.m. last evening, was short and simple. He didn't believe his son had a stomach bug. Chase should call immediately.

The second message had been left close to midnight. Panic gripped him and fear raced up his spine as he listened to Dick Donovan's incensed voice and digested his words.

He downed an entire glass of whiskey in one gulp, and replayed the message.

"Chase, what the hell are you doing?" Dick ranted. "Didn't I tell you to stay out of that woman's situation? Why don't you ever do what you're told? Chase, sometimes you're more trouble than you're worth. Call me immediately!"

*

Laura stared at the green sweatpants, imagining them as Chase's neck. She took the garment between both fists and wrung tightly. How could he be so blind? The evidence against his father was right under Chase's nose. Why didn't he see it?

After a final, deadly squeeze, she stepped into the sweats, crawled into bed, and yanked the bedcovers over herself.

She enjoyed the boat's gentle rocking motion, but sleep eluded her. Her anger at Chase's credulity evolved into her own frustration. She wished she had paid closer attention to Daniels' invoices and packing slips, but after staring at one too many invoices, apples were apples, pears were pears, and zucchini was zucchini.

She heard Chase enter the room and kept her eyes closed. They had decided at dinner he would sleep on the window seat. She heard him ease the closet door shut and step into the head. Sweats were a handy substitute for sleepwear.

She smiled, recalling how handsome he had looked at dinner, how the shade of blue he wore brought out the vibrant blue in his eyes. Laura was female, so naturally, she had enjoyed looking at Chase these past three years. She had kept their own office conversations genial but noticed his interaction with others. Where Dick's exchanges with people depended upon their status or how the association benefited him, Chase was consistent with a greeting, joke, and hearty dialogue for everyone from the most valued customer to the janitor who swept the floor.

Last night Chase had saved her life; tonight, as a delightful dinner companion, her sanity.

A low sigh passed through Laura, calming her entire body. She had to remember Dick *was* Chase's father. Accepting his father as a heinous individual wasn't easy. Chase had been attentive, patient with her last night. She had to return the gesture and be patient with him—even if his dim-wittedness riled her.

She heard him return and settle on the window seat. The ledge wasn't long enough to recline, but at least he could stretch his legs and press his back against the wall. Before Laura had climbed into bed, she had placed the extra blanket on the window seat. He shook it out, then covered himself.

She remained motionless, not wanting to disturb her roommate. Her mind was weary, but sleep wasn't forthcoming. She closed her eyes and started counting zucchini.

She was up to zucchini number 212, and still not sleepy.

Drip . . . drip . . . drip . . .

Laura's eyes flew open.

Drip . . . drip . . . drip . . .

She sat up in the bed. The moonlight's glow flowed from the uncovered windows, brightening the room. She listened more intensely.

Drip . . . drip . . .

Prickly rain had started falling. The third window wasn't closed entirely. The rain fell on the window seat, Chase's head, and his shoulder. He slept soundly under the unexpected shower.

Laura slipped out of bed and padded across the room. She leaned over him and pulled the window shut. The contraption slid open. She repeated the action, but the window refused to cooperate. The water seeping in wasn't enough to flood the cabin, but annoying to anyone sleeping on the window seat.

"Chase," she called in a low voice. No response, she gently shook his shoulder. "Chase, you can't sleep here."

His eyes opened, blinked but didn't focus. "Why not? You still mad at me?"

He must have assumed she didn't want him sleeping in the room with her. "You can't sleep on the window seat," she told him. "It's raining, and the window's broken. You're getting wet."

"I'm fine." He closed his eyes. A water droplet hit his nose.

"Chase, you can't sleep on the window seat," she said, her voice stronger.

"I'm fine."

"Sleep on the floor." She tugged the blanket. He tugged back.

"Chase. You'll get sick." *Why were men so stubborn?* "Chase!" The floor was hard, but at least it was dry.

His eyes remaining closed, he waved her away and struggled to stand. Dragging the blanket behind him, he staggered to the bed, plopped down on top of its quilt, and pulled his own covering over him.

She stared at the immovable form that appeared quite comfortable. He hadn't opened his eyes or lost a minute of slumber. She could sleep on the floor. That idea was quickly scratched. The surface was hard under the soles of her feet. Imagine how stiff a person's back would feel in the morning. She couldn't blame Chase for not wanting to sleep on the floor.

Laura slid beneath her neatly arranged covers. This would work for one night. He was on top of the blanket and quilt, and she was beneath. This was an emergency. They were adults.

Lying on her side, her hands tucked beneath the pillow, Laura listened to the droplets tap, tap, tap on the windowpane. She actually enjoyed the sound of rain, found the steady pitter-patter soothing.

"I'm cold," he said simply.

His weight shifted as he turned and one hard arm looped itself around her waist. Her slim frame stiffened, his movement more surprising than offensive. He pulled her closer, drawing her tightly against his chest.

"Chase." She didn't move a stunned muscle.

"This is better," he muttered.

She hadn't the chance to reply as his light snores mingled with the rhythmic raindrops.

Chapter Six

The foghorn blare roused Chase, intruding on the best night's sleep he'd had in months. Chase was generally a toss-and-turner during the night. Opening first one eye, then the other, he frowned. The sun flooded three luminous cylinder beams through the windows, the brightness stinging his eyes. He had been enjoying his slumber.

Yawning, he stretched overhead, tossing his legs over the side of the bed. An inert form caught his attention. He turned his head slightly, glancing over his shoulder. Laura, lay on her side, sleeping effortlessly. She was curved toward him, her golden locks spread across the pillow, eyes closed, breathing lightly, contentment smoothing her features.

He swallowed hard. What the hell were they doing in bed? Together? He was supposed to be on the window seat. He groaned, feeling a deadly unease crawl through him.

No, he didn't.

Did he?

He hadn't had much to drink last night, wine at dinner and a few whiskies when they returned to the boat. He had consumed more alcohol during one night in an Atlantic City casino and drove back to Philadelphia without incident. He had bedded less attractive women and recalled every detail. God . . . please tell him he didn't take advantage of Laura. Not after what she had been through.

"Laura, wake up." He waited. "Laura."

Long-lashes fluttered and her sparkling emerald eyes opened, then stared. "Somebody die? You look grief-stricken."

"How did I get in bed?" He paused. "With you?"

"A window is broken. It started raining, and you got wet on the window seat."

Flinching with self-loathing, a low moan escaped him. Was

that the lame excuse he had offered to get into bed with her?

"I suggested the floor, but you plopped into bed. I didn't have the heart to throw you out. If I offended your modesty, I apologize." She chuckled, lifting the blankets and quilt. "Look. We had plenty separating us."

I didn't have the heart to throw you out, she had said. He remained dumbfounded.

"Your virtue is still intact." She laughed and rolled over, presenting him with her back. With a contented sigh, she snuggled deeper beneath the bedcovers.

Chase shook his head, amazed. Wasn't this a new one? At least, for him. Sleeping with a woman—only sleeping. For Chase, if there was no copulating, there was no reason for a woman taking up space in his bed.

He admired the willowy form wrapped in the down quilt. He liked this woman, and not because he appreciated how pretty she was after having sat across from her for three years. There was something about her he just hadn't pinpointed yet, a quality that made him enjoy sharing a meal with her, sharing the boat, and sharing the bed—even if only to sleep.

He remembered their conversation the previous evening, before she had stormed off to bed. If she had prevented him from a soaking, she couldn't be too angry. He smiled at the thought.

After he showered and changed into jeans and his college black football jersey with the yellow number 5, Chase guided *Madre* back into the bay. He checked his cell phone messages. Two more from his father, both berating and shouting a stern "Chase, call immediately." He laughed. Good, maybe his father was worried that Chase had taken Laura to the FBI. He got perverse pleasure in ignoring the messages, aware the older man was seething back at the warehouse.

Yet he wasn't ready to tell Laura. How do you tell a woman that your father tried to have her killed? Chase still had difficulty understanding and accepting the situation himself.

"Hi. Want a granola bar?"

Laura stood next to him, chewing on one bar, offering him another. No other woman was seductively sexy in green sweats. Her golden locks were pulled back tight in a rubber band, the bruises had faded into a light blue stain, and apple red blushed her cheeks. Man, he loved looking at her.

He winced, rejecting her food offering. Even the sweet, honey scent of a granola bar turned his stomach. Her jovial laughter had a smile tugging at his mouth.

"Don't you have any real food?"

"During the summer months, I do. I use the boat more."

She munched on the sweet treat, looking serene and content.

"Chase, about our argument last night, about your father's involvement," she said. "I'm sorry. I—"

His reply was quick. "Nothing to be sorry for." He didn't want to discuss his father, knowing she was right about his connection with her assault and not ready to tell her. He found a distraction. "Want a lesson on navigating a boat?"

Her face brightened. "Sounds like fun." She tossed the last bite into her mouth. "How much longer until we reach the Chesapeake?"

He slid off the stool and nudged her to sit. "Another day or two, depending how long we drop anchor at night. You'll be safe there. My Aunt Lonnie will enjoy having you."

"How long do you think I'll have to stay? I don't want to impose on your aunt, or leave my condo unattended for too long."

His aunt would welcome her for as long as Laura wanted to stay. Especially after he clued Aunt Lonnie in on why they were popping up at her door. He struggled with how much he should tell his aunt about his father's involvement. To say that Aunt Lonnie had never liked her brother-in-law was a polite way of phrasing it.

Also, something else that hadn't occurred to Chase . . . Laura's life in Philadelphia. She had a home, friends. If someone were trying to call or visit her and be unable to find her, to them it would seem as if she disappeared off the face of the earth. Although her mother had passed away, there had to be someone who would be concerned about Laura if she wasn't heard from for a few days. There had been some guy he'd overheard her talking to on the phone on occasion . . . Jim, John, something or other. She had been setting up a time to meet him for dinner.

Was Laura's relationship with this man serious? Was he waiting to hear from her? Wondering where she was? Should Chase suggest that she call him?

A nagging instinct told Chase Laura should stay hidden. For the time being, he shouldn't encourage her to call anyone.

"You should stay with Aunt Lonnie for however long it takes me to look through the warehouse files and figure out what's going on."

He stood behind her, an arm along each side of her waist, cradling her, and explained the control panel. His chin brushed her cheek, jump-starting his heart. She had used his dandruff shampoo, the only type aboard. Menthol had never smelled so erotic.

She listened intently as he described the mechanics. She asked questions, eager to try out her new knowledge, and admitting her minor errors with humor.

Madre passed through a narrow, watery strip that demanded their undivided attention.

"You're doing well, skipper," he said. She was a quick learner.

Laughter pinched her voice. "Yeah, I haven't rammed into another boat, yet. Of course, there are no other boats in the ocean."

"What will you live on until you find a new job?" He felt uneasy that she might suffer financially from a situation not of her making.

"My rainy day money."

He raised an eyebrow. "Your what?"

"My father died in a car accident." She explained the drunk driver, the ensuing lawsuit, settlement, and the trust fund her mother had set up.

"We were fortunate financially, not overwhelmingly wealthy,

but Mom and I never hurt for money," she said. "I was lucky to get a full college scholarship. The trust fund money has sat for years, untouched, collecting interest." She paused, then sighed. "Maybe now is the time to open my antique shop."

"Your what?"

She tossed him a quick glance over her shoulder. "When I was little, my mother and I enjoyed going to flea markets. I wanted us to open an antique store. With Mom's death, the idea got put on the back burner."

She was quiet, and Chase was at a loss for words. He had the feeling nothing had been the same for Laura since her mother had died. Her starry-eyed look, the green glitters dulling, reminded him how much she missed her mother, an emotion he understood.

"I don't know, maybe the shop's just a dream," she said.

Nothing wrong with dreams, he wanted to tell her. But perhaps talking about the shop and her mother hurt too much. Instead he said, "You're doing so well with this boat, you should consider starting a boat charter service."

Her tone was cheerful. "I'm still learning. I won't be an expert until tomorrow."

They laughed, both enjoying the lighthearted exchange.

"How long have you been a sailor?" she asked.

"Since law school."

"Why aren't you practicing law?"

"You'll say I'm strange. My father did."

"I'm not your father. Try me."

"He had wanted me to go into corporate, do something like mergers and acquisitions. But I chose constitutional law."

She nearly spun all the way around to face him. "You're kidding?"

He nodded. "I naively thought I could right the wrongs, stick it to the bad guys, and do right by the good ones," he said. "Until I clerked. The law is a game. Too few people care about what's fair or right. When you're a crusader, after a while, your head hurts from hitting that brick wall."

He considered for a moment, then went on. "It's about winning, and trying to one-up the next guy. It's supposed to be about justice."

She turned back to concentrate on the open sea. "More people should share your convictions."

"I didn't see many of those folks practicing law."

"Chase, what was your mother like?"

He took a minute and reflected. Growing up Michelle and Dick Donovan's son had been like being the rope in a tug of war, his mother's virtue versus his father's irreverence. "My mother was a quiet woman. She died while I was in college. Cancer. Painful, but mercifully quick. I used to tell her why I wanted to be an attorney."

"She encouraged you?"

He shook his head. "She didn't discourage either," he said wistfully. "My mother kept her opinions to herself, especially if they differed from my father's. She had a good heart and a kind word for everybody. I remember her buying coffee and donuts whenever she saw homeless men on the grates. Whenever I see these men in single-digit weather, huddling over a steam vent, I hear her say, 'Chase, get those men some coffee.'"

Laura's voice was gentle. "Your mother sounds like a very special person."

"She was. My parents, two totally different people. Caring for strangers. Not a Dick Donovan-like trait."

"Caring for strangers, a Chase Donovan-like trait."

"If you're referring to yourself, you're not a stranger."

"I hope not," she said with mock astonishment. "We shared a bed last night. I couldn't let you stay on the wet window seat."

He shook his head. "I must have been totally out. I don't remember you waking me up."

"Oh, I carried you." She coiled her right fist and flexed her arm in a bodybuilder's gesture.

They both laughed, and Chase impulsively made a move that shocked him. His arms encircled her waist. He pulled her back against him and squeezed her tightly. Although he expected Laura to tense or shy away, she reached up and gently patted his cheek. She had interpreted his gesture as two friends sharing a warm exchange, he assumed. Only for Chase, friendship had nothing to do with his actions.

"Oh, Chase, look!"

Saved by the dolphins. Six dolphins, sleek and powerful, played alongside the boat. Bobbing in and out of the water, they appeared aware of being admired.

"They're probably heading north from Florida, or maybe from Mexico," he said.

She was totally immersed. "They're a magnificent sight."

Focused on the mammals, she was unable to see Chase staring. Her face radiated, her smile widened, her eyes sparkled. "Yeah, a magnificent sight," he said. He wasn't referring to dolphins.

Laura was more than magnificent. She was breathtaking.

Chase realized that the "something" drawing him to her *was* her. Funny, beautiful, bright, genuine. That "something" that astounded and delighted him was simply her being Laura.

One last graceful swirl, and the parading dolphins pranced off in another direction.

An idea came to Chase. "Given we have another day or two on the boat, and you need some clothes, let's stop in Beach Bay. It's not far." Prolonging the trip gave him more time with her. "While you shop, I'll grab some decent food."

She agreed. "That reminds me. Your laptop. Do you mind if I get online to pay my bills? I would hate to return home and find my utilities turned off."

"Sure." He gave her the necessary computer information. "We'll dock in about a half hour."

*

Laura hopped on the bar stool and waited while the laptop hummed. She had heard the stories, mostly from Rachel, of Chase Donovan's revolving door of women, his gambling nights in Atlantic City, his "good-time-Charlie" persona. She already knew he didn't really have a job, unless one called taking customers and suppliers to dinner a job. Many times he sat at his desk feigning a business task while merely scanning the Internet. This was a man in his thirties who basically made a career of not having a career at all.

Who would have guessed he had wanted to be an attorney to help others? Who would have guessed he even was an attorney? Or that his eyes would get misty when he talked about a repulsive individual beating a defenseless horse? A few weeks ago, Laura would have imagined Chase's only link to homeless people had been a monetary donation for a tax deduction. Like his late mother before him, he bought these unfortunate souls coffee.

The computer found its connection, she tapped the keys bringing up her bank account, and started rearranging the funds. First on her mental list was paying her telephone bill. She tapped a few more keys, stared at the screen, and frowned. The telephone company line was down. *Please stay online,* the words flashed from the blue screen. *We'll be with you shortly.*

Laura's mind wandered and she felt two imaginary arms envelope her. Chase's earlier unexpected bear hug had seemed natural. She liked his pleasant gesture, his embrace. She especially liked sleeping next to him, how they had cuddled together to ward off the cold.

Chase made her feel all warm and fuzzy. She shook off the pleasant sensation. She had to put aside this foolishness. He was a human being who helped her through an ordeal. She shouldn't romanticize their situation.

Back in business, Laura hit the keyboard. She paid her telephone bill, the gas bill, then logged into her ATM account, checking available cash for clothes shopping. Luckily, she had plastic in her purse.

The numbers staring back were puzzling and weird. Stroking a few more keys did nothing to improve the figures. There should have been much more money in her account.

Behind the bar was the box with her desk items. She knelt down, shifting the contents until she found the envelope. Dick Donovan had been stuck in the seventies and used the term "paycheck," but thanks to direct deposit and computers, paychecks were pay vouchers. When Dick had given her the envelope, she hadn't opened it, but had merely slid it in the box. To open the envelope and check the amount—which included two weeks of vacation pay and he had promised two weeks of severance—in front of him would have been rude. Laura was far from rude . . . which her boss was well aware.

She ripped open the envelope and let out a gasp.

"What's the matter?"

Seeing Chase in the doorway, she bounced to her feet.

"Nothing." She forced her best synthetic smile.

His brow wrinkled. "We're docked. I came to see if you were okay with the laptop, and you're a lousy liar."

Her smile remained set, but she flinched.

"Laura, don't lie," he said.

"I don't want to hurt you."

He lifted an eyebrow. "Lying to me doesn't hurt?"

She dreaded her words. "Before I got into the car with Ron, your father gave me an envelope. He told me it contained my final wages."

"The money is short?"

"Chase, there is no money," she said quickly. "There is no pay voucher. The envelope contains nothing but blank white paper to make it look full. Your father never made the deposit to my bank account." She held out the envelope.

He took the envelope, eyes set on her, staring apprehensively before looking inside.

White paper. His eyes remained on the blank sheet as if waiting for print to miraculously appear. After a few moments, he sighed. "Dad knew you wouldn't open the envelope in front of him."

Chase handed her the envelope. His blue eyes, a short while ago bright and animated, dulled with pain. She felt his ache, a stab in her chest almost as if Lou were slicing her flesh again.

"No money." His fingers raked his wavy hair. "The bastard knew you wouldn't get to spend it."

"Chase, I'm sorry. You hoped your father's involvement was a misunderstanding."

He shook his head. "I wasn't hoping." He inhaled, then exhaled deeply. "Last night I listened to my voicemail." He detailed the messages. "I didn't know how to tell you."

"Oh, Chase," she said, her voice barely a whisper. She ached to throw her arms around him, to comfort him, take away the ugliness as he had done for her.

She expected him to swear, to shout, to throw something. His father's deception should rile him.

Instead, Chase quietly smiled. "Finished with your bills? I'm looking forward to taking you ashore. You'll like Beach Bay."

Chapter Seven

Walking on concrete felt good. A damp chill nipped the air, and Laura tugged up her coat collar. The weather offered a chilly, musty April shower's preview. Chase's monologue seemingly well prepared, he entertained her with the history of Beach Bay, a small town with an even smaller population.

They stopped at a picturesque café overlooking the bay. Chase ordered a cheeseburger with fries, Laura a turkey on rye. Attentive, cheerful, his playful mood turned on in full force, he promised to teach her blackjack. A jovial Chase focused on their time together, as if their conversation before leaving the boat had never occurred. Laura had noticed that trait about Chase. How he could easily pretend something unpleasant hadn't happened. With Dick Donovan as a father, she decided the pretense served as a survival mechanism. For Chase's benefit, she happily pretended, too.

They strolled along Bay Street, the town's main street. The sidewalk was littered with a bakery, a bookstore, cafés, gift shops, and on the corner, a charming boutique. Laura focused on the adorable blue sundress in the window. Unfortunately, she was in the market for more practical attire.

They stood outside the boutique. "Anything special you want from the supermarket?" he asked.

"No thanks."

"What's your cell number? In case I need to get you."

"I don't have a cell phone. It's ridiculous to walk down the street talking on a phone."

"No cell?" He arched an eyebrow. "What year do you live in?"

She smiled at his quip. "This one. I never saw a need for a cell phone. Any phone calls I have to make can be done from home or the office."

He shrugged nonchalantly. "Well, I'll pick you up right here in an hour. Have fun." He tossed her a huge grin and started down the street.

Laura needed no excuse to go clothes shopping, and the tiny boutique had some charming designs. Few patrons scanned the shop. The lone sales associate, a freckled-faced bored teenager, eagerly assisted. In the end, and to the associate's pleasure, Laura had purchased ample lingerie, two nightshirts, one yellow satin, the other a soft plum fleece; two V-necked, long sleeved, combed cotton tees, one black, the other a dusty pink; a pair of denim jeans and a pair of charcoal cotton/spandex leggings with a matching tunic sweater; a pair of black flat shoes that she immediately changed into—her heels weren't made for walking.

When they returned to *Madre*, dusk skimmed the harbor. Laura was hanging her new clothes in the closet when Chase stepped into the room. His hands were concealed behind his back.

"I got you a present," he said.

She was taken aback. "Present? For me?"

"Yes. Something nobody should be without."

"What is it?" Laura's tone mirrored her curiosity.

His answer was a lift of an eyebrow and an impish eye twinkle.

"I like getting presents," she said.

His hands came from behind his back. In his right, he held a silver cellular phone. "Nothing fancy or overly tech. And you don't need to walk down the street scheduling your next hair appointment. But you should have this at all times. For emergencies."

He pressed a button and the screen glowed. "I have all the paraphernalia in the galley, your phone number and battery recharge and stuff. I've done the important programming, speed dial." He pointed to the buttons. "One is for my cell. Two, for me at home. Three, the office. If you're in a jam and need someone, call me."

She took the gadget, inspecting the details. Tears stung her eyes. "Oh, Chase. This is so sweet." Her mother, girlfriends, even Jack had ribbed her for not having a cell phone. But to Laura, if you had a cell phone, you had to keep it turned on, and people generally called you when you weren't in the mood to talk . . . like on a bus. She was often annoyed, at the end of the day, taking the bus home and being forced to listen to all of the personal business of the person sitting next to her.

Chase's words rushed out. "I don't expect you to get into any more jams. You probably won't need to call." He paused. "You should keep the phone on you."

His thoughtfulness was overwhelming. Her arms instinctively slid around his neck, and she hugged him tighter than simple friends should hug. His arms wrapped around her waist, returning the embrace.

"Thank you." Something brushed her hair, and she realized it was his lips.

"You're welcome," he murmured, and Laura thought he hesitated before releasing her.

She sniffed the air. "What's that great smell?"

"I picked up a rotisserie chicken for dinner. All prepared with the trimmings. It's warming in the microwave."

"I love rotisserie chicken!"

"I knew that."

"You did?"

Chase joked of his psychic abilities.

"Oh, you." She laughed. He had no idea she liked rotisserie chicken, but simply enjoyed teasing her.

"By the time you're finished hanging your clothes, I'll have the food ready," he said and left the cabin.

Laura held the cell phone in one hand, stroked it lovingly with the other. He wanted so much to be a considerate friend to her, and he was.

But Laura had a real big problem with his friendship.

She just might be falling in love with Chase Donovan.

*

Since he had cooked, Laura insisted her job was to clean up. While she was busy with her task, Chase picked through the can filled with bolts and screws. He had tried three different spring catches, but none seemed to do the trick. The entire window needed to be replaced, a deed that couldn't be accomplished tonight. If the Beach Bay supply shop didn't have a replacement in stock, one needed to be ordered. Continuing on without a secure window meant major water damage if they ran into a severe storm.

"Not much can be done tonight," he said as Laura entered the room. "Luckily, despite how dreary it's been all day, the Coast Guard weather forecast isn't calling for rain." His brow crinkled. "Although they are warning of a dip in temperatures. I can cover the window with plastic trash bags. Some extra blankets and quilts are in the storage area."

He found one extra blanket, which wasn't enough to keep them both warm if he intended to sleep on the window seat.

"I must have sent the quilts out to be dry-cleaned, and forgot to bring them back."

She pulled the plum fleece nightshirt off the wooden hanger. "Chase, you're not freezing on that window seat. We'll sleep the way we did last night. I'm beneath the quilt and you're on top with the blankets. I won't be responsible for you catching pneumonia."

Before Chase had a chance to reply, Laura was in the bathroom, and he stared at the closed door separating them. He sighed and popped the plastic lid on the can. So, here they were. Sharing a bed again tonight. What she had said, one sleeping on top of the quilt, while the other slept beneath, made sense. And they were adults.

Since he had bought the cell phone that afternoon, he couldn't help but notice that there was a little too much togetherness going on between them. *Emotional* togetherness. As he had stared at the electronic gadgets in the store window, he couldn't help but wonder if her abduction could have been prevented if she'd had a phone that evening.

Probably not.

But he was concerned about her. Probably because of the last few days, but her welfare consumed his thoughts.

Plus, whether intentional or not, he was letting Laura see a side of him that he never revealed. Being with her stabilized him, softened him. His mother would have called it his human side. With Laura, his guard was down. He was comfortable.

And he liked it.

Being around Laura also had another, more unsettling effect; when she stood near him, when he caught a trace of her fresh scent, he found keeping his hands off her a challenge.

The last thing he had needed tonight was her throwing her arms around him, even if the gesture had been one of gratitude.

His connection and tenderness toward Laura was growing, increasing by the hour. His common sense reminded Chase that his affections were the last thing she needed right now. But when he took her delicate hand to help her on and off the boat, or heard her jovial chuckle as they exchanged good-natured barbs, he never wanted their time together to end.

*

She turned over. A sandpapery item scratched her cheek and something bumped her nose. The room was enveloped in complete darkness. The outside breeze caressed the waves, swaying the boat back and forth. Her senses half dulled by sleep, Laura lifted an arm from beneath the quilt. She patted, trying to distinguish what lay in bed.

"Looking for something?" He was completely awake.

She shook off her grogginess. "I didn't hear you come in." He had been in the galley, on the phone with the marina's office and talking windows, when she retired.

"I did my best not to wake you. Go back to sleep."

"Why aren't you asleep?"

After a long pause, he said, "I'm thinking."

She wanted him closer. Last night his body had been so snuggly. She wanted to feel him again. Her other arm shot out from beneath the quilt, and both her limbs encircled his neck. She didn't care if she was proper or not. She wanted to be near him, feel his snug body tight against her. His arm slid around her shoulders, but she couldn't get close enough. She kept pressing, but she couldn't feel him, his body, his warmth, his touch. How frustrating.

"What are you doing?" he asked.

"You're so warm and cozy. I want to be near you."

"Then get rid of these damn blankets," he grunted.

One quick movement on his part, and there were no blankets or quilts separating them. Her taut breasts strained against the nightshirt, brushing against his chest, as he eased her back into the mattress. His hands clung to her hips, and her arms wrapped around his neck.

"Laura, when I said I was thinking," he murmured. "I was thinking about how beautiful you are, and how much I want you."

He bent his head and kissed her with a passion that warmed her entire being. She pressed against him, holding him tight, her arms clasped around him. His mouth left hers, his lips traveling behind her ear and down her throat, nibbling, sucking, teasing. Laura was dizzy.

He lifted his head. Her right hand reached up and she ran her fingers through his thick, wavy hair. "I wanted to do this for such a long time."

"What? Kiss?"

She laughed. "No, run my fingers through your hair. It's so wavy and thick."

He feigned injury. "You hurt my feelings. You didn't like the kiss?"

"Hmm. Let me see." She paused. "I'm not sure. Do it again."

His mouth slid over hers, and his arms tightened around her waist. His lips were warm, soft, arousing, and she parted hers instinctively in response. Yes, she liked his kiss very much.

"That *was* good," she said in a soft voice.

"Laura, if you want me to stop, tell me." His tone was no longer teasing, but gently serious. "I'll understand."

She kissed him. "If you want me to stop, tell me," she said warmly. "I'll understand."

He replied with another kiss. This time his mouth was strong and intense, his tongue sliding inside, tantalizing, enticing her emotions. She was tight against him, his chest pressing hard to her breasts, her peaks hardening. His mouth left hers, his tongue tracing an outline of her lips before he planted a gentle kiss where a knife had once sliced her jaw.

Laura shivered, his mouth covered hers again, and he kissed her deeply and completely.

He eased himself off her a bit. His mouth moved along her neck. A hand slithered from her waist up to her breast. His palm pressed against her, petting, cupping, caressing with an intensity that had her nipple throbbing. Laura arched into him.

Chase reached down and bunched the nightshirt's hem. She raised her arms, and he pulled the garment over her head, tossing it to the floor. His hands ran along her bare body, fondling, stroking, learning every outline and curve.

She yanked off his sweatshirt. It joined her nightshirt. Laura's lips moved along his muscular shoulder, up along his throat, then found his mouth again.

"Why didn't I admit this to you before?"

Laura stroked his cheek. "Admit what?" With darkness all around them, she couldn't see his face.

"How much I wanted you." His head dropped to her breasts, he took one, sinking his lips and twirling the erect nipple.

Laura lay dreamily, soaking in the exquisite sensations. "Chase, I want to touch you," she said.

He shifted and shrugged out of the sweatpants, kicking them

to the floor. Her hands clasped and kneaded his buttocks while his mouth returned, hot and wet, to her breasts. She sighed, the sound curdling deep in her throat. His flesh, hot and strong against her fingers, along with his mouth caused a quick, pounding sensation clamoring in the pit of her stomach.

Hands roaming, Chase found and caressed the softness between her thighs.

"No," she gasped, jerking back. She scampered away from him, recoiling in the corner of the bed.

"Laura? What is it, honey?"

Silence hung heavy as he waited.

She muttered her lie. "Nothing."

Neither spoke. Fists clenched at her side, Laura cowered in the corner. She closed her eyes, trying to shut out the brutal memories.

"Did they hurt you there?"

She continued shaking, part fear, part anger, part humiliation. The shudders refused to stop.

"Come here." Taking her hand, he gathered her quivering body in his arms. He tucked the blankets and quilt around them both and simply held her.

After a long silence, Laura spoke, her voice low, timid. "I'm embarrassed."

"Why?"

She nestled closer. "They took turns pinching me until I screamed. Ron and that man. The same spot you just touched. They made a game. Seeing who could pinch me the hardest and make me scream the longest." Clamping her eyes, Laura tried to shut out the vivid image, not feel the wincing pain as each man had taken her tender flesh between his fingers and squeezed. "I tried not to give in, not to scream, not to give them the satisfaction," she said, her voice barely audible. "But it hurt."

His body flinched as if stung by a wasp. He said nothing, but simply held her. He wouldn't hurt her, she knew, and the tender area wasn't sore any longer, but when he had touched her, even though it was a gentle stroke, she felt the stabbing, twisting squeeze, and heard the wicked laughter.

Chase's lips pressed her temple. "You're with me. Nobody is around to hurt you. I promise."

Their silent intimacy continued. Chase held her close, occasionally brushing his lips against her temple or cheek while his hand stroked her hair. She liked how he held her.

She was relaxed, ready, and tilted her head upwards for Chase's tender kiss. His kiss turned passionate, insistent, needing. She answered his need with her own urgency.

His arms tightened around her. This time she wasn't resisting the safe, secure cocoon as she had when he had caught her in his arms, stopping her flight from him that first night. Now she welcomed his embrace.

"Don't ever be embarrassed. You were strong. You survived." He kissed her lips lightly. "Remember, you can tell me anything. Anytime." His hand caressed her cheek. "Better?"

"Um-hum." She lovingly patted the hand stroking her skin. "Thank you."

"My pleasure." His mouth covered hers again.

His lips left hers, leisurely traveling down her throat, along her right shoulder, roaming freely over each of her breasts. He waited for unspoken permission before stopping to nuzzle and suck each rigid nipple, then continued his journey downward.

Laura sighed, never before feeling so worshiped, so desired, so special . . . so loved. But she needed to remember Chase didn't love her. They were two people who needed each other's comfort and a respite of pleasure. When daylight arrived, she must not make him feel uneasy or awkward. But for tonight, she delighted in the essence of him.

His lips continued wandering, teasing and playing along the way. Laura was unaware of everything except the pleasure he gave her, the amazing way he made her feel.

When his gentle kisses found that vulnerable place between her thighs, that soft spot where she had been abused, his lips brushed tenderly . . . once, twice, three times. He moved upward and kissed the sensitive stomach area where that bastard had cut her. His cheek lay against her stomach, his faint breath soothing the area that had her crying out in brutal agony not so long ago. Chase was so sweet, so tender, Laura decided she could lie like this with him forever.

Eventually, she reached for him, and her fingers ran lovingly through the waves of his brown hair as the two bodies lay still, calmly, peacefully. After a tranquil interval, Chase kissed her special place again. His hand caressed, and when the contented moan passed through her lips, he slipped a finger inside. Laura remained unflinching, relaxing against the mattress, soaking up the tantalizing sensations his touch produced.

Chase worked his way upwards and Laura's hands, followed by her lips, glided over his chest. She loved his chest, smooth yet firm, with only a little bit of hair that was light and fuzzy. Her lips nuzzled his stomach, her hand slid between his thighs, stroking his swollen flesh that was hard with desire and begging for them to join together. He groaned at her touch, a cutting, deep, echoing sound.

Bending her head, Laura kissed the focus of her attention, her lips lovingly caressing the hard, yet sensitive part of his body before starting back up his stomach and chest.

Chase, entwining his fingers in her hair, lifted her head and his mouth took hers greedily in a blazing kiss. He rolled her over on her back. He was burning, pulsating, ready, and pressed against her thigh.

"Chase."

"Honey, are you okay?" he whispered against her ear.

"Yes." She chuckled. "Are *you* okay?"

"I'm with you. I'm fine," he said tenderly.

She spread her thighs, anxious, wanting, needing him.

His arms clasped around her, drawing her body close, he eased inside her. They lay for a moment, not moving, simply soaking up the contentment of being a part of each other. Slowly, he began moving, thrusting gently at first, and then little by little building up speed. Laura sighed with each increasing stroke. Heated tingles glided through her body. Her legs clamped around his waist, taking him deeper, and she shook with the hot bliss as he moved powerfully, up and down, in and out.

She clung to him, rocking with him, answering his rhythmic strokes. His breathing was ragged and panting. His tempo increased, bringing them both to their ecstatic edge. Laura arched against him, moaning his name. Chase continued driving, steady and swift, until with a jolt and lunge, wave after wave of his burning release spread quickly through her.

He cried out her name and she held him, floating away on a cloud.

Chapter Eight

The morning's first glow struggled to break through the dark plastic that covered the windows against the season's late chill and early morning light. Chase blinked open first one eye, then the other. Laura was on her side, pressed against him, her hand resting on his chest, completely at home. Her eyes closed, soft breaths escaping through her slightly parted lips, she was the most alluring woman he had ever seen, let alone been with. Hot damn, he hadn't been dreaming. Nor had he been drunk, mildly irrational, just trying to get his rocks off, or all of the above.

He had no intention of analyzing how last night had happened. When her arms had glided around him, all he cared about was having her. His need so strong, he had feared leaving the bed for those blasted condoms. She might have changed her mind, and he wasn't taking the chance.

Now Chase selfishly wanted to wake her and make love all over again. Had she been some broad he had picked up at a bar, that's exactly what he would have done, since everything had always been about Chase.

Laura was different. Or rather, he was different with Laura. Solely indulging his own lust brought him little satisfaction. His complete fulfillment came from her tender smile, light moans, and soft murmurs when he touched her. From the easy way she stroked him, whispered his name, caressed his skin with her lips, he felt at home with her.

His heartbeat quickened as he watched Laura in gentle slumber. After what had happened to her, reaching out last night was important. Being with Chase, or any man, was a major step after her assault.

Only Chase didn't want Laura with any other man. He wanted her with him.

Her effect on him was a strange and unfamiliar one. But right now, gazing at Laura, he felt a little ember spark inside him, growing into a flame and melting the block of ice he considered his heart to be whenever he decided a woman was getting too close to him.

For Chase, women had been the proverbial dime-a-dozen. He went through periods where he had different women every night. He picked them not for their intelligence and congeniality, but for how they looked on his arm and took to his bed. When he spent too much time with the same woman, he cut the strings and waved goodbye.

As with his job at the warehouse, with women, Chase enjoyed coming and going as he pleased. No demands, no commitments.

But then there was the other side of his life. Although he still lived in the family home he grew up in, weeks could go by and he never saw his father. He saw Millie, the housekeeper more often, and she wasn't even a live-in. And they'd simply smile at each other in passing, or she'd tell him she'd put clean towels in his bathroom. As much as Chase enjoyed his solitude on the boat, the silence was sometimes disheartening. He often wondered what life would be like with a wife, kids, a specific time to eat dinner every night, and a mortgage.

Now, there was Laura, who was beautiful, funny, bright . . .

For the first time in his life, Laura was a woman he wanted to be close to. Chase couldn't imagine being without her.

Was he in love? With Laura?

That he could fall in love with a woman had never entered Chase's mind.

"Mr. Donovan. Chase Donovan." The faint, gravely male voice came from outside the boat. "Chase Donovan!" The voice shouted this time, and continued repeatedly.

"Who's that?" Laura, awakened by the mysterious voice,

grabbed for Chase as he shrugged into his black sweatpants.

"Probably someone from the marina office." The bedcovers were on the floor. He picked them up and tucked them around her. "Hopefully, somebody's got a window. Go back to sleep."

Climbing the steps, Chase shivered as the early morning wind brushed his bare upper body. His hand shielded his eyes from the sun. He recognized Harry, the portly, middle-aged security guard. Harry stood on the dock, hanging over the rail and looking down into the boat.

"Morning, Mr. Donovan. Sorry to wake you."

"You didn't," Chase said.

"I have an urgent message from your father."

Chase's voice was sharp. "My father?"

"Yes." Mistaking Chase's curt tone for concern rather than irritation, Harry went on. "He can't get you on your cell phone, and is calling marinas where he knows you dock. He sounds real worried and wants you to call him. Right away. If your cell's not working, you're welcome to use the office phone."

"My cell phone is fine. I had it off."

Harry winked. "I don't blame you, Mr. Donovan. I've seen that pretty sweetheart you're with. You should call your father," he advised. "As a father myself, your kids never get too old and you never stop worrying."

Chase was courteous. "Thanks, Harry." The man was being polite, doing his job. Fatherly concern had nothing to do with Dick Donovan's persistent search. "Hey, did you hear anything about a window?"

"The shop was already closed after we spoke," Harry replied. "I left the information with Marie. She's the secretary in the office. Stop by in about an hour, and she'll have something to tell you."

Chase thanked the man, bid him a nice day, and watched him walk down the dock and fade into the parking lot.

When he returned to the cabin, Laura was clad in her plum nightshirt. She stood in the doorway, her arms folded across her chest, having heard everything.

"Is that a smirk I see on your pretty face?" he asked playfully. She did have her cute nose turned up at him.

"Call your father." Her tone was much nicer than the facial expression she wore.

"Can I have a kiss first?"

Her lips curled upwards, and a crooked index finger beckoned him.

Smiling, Chase followed that finger, dipping his head and meeting her lips in a gentle kiss.

As she drew away, her hands cupped his face. "Call your father." It was more an order than a suggestion.

Chase was wickedly unrelenting. "Okay. Let me take you back to bed, we'll fool around, and then I'll call."

Laura wasn't deterred. "Chase, please listen."

"What?" He took her hands from his face and held them tightly in his. She didn't pull away.

"Can't you see what you're doing?"

"Yes, I can. I had a beautiful woman in my bed last night, and I'm trying like hell to get her back in there."

She disregarded his playfulness. "Just because you're not returning his calls, doesn't mean your father's involvement isn't there. It doesn't mean you won't have to deal with it. Ignoring him makes the situation worse."

"Laura, the—situation—isn't one that can, or should be, discussed on a cell phone."

"At least, call him," she said, her eyes pleading. "Tell him you're not ready to talk. Please don't ignore him, and what's happening around us."

There was a significant pause. "If I call my father, do you promise to get back in bed with me?" He smiled.

She crawled back onto the mattress. Drawing her knees to her chest, she draped her arms around them. "I'm here." She grinned devilishly. "Let me see you do your part."

Chase picked up his cell phone from the desk. A half smile, half smirk covered his face. "Having sex sure does make you a bossy little gal."

"You're not pushing the buttons on your phone."

He flicked the top of the phone with his thumb and entered his father's private telephone number at the warehouse.

Dick Donovan answered on the second ring. Chase figured he recognized the telephone number on the caller ID.

"Chase, what the hell are you doing?" Dick barked.

"It's a pleasure to speak to you, too, Dad. I can't believe you're tracking me down like I'm some wayward teenager," Chase said tersely. He wanted to be careful what he said, not wanting to upset Laura.

Dick made no reference to Chase's comment. "I want you to listen." His tone was rigid. "The guard said you have a woman with you. It's her, isn't it? You have a lot of explaining to do. Why did you interfere, Chase? There are plenty of women around for you to screw. I want you to bring that one back. Now!"

"Excuse me?" Chase took offense to the command and clipped manner. And his father was the one with a lot of explaining to do.

"I can't believe what you pulled," Dick fumed. "You were supposed to be having dinner with me, damn it. You have no idea what you've gotten us into, the trouble your interference caused. You turn that friggin' boat around and get back here. With that woman!"

This was crazy. What Chase had interfered with, thank God, had saved Laura's life. He swore under his breath.

Lucky for his father, Chase couldn't bring himself to have Laura visit her new FBI friends. If so, the old man might be sitting in a jail cell instead of them having this conversation. Despite an interest in whatever Laura had to say, Chase wasn't convinced the FBI had her welfare at heart.

It was up to Chase to protect her, from Special Agent Saunders and from Dick Donovan.

"Chase, do you hear me?" Dick was practically foaming at the mouth. "You're not a little boy anymore, and she's not some pathetic stray dog you picked up off the street."

Chase lips tightened. No, Laura wasn't pathetic and she wasn't one of the homeless, defenseless strays Chase had encouraged to follow him home so that he could care for it—only to have his father cart the poor animal off to the animal shelter where most likely it ended up dead.

Protecting the vulnerable was a trait Chase figured he acquired having grown up watching his father's mean-spirited tactics toward others.

Dick fought for control. "Chase! Do you hear me?"

Chase's gut tightened. He was on a cell phone, and conversation was a challenge. Laura stared at him as he spoke, her eyes wide and questioning. Chase didn't want to alarm her.

Expelling a deep breath, he stopped himself short of telling his father exactly where to get off. The man seriously expected Chase to return with Laura, fork her over, wipe his hands, and walk away without looking back. She was a woman.

The woman Chase loved.

As usual, the idea popped into his head and Chase ran with it. His voice was strong into the phone. "That woman, as you call her, is my wife, and the mother of your grandchild. When you speak of her, kindly show some respect."

Chapter Nine

Finished with his call, Chase placed the phone on the table. He stared at Laura, not saying a word, not blinking an eye. She held her breath, afraid to speak and at a loss for words anyway. She had slept with another woman's husband? When had Chase gotten married? And why hadn't she heard? Surely, Chase's marriage, and the woman who snagged him, would certainly be hot gossip items for Rachel.

"How fast can you get pregnant?" he asked bluntly.

Her green eyes widened. "What?"

"Any chance you already are?"

"Are what?"

"Pregnant."

"No."

"In the office, didn't I hear you on the phone with," he paused. "What was his name? Jeff? Joe?"

"Jack," she corrected. "We broke up a few months ago."

"Really?" His interest piqued.

"Yes. And I haven't been with anyone . . . until last night."

His eyes lit up and he cocked his head sideways. "You're kidding?"

Laura equated a man in her bed with an exclusive, serious relationship. That was her rule until last night. "I can count the number of men I've been with on one hand, and have fingers left over." She didn't know whether to feel proud or slighted.

He was amazed. "Wow." He quickly regained his purpose. "Well, we have to get you pregnant."

The man had lost his mind.

She laughed, convinced he was teasing her again. "Chase, be serious."

"Didn't you hear the conversation with my father?" He stepped toward the bed. "I told him you and I are married. You're pregnant.

We're on our honeymoon."

Laura's jaw dropped. *She* was the wife? His child's mother?

Chase smiled, obviously pleased with his quickly conceived idea. "What do you think?"

The honeymoon part she had tuned out, probably when she had tried figuring out the dynamics of his marriage. "What do I think?" she repeated. "I think you've been snorting the salty sea air. Whatever possessed you to tell your father we're married? And I'm pregnant?"

His lower lip fell open, and he cocked his head to the side. "You don't want a baby? You're a caring person, Laura. You should have a baby," he emphasized with a nod. "You'll make a great mother."

"Thank you. Sure, I'd like to have a baby someday. But it's not my intention to have one in the near future."

"I'm not talking near future. It takes nine months. Near future is more like a week or two," he reminded her.

"Chase, stop clowning," she chided. "This is serious."

He turned somber. "I am serious. That old man insisted I bring you back to Philly."

"We won't go."

His brilliant blue eyes widened. "Look, I don't have a clue to what's going on back there, or who the players are," he said. "Whatever the reason for finding you on this boat hasn't gotten changed, it is merely postponed."

Her stomach gave a nauseating leap. Someone, for some unknown reason, still wanted her dead. She had been so excited, so caught up in spending this time with Chase she had forgotten why they were sailing the Atlantic.

"What do you accomplish by saying we're married?"

He folded his arms across his chest. "In Dick Donovan's mind, that I've kept you from the police means I'm willing to play his game. He believes I'm getting off on aggravating him, and while I'm at it, keeping you around for a few quick tumbles. He's

demanding I bring you back and go tumble with somebody else."
His tone turned lethal and emphatic. "I'm not doing that, Laura.
I'm not handing you over to anyone who wants to hurt you."

For that she was grateful. However, he wasn't solving one
problem, but creating another. "Chase, we can't keep on running."

As if he didn't hear her, he continued. "My father believes the
only means of support I have is the business, and is gambling on
me not bringing it down."

"Married? And a baby? A *baby*, Chase?" Her words weren't an
inquiry, but to force him to see the absurdity.

"Buys us time. There's no way my father will hurt you if he believes
you're carrying his grandchild," he explained. "The old man has been
bugging me for the last five years to get married and give him a
grandson. He wants a little Richard Chase, the fourth, desperately."

"A what?"

"Richard Chase Donovan. Expand the line," he said. "My
grandfather was Richard, my father Dick. My mother called me
Chase because she didn't want me called Dickie. I'm sure it was
the only time in her married life she got what she wanted."

Laura shook off an anxious shiver. "Chase, I've hesitated
bringing this up . . . "

Suspecting her suggestion, he was explicit. "No. We're not
going to any authorities. Especially the FBI."

"For heaven's sake, I'm the one these people want dead!" She
knew how a deer felt during hunting season. "Why no FBI? It's
their job to protect me and investigate wrong-doings." Bringing in
law enforcement was the most logical solution.

Anger darkened his eyes. "I don't trust them. There was no
reason for the big, dramatic diner scene. They used you to toy
with their real target. Those Saunders types get a kick out of using
and frightening unsuspecting souls like you."

"What's happening now isn't frightening me?"

"Laura, you *know* something," he said emphatically. "Something you don't even realize you're aware of." He took a step toward the bed. "Something that unnerves the hell out of Dick Donovan and Oliver Daniels. Until we know what that is, I want to stay clear of any badges. I don't want the FBI using you as bait for their fishing expedition."

"If your father believes I'm already pregnant, I would have to be at least a month," she pointed out. "If it takes another month . . . Chase, this won't work. He'll do the math. I believe your heart's in the right place, but we can't do this." Why couldn't she make him see this notion was lunacy?

He chuckled, his expression turning mischievous. "It's not my heart that needs to be in the right place."

The blush spread over her entire body. "Chase, I—this—you are—"

He reverted back into playful mode, his blue eyes gleaming and his lips twitching upwards. "The thought of having my baby leaves you speechless."

"Chase." She laughed, finding his jocular moods hard to resist.

He eased on the bed and crawled toward her. "The thought of having my baby leaves you repulsed?"

She never wanted him believing that. "No, not at all." Laura sat cross-legged. Chase knelt over her. She couldn't help but grin as he leaned in to kiss her. "Although the thought of having your brain examined leaves me intrigued," she added.

His hands on her shoulders, he pushed her backwards. "You want to have my baby." He placed a hand on each of her legs and straightened each limb. "Getting pregnant is one of those daunting tasks that if at first you don't succeed, you try, try again." He stretched his long, firm body over her slender one.

"Chase," she whispered doubtfully, but her arms went around his waist.

His arms encircled her head and he entangled an index finger in her hair. "Please don't bruise my ego and tell me you find the task a dreary one." He grinned impishly.

The actual *task* had nothing to do with the misgivings nagging

Laura. "Chase . . . "

His lips brushed hers. "I kept my part of the bargain. I called my father, and if I remember correctly, you promised we could fool around."

Her eyes widened. "Chase, we need to discuss your crazy notion."

His thorough kiss cut off any more of her words.

How quickly the man ignored what he preferred not to deal with—as in reasons why this wife with child idea was an insane one—and how quickly she went along with him.

"We'll get married later," he whispered against her ear. "Let's start on the baby now."

He didn't give her a chance to answer. His hand glided up her nightshirt, not stopping until he cupped a breast. His other hand cradled her head as his mouth came down on hers. His kiss was soft, then turned more insistent, his tongue creating a seductive rhythm.

When he came up for air, his gaze passed over her face. She smiled at him. He simply had that effect on her. His grin matched hers, and his lips brushed her temple. She moaned a soft, contented sigh.

"Chase." Her predicament wasn't his to carry. Their conversation wasn't finished. "We have to talk."

"Shh." He gave her a quick kiss. "This is your ship's captain issuing an order. No talking."

He kissed her again, and she responded with ready eagerness. His body moved against her. As their kiss deepened, she felt his passion. Chase wanted her this instant, and it had nothing to do with making a baby. He was hard and ready, and wasn't about to be gentle and patient. She grabbed a fistful of black fleece and tugged down his sweat pants. Her desire synchronized with his, burning, aching to be a part of him.

His kisses deepened, a demanding need that she matched wholeheartedly. He pulled the nightshirt over her head, almost ripping the fabric.

"Laura," he panted.

She felt his need pressed against her. He had to take her this instant. "I'm not glass. I won't break." She clung to him.

Her urgency reflected his. Laura pulled Chase to her, pressing her breasts against his chest. Her lips met his, their kiss intensifying their desire. Instinctively, her mouth opened to his probing tongue. She was ready for him, too. Spreading her thighs, she opened herself wide.

Without a word, without pause, he was inside her, plunging deep. Sighing, Laura arched against him, welcoming the vigorous, driving force. He panted, moaning her name against her ear. More than lust compelled him. Chase thrust as if branding her, momentum pushing him feverously toward the edge. They were locked together, neither wanting to let go.

She sensed his powerful urgency, matching his hearty speed stroke for stroke, trembling with the threat of her own release. Their excitement climbed and peaked, reaching higher and higher for their plateau. A hot, feverish sensation surged throughout her entire body.

Chase, nearing the brink, plunged wildly while alternating between kissing Laura and murmuring her name. As her body jerked with ecstatic tremors, he lunged and tensed one final time before shaking with his own burning relief.

*

Laura lay beneath him, her arms clasped around his waist.

She liked Chase sprawled on top of her. His arms encircled her head, his own head resting on her shoulder as he dozed. His cheek was warm and sweaty pressed to her bare skin. She rubbed her chin on his soft, wavy hair.

She had always thought he had a nice body with his clothes on. Her hands roamed over his muscular shoulders. A shameless grin curled her lips as she traveled lightly over his smooth, broad back, hard thighs, and firm buttocks. He was much more appealing with his clothes off.

They hadn't discussed last night, their feelings, the ins and outs of what had occurred, and yet they had made love again. He wanted to get married and have a baby. All to protect her. Chase bit off much more than he could chew, taking on the responsibility of protecting a wife and child.

Still, Laura had always wanted a baby. Of course, with the right man. Only that man wasn't coming along. From the very beginning with Jack, she knew he wasn't "the one."

She had never been a career "go-getter." Never looked for the next rung on the corporate ladder. Her job was just that, a job to pay the bills and keep busy. What she had really always dreamed of, besides her antique shop, was a husband, a family, the PTA. Aspirations she had shared only with her mother because in the twenty-first century, there seemed to be something atypical with wanting those simple things in life.

A baby, a little person to love and nurture. Her eyes misted and she smiled, hearing a small, soft voice call, "Mommy." Laura yearned for a baby, someone to be close to, a precious little darling who would be a part of her.

This one would also be a part of Chase.

His borderline insanity was contagious.

She had to marry Chase. They not only had to worry about his father, but also Oliver Daniels or whoever else was a part of this racket. If the ringleader, be he Daniels or whomever, discovered Chase had lied, that Laura wasn't his pregnant wife, it was unlikely even his father could keep Chase or her safe. Chase had put his life on the line with his tall tale. She had to stand with him.

Chase . . . her Chase . . . her very special Chase. She couldn't deny her feelings for him, partly because they had surprised her. While Chase was charming and fun to be around, his compassion for others and sensitivity amazed her and drew her straight to him.

But Chase didn't want a wife. What he did want was not to have her death on his conscience . . . or on his boat. And she didn't want him endangering himself for her. Despite her growing feelings for him, she wasn't about to saddle him with a lifetime commitment when all he wanted was to protect her.

Laura's fingers tap-danced up his back's perfect cords. "Chase," she murmured. He didn't respond, and she called his name again.

His eyes blinked open, and anticipating her desire for more intimacy, his lips covered hers. Laura was more than willing to oblige, but she had an answer for him first.

"Chase, I'll marry you and have your baby. On one condition."

His eyes met hers. A wayward golden lock hung on her forehead and he twisted it around his index finger. "What?"

"You don't deserve to be saddled with a wife just to protect me. When this is over, we get divorced."

He took no time to consider. "I have a condition for you."

"Yes?"

"You will not keep me away from my child."

She kissed his cheek. "You always will be my baby's father. You can see our child any time you want." She blinked back tears. The simple thought of keeping their child from him was repugnant. "Any time, day or night, with or without notice. I promise."

"Good," he said softly. "We've been through too much not to be fair to each other."

Chapter Ten

The following day, shortly before noon, perfect results on their blood tests, the ink still drying on the paperwork, and dressed in jeans, Chase and Laura married at the Beach Bay Courthouse. The mailroom clerk, serving as best man, kept disposal cameras in his desk. He took several pictures of the smiling couple before Chase purchased the camera.

The day's events seemed surreal. A quick wedding ceremony, a leisurely lunch, including slices of vanilla cake substituting as wedding cake, followed by a peaceful stroll along the bay, Laura hadn't had a minute to second-guess their actions. She had never been so content.

Later, in the darkened cabin, Chase lay across her. The man was wearing them out, and if she didn't find herself pregnant quickly, they would literally copulate themselves to death. The image shook her body with a giggle. Without disrupting his snooze, Chase eased off her length. Laura snuggled up against his side and he turned toward her, his chin brushing the top of her head. She gazed at her husband's left hand, resting comfortably on her breast, a gold band on his third finger. That morning in the jewelry store, she had been astonished by his genuine desire for her ring's mate.

She pressed his open palm to her bare belly. On their way to the courthouse, they had stopped at an ATM and Chase noted their wedding date on his receipt. In the courthouse ladies' room, Laura had rummaged through her purse, finding the small calendar she carried. Forget that she had missed lunch the previous day with Kate—she would email her friend regrets from Chase's laptop— Laura had always kept track of that dreaded twenty-eighth day every month so she could curtail her caffeine intake. As she had stared at the date with the red felt-pen circle, she counted backwards.

*

The next afternoon Chase strolled down the dock, holding the window above his head. The weather had clouded up again, but the temperature was quite pleasant. A light wind whisked the waves. Laura, stretched out on a deck chaise, wore her jeans and a T-shirt and flipped through a magazine.

Installing the window proved a challenge for Chase, probably because he concentrated more on sneaking glances at his beautiful wife. *Laura, his wife.* He liked that.

Their marriage had been no idealistic whim. Nor had he been playing games when he told her his father would protect a pregnant daughter-in-law. This marriage, along with the baby proposition, solved a dilemma. As Mrs. Chase Donovan, Laura was safe. He got to hold on to the woman he was crazy about. And her pregnancy? Well, at this point, all that really mattered was that Dick Donovan thought Laura carried his grandchild. Planting that idea in his father's head was the only way Chase could count on to protect her.

She would be safe with his aunt. What he expected to find in the warehouse invoices, how he would handle the discovery and what he would say to his father still preyed on Chase's mind. But one detail at a time. Right now the priority was getting Laura, his wife, to Sea Tower.

He gazed out the brand new window, picked up his cell phone from the desk and pressed a digit. She jerked forward, startled, and then realized she had her phone on vibrating mode. Placing the magazine facedown across her thighs, she took her cell phone from her jeans' hip pocket. She glanced at the caller ID, and put the gadget to her ear. His eyes fixed on the kittenish smile spreading across her face.

"Hello, husband."

Husband . . . Chase's heart did a flip, delighted to hear how she addressed him. He never considered a woman addressing him as such. He liked hearing the word. "Come see the new window," he said.

"I'm comfortable. If you want me, come and get me." She barely hid her lighthearted laugh.

"If you make me come up there, you'll pay, my beauty." His voice lowered, mimicking a ruthless privateer.

"I'm scared," she taunted and ended the call.

Chase took the stairs two at a time. The boat was docked tight against the pier, swaying in the sparkling bay water and surrounded by bright sunlight. Laura's face was buried in the magazine, and she never looked more desirable. Her golden hair windblown, cheeks rosy, Chase couldn't help himself. He wanted her. Plus, she did disobey the captain's direct order.

She focused on her reading, paying him no mind when he stepped onto the deck. He scooped her up in his arms. Laura screamed, more startled than frightened. He dipped her over the side. She shouted a loud protest and smacked his shoulder with the rolled-up magazine. He dipped her again. Her feet kicked the air.

"When we get inside, I'll show you what happens to naughty wenches who disobey a captain's orders."

Laura half screamed, half laughed as he carried her down the stairs. She slapped his chest with the magazine, wriggling in his grasp.

She was still laughing—at his amateur buccaneer voice she insisted—as he dropped her onto the soft mattress.

"You're a very bad lass to make sport of the ship's captain," Chase croaked.

He plopped down beside her. Laura's attempt to roll away from his reach proved fruitless. His hands closed around her waist, pulling her against his body. His mouth took hers, cutting off her laughter. Laura returned the hungry kiss. His mouth traveled to a cheek, down her throat, and back up to take hold of her mouth again. His tongue slid inside, meeting hers, and Laura's soft, slender body relaxed against him. He gentled the kiss, brushing his tongue over her lips.

"That's what you get for being a naughty wench," he said drawing away, his voice husky.

She met his gaze and smiled demurely. "I like being naughty."

Chase liked her naughty, too. He lowered his head and kissed her again. Teasing, caressing, his mouth parted her lips, his tongue sparring with hers. He was lying on his side, facing her. His hand found her left breast and closed over it. His hand kneaded, a thumb grazing her nipple, his teeth gently biting the side of her neck. Laura sighed, pressing closer. Desire soared through him, enjoying her nearness. She was soft, warm, passionate, tantalizing. His mouth moved lower, kissing the soft mounds of her breasts through her shirt. She sighed, her fingers weaving themselves in his wavy hair. His mouth crept lower, his fingers clenching the zipper of her jeans. Damn, would he ever get enough of her?

"Time for this later," she breathed into his ear. "First, I want to see our new window."

He rolled off her and flipped over on his back. "You sure can kill a mood."

"I'll be back." She slid off the bed. "I want to see our window."

"No, too late." He propped himself up on elbows and looked down at his pelvis. "You ruined it."

"I can fix that easily."

She knelt on the window seat, staring out the casement. Chase loved hearing her say *our window*, jointly, together, like regular, sharing, married people. It felt right. Her divorce notion . . . he had gone along with her because it was the easiest thing to do. But Chase was convinced he and Laura were good for each other. He had at least nine long months to convince her.

"Chase," she said, her voice wary.

"What? Did I forget a nut or bolt?" He swung off the bed and stood beside her.

She whirled and looked at him, her previously amused green eyes now alarmingly wide. "Chase, there's a man watching us."

Chapter Eleven

Fear, an all too familiar sensation, returned to Laura. "I didn't pay him much attention. I thought he was taking in the day, enjoying the water," she said, her voice cracking.

Chase stood next to her, fixated on the outside. "Honey, no one is there. Did you see him the entire time you were on deck?"

She stared back out the window. There was no one in sight. "Not until you picked me up. When you spun me around." Her words pushed through the tightness in her throat. "I saw him. He was on the dock. I thought he was enjoying the water," she repeated. "He was by the newspaper box. *He was there.*"

Chase made light of her anxious concern. "He was probably watching you because you're so damn beautiful."

Laura's dismay remained. "You don't understand. When I looked out the window, he was closer. To get a better view of the boat." Panic gripped her. "That's how I know. He's watching us."

His eyes hardened into steel flecks. Laura grabbed for him, but despite her efforts, Chase ran out the door. She feared for his safety as he raced up the stairs. She watched through the new window as he leaped over the boat's side, and flew down the wooden boards. His sneakers hardly hit the planks. She watched his image fade, and her heart pounded. Terror sped through her body. She was afraid to go up on deck, afraid someone might be waiting to snatch her. Then she saw Chase's cell phone on the desk and dread overpowered her.

Vivid images ran wild. Suppose they waited for Chase at the end of the dock. Or in the parking lot. Suppose they grabbed him, overtook him, and stuffed him in a car trunk. He didn't have his cell phone to call for help. Chase had told her, always have your cell phone. He didn't have his.

Bile rose in Laura's throat, choking her. Her introduction to *Madre*, the panic and fright as she had lain bound and helpless, returned.

"Chase," she croaked.

They were going to kill him. They were taking him from her, and he wasn't coming back.

She sobbed uncontrollably. Her chest grew heavy, she gulped for air and her legs weakened. Her lungs struggled to take in air. She crumbled to the floor in a heap of wretched tears.

Which was how Chase found her as he rushed back into the cabin.

"My God." He hunkered down and gathered her in his arms. "I got you, honey. Little breaths, Laura. Take little breaths."

He held her, murmuring soothing words. Laura wished she could stop crying, but she shook with fear. Her tears refused to let up. Driving sobs heaved from her throat, piercing the tiny space. Her cries clogged her airflow, and she gasped for breath.

Chase repeated, "Little breaths, little breaths" until finally her tears eased, and she took in air again. Gently, with his arms locked around her, he lifted her into a standing position, resting her head on his shoulder.

"I'm with you, honey," he whispered, stroking her hair.

She yanked her head back. Wet eyes focused on him. Bitter anger replaced her distress. "You dumb jerk," she spat. "Your cell phone. Always have your cell phone. You ran after him, alone."

She clenched both hands into fists and pounded his chest. "Suppose there had been more waiting for you." Again, the powerful wails began.

"Honey," he whispered.

"You-didn't-have-your-cell-phone." She emphasized these last words with harder blows, then collapsed against him once more.

"Laura, I'm sorry. That was a stupid thing to do." His arms tightened around her. "I ran out without my cell, without a weapon. You're right. Always have your cell phone."

"If I have to obey the rule, so do you," she garbled, sucking in air.

He held her close. "You're absolutely right."

They stood in the center of the room; Laura locked in Chase's arms. After a while, she calmed, her tears diminished, and the only sound as he held her was the ocean waves slapping against the boat.

*

With Laura resting, and the window replaced, Chase guided the boat back onto the open sea. He had read about Laura's breakdown in one of the Internet articles. How people, men and women, who endure a trauma seemed fine, living life as if the nightmare had been put behind them, then one small, trivial incident occurred, and the agony and horror returned.

Chase had expected Laura's emotional crash would come the first night they made love. After her initial hesitancy, she was fine. They continued making love, and they were fine. No, they were more than fine. They were fantastic together.

But her collapse circled, lingering and waiting to show itself. A forgotten cell phone was Laura's breaking point.

Chase had sprinted to the end of the docks, but no man—or woman, for that matter—had been anywhere in sight.

On the other hand, his father knew *Madre* was docked in Beach Bay. The stranger, possibly dispatched by Dick or Oliver Daniels, perhaps wanted to ascertain that Laura was with Chase. Perhaps the intention wasn't to harm her, at least not in broad daylight, but to confirm Chase's story and regroup for the next step. If that were the case, Chase was more than relieved that *Madre* was back on open water.

"Chase."

His wife stood in the doorway. Her buttery blonde hair attractively tangled, she chewed nervously on her bottom lip, her eyes still raw and spent from her earlier tears.

"Did you have a nice nap?" he asked.

She nodded, remaining set in the doorway. Her timidity and vulnerability wrung his heart. Helplessness overwhelmed him, wishing he could make all the bad that had happened go away.

One hand on the wheel, he held out his free arm, beckoning her. "Come here, honey."

Her footsteps were swift. When she reached him, her arms slid around his waist. Chase pulled her close.

"I'm sorry. The way I acted earlier. My hysterics." She nestled against him. "I'm sorry."

"Nothing to be sorry for."

"I don't know what got into me," she whispered, her tone embarrassed. "I never carried on like that."

"You saw someone who frightened you. You were frightened when I ran off, that I would be harmed. You were worried. A wife being worried about her husband's welfare, what a novel concept," he quipped.

Chapter Twelve

Wind gusts assaulted *Madre's* deck, and rain pounded against her sides. A violent storm raged along the coast, nature's rampage forcing the vessel to dock at a lakeside marina in Fisherman Point, Maryland. The newlyweds, secluded for three days, barely noticed the outburst, spending their time talking, joking, and making love. Caught up in being with Chase, and enjoying being his wife, Laura forgot the stranger on the pier.

By dawn on the fourth day, although a light drizzle remained, the Coast Guard gave the "all clear" for travel. Chase was confident they would reach Sea Tower, the small town where his aunt lived, before dark.

Laura found him in the galley. His back to her, he was hunched over the bar, scanning a map. Coming up behind him, she pressed into his solid, muscular frame, her slender arms sliding around his waist.

"Remember the day we were married?" She laid her cheek against his shoulder. "I stopped at a pharmacy?"

He turned and faced her, wearing a wide grin. "You insulted my toothpaste. Claimed it wasn't minty fresh and you wanted your own."

She eased back and held up a thin, long rainbow-striped box with a torn lid. "I also got a few of these."

Chase fingered the box, focusing solely on the big, red print. "The 'ES' means extra strength?"

"Extra sensitive. Most home pregnancy tests instruct you to take it ten days after you sense conception."

His eyes widened. "Home pregnancy test?"

She smiled. "For two dollars more, and since you're not married to a cheapskate, I got the extra sensitive. Gives results sooner."

His features bore a blank, vacant stare. "Laura . . ."

111

Her grin faded. Perhaps, he had reconsidered. He realized that even after they were divorced, he remained tied to her, along with the real responsibility of providing for a child.

Anxiety replaced her enthusiasm. "The nuns at Saint Theresa's lectured us it only took one time," she said plainly. Saint Theresa's was the Catholic high school that Laura had attended. "For you and me, the first time was it."

Laura held her breath.

"You're kidding? Right?" he asked.

His expression remained blank. Dread crept through her. If he no longer wanted a child, she would raise and love this baby on her own. She and her child didn't need a man in their lives.

"I'm not kidding."

With one huge scoop, Chase enveloped her in his arms. "Hot damn!" He pulled away. "Oh, wait a minute. Here, sit down."

He pulled out a stool and nudged her to sit. "Are you sick? Throwing up? Any pain? You need vitamins, right? The first time, you say? Isn't that something? Did you have breakfast? What did you have?" His brow crinkled. "You didn't eat a granola bar, did you? They're all sugar and no nutrition."

Laura studied her child's father and sighed with relief. The man beamed.

"I'm not sick, or in pain, or throwing up. Nothing."

"Are you sure?" His thoughts came in a rush. "What's the first thing we need to do? I guess get you to a doctor. You got a doctor? Never mind, we'll get you one. When's the baby due?" The crinkled brow returned. "You probably won't know until after you see the doctor."

Laura gently ran her fingers through his hair. He was so adorable. He had to calm down. At this rate, the doctor would prescribe vitamins for her and Valium for him.

"I'm fine. I figure the baby's due around Christmas," she said.

"Should you take that test again? To be sure?"

"I took two. The instructions state I should take it again in two days. By then we'll be at Aunt Lonnie's, and I can see her doctor. A blood test will confirm."

"You mean you could be wrong?" His voice held a hint of panic. "Maybe you're not pregnant?"

If she were wrong, his letdown was evident. "I've had friends who've used this exact brand. I don't know anyone who had a positive turn out to be a negative."

"You're getting the best. The best doctor, the best hospital, live-in nurse. We'll get you the best."

"Chase, Aunt Lonnie will recommend a doctor. She won't send us to a quack."

Chase had spoken so fondly of Lonnie during the journey, to Laura his aunt already felt like her family.

"You haven't changed your mind?" Laura palmed her stomach. "I mean, sure, we're married for convenience's sake, but there will be a baby. You want to be part of the baby's life?"

His eyes held her. "You bet. I'm happy to be a father. I'm happy to be *your* baby's father. When we first discussed having this child, I told you I wanted to be part of my child's life. You want a divorce once we get to the bottom of who wanted to hurt you . . . "

" . . . because you shouldn't be stuck with a wife you only married to solve a sticky problem."

"But my child isn't a problem." He pulled her close. "I'm not going to bring a child in this world and move on whenever it suits me."

*

Many people, unfamiliar with the area, considered the Chesapeake a town on a bay. The Chesapeake Bay, a long water mass, stretched for miles with petite towns and major cities littered along the way.

Sea Tower was a tiny community filled with acres of trees and perfectly landscaped gardens, two-story, white picket fence houses, and cobblestone paths. Aunt Lonnie, older sister to Chase's late mother, was a slight, petite woman in her early sixties with short pixie-styled brown hair. She and her nephew shared the same sapphire blue eyes.

On a cloudy late afternoon, the three stood on Lonnie's white-painted porch passing around greetings, hugs, and well wishes.

"A baby, too!" Lonnie hugged Laura for the third time, then Chase. "I should have known you'd pull this, Chase," she scolded him affectionately. "I don't have a chance to recover from the news you're married, and you spring a baby, too."

"Aunt Lonnie, Laura and I want to stay in Sea Tower, at least until after the baby's born," Chase said. "Can you recommend a doctor? Laura hasn't seen one yet."

If Aunt Lonnie thought the couple showing up on her doorstep, out of the blue, and announcing an intention to stay in Sea Tower was odd, she didn't let on. "Of course, I can." She smiled at Laura. "Sea Tower isn't John Hopkins, but we have good people. Dr. Dora Silver. You'll like her."

She ushered the couple inside. Laura admired the house's style with its walnut hardwood floors and the living room's brick fireplace. She particularly loved the gigantic front porch, complete with swing and rocking chair. She saw herself on a sunny, pleasant spring day, sitting on the porch and rocking her baby.

Lonnie insisted they have tea. She must have sensed their visit, she told them, because she had apple/blueberry muffins fresh from the oven. The kitchen was homey with a bright orange glow burning in the small brick and stone fireplace. The fireplace added to the room's coziness. The cabinets and wall paneling were walnut, as were the round table and chairs.

Over tea and muffins, Lonnie wanted all the details, where the couple had met, married, why the big secret. Since Laura had been the company's bookkeeper, they had kept their relationship quiet, Chase concocted. They wanted their wedding the same.

"I never fantasized a big, flashy wedding," Laura said. She wasn't fibbing, either. A parade of bridesmaids and securing a small bank loan to purchase a designer gown had never appealed to her. "Our wedding was simple and perfect." She had always concentrated her efforts on the life afterwards.

Lonnie beamed, not hiding her excitement for them. "As long as you're both happy and the baby's healthy."

"We are happy," Chase said. "And the baby will be healthy. That's why we want to stay here. Sea Tower has a lot of good karma."

Dr. Silver had a ten o'clock cancellation the next morning. After snapping up the appointment, Laura and Chase set out in Lonnie's Toyota compact for a Chase Donovan-guided tour of Sea Tower. Extremely charming, Laura felt what he called the town's "good karma" instantly. The houses, nearly all like Lonnie's, were narrow, two-story colonials with similar wooden porches. Everyone had a garden, and with the onslaught of spring, was involved in the planting process. Rakes and hoes were left wherever they had dropped, waiting for the gardener, whether an amateur or professional.

They picked up Lonnie for dinner, a seafood house called, aptly, *Seafood Shack*. The most delicious crab cakes in all of Maryland, Chase promised his wife. He wasn't wrong.

Laura was exhausted. She headed for bed while Chase and his aunt took to the kitchen to end the day with a shot of Irish whiskey. Decorated in pink and white, the bedroom had a summer cottage feel. Laura struggled to stay alert, wanting to be awake when Chase came to bed.

She glanced at the clock on the night table; eleven p.m. Muffled voices from the kitchen drifted up the stairs. How long did he intend to stay in the kitchen? Was he avoiding sharing a bed with her? Since she was pregnant, perhaps he no longer saw a reason for being intimate with her. This was the larger of the guest bedrooms, but there were two smaller ones. Perhaps he was explaining to Aunt Lonnie why he needed to sleep in another bedroom. Yes, they had enjoyed each other, but their intimacy had a purpose. Making a baby.

She glanced at the small, round clock on the nightstand; eleven twenty-five p.m. Laura tried to keep her eyes open, but she was dozing . . .

Everything was dark. Rising through a fog, a haze surrounding her. Laura's senses were dull. Groggy, tired, she drifted into the shadows, the salty sea air tickling her nose. The gentle dipping— *Madre* swaying?—lulled her. The bed's weight shifted, and a hard form nestled against her back. An arm hooked around her waist and a protective hand rested on her belly. The body, snuggling beneath the bedcovers, was pleasantly familiar. Warm lips brushed her cheek. Even if only in Laura's dream, her husband slept with her tonight.

*

Chase was leaving for Philadelphia tomorrow. She wished he wouldn't leave Sea Tower, wished everything that had happened since the diner and the FBI were all forgotten. Except, of course, for Chase making love to her, her pregnancy, and their marriage. She wanted him with her, but Chase had convinced himself that the puzzle's answer remained locked in the warehouse files. He had also convinced himself that his job was to solve the mystery. He planned to gather whatever information he could, confront his father, then head back to Sea Tower and sort out the mess. Earlier, Dr. Silver had confirmed what the couple already ecstatically knew. Laura was pregnant.

Tonight Lonnie attended her book club meeting. The couple sat on the sofa watching a DVD, something featuring Kevin Costner and baseball. Their feet shared the ottoman, Laura sitting close enough so that Chase could wrap an arm around her shoulder. She enjoyed any excuse to snuggle against him.

He concentrated on the movie while she fought sleep. This baby really snapped her strength. Convinced she carried a boy, if the child made her this tired barely weeks into the womb, imagine how exhausted she would be mothering an energetic toddler. A DVD slow motion image of Laura, chasing a curly-haired little replica of Chase in fast-forward mode, gave her the giggles.

"I've been quiet for almost two hours. You can't be laughing at something I said," Chase chuckled.

"I'm tired. That's all." She noticed the closing credits rolling.

Pressing the remote, he turned off the television. "Ready for bed? Yes or no?"

She couldn't hold back her yawn. "I guess."

Chase stood, and the warm snugness she took pleasure in left her. He held out his hand, tugging her to her feet. Laura's legs, stretched in one position for too long, gave way, as if they no longer had the strength to support her, and Chase's hands were immediately on her waist.

"You need some help?" He didn't wait for her response. Sliding an arm around her waist and the other beneath her knees, he lifted her. "How 'bout a ride?"

"Sure."

With long, powerful strides, he carried her up the stairs. Laura closed her eyes, her head resting comfortably on his shoulder. Inside the bedroom, he sat her on the bed.

"I need some help getting undressed." A smile curled her lips. "You're the only one around to assist."

He grinned wickedly, his blue eyes blazing. Laura delighted at that look. Only when directed at her, of course.

"I thought you were tired," he said.

"You carried me up the stairs. I'm wide awake." She raised her arms. "Help me undress? You won't be sorry."

There was a long silent pause. Passion left his eyes, and his features took on a serious expression. "Laura, you're pregnant," he said, his tone flat.

Those words, with their deadpan tone, hurt more than any slap delivered. She was pregnant, no need to make love, no need to be close, no need to hold her.

Quickly, her arms came down. She need not embarrass herself any further. If that was desire she saw in his eyes, it was only there because she had wanted it to be.

"I'm sleeping in my clothes." She stretched out on the bed, turning her back to him. "Goodnight."

"Laura." He lowered his head, eyeing the hardwood floor. "I—I—you—listen—" Pausing, he inhaled, then exhaled loudly.

Tears stung her eyes. He didn't need to explain and cause her further humiliation. They had reached their goal. "I'm pregnant." She spoke to the wall. "I need to go to sleep."

She held her tears until she heard the door close.

When Lonnie woke Laura the next morning, Chase was gone.

Chapter Thirteen

The small commuter plane left on time. Before boarding, Chase had called a casino bartender he always tipped generously. The man agreed to meet Chase at the Atlantic City airport and drive him to Magic Lake Island. Chase's next call was to Mac. The security guard, who had been looking after the BMW, promised to be waiting when Chase arrived. Adrenaline pumped through him at full speed. His objective: get to Philly and get back to Sea Tower as fast as he could.

By mid-afternoon, Chase in his BMW exited the bridge connecting New Jersey and Pennsylvania. He drove along the expressway toward his father's warehouse. An acidic feeling wrangled in his stomach. Now that he was here, he hated being back in Philadelphia. He dreaded a confrontation with his father, who was bound to be a nasty son-of-a-bitch, berate Chase for getting involved, tell him shit about what was going on, and have a fit for Chase's marrying Laura.

Chase sighed. Maybe Laura was right. They should just let the FBI deal with this crap.

But his father was his father. Chase's conscience wouldn't just let him hand his father over to the law without knowing exactly what the old coot was involved in.

On the other hand, Chase's concern was protecting his wife and unborn child.

He missed his wife.

Laura. He recalled her peaceful expression that morning, her delicate form curved around him. The woman slept like the dead. Both nights, she hadn't even stirred when he had gotten into bed. Perhaps the heavy sleeping was from her pregnancy. He had chosen not to wake her this morning, and after a light kiss, he was off.

The grin tugged at the corners of his mouth, recalling the wantonness covering her dainty features last night. Even now, his lust stirred in all the right parts. They had made their baby, their mission accomplished. Chase had assumed their lovemaking days were over. Hadn't the first time been just a fluke?

Maybe it wasn't?

Could pregnant women have sex? Chase wished he had paid more attention to his high school biology. He considered the lunging, pushing, and thrusting could hurt the baby, and Laura's tender insides.

Maybe not?

Damn, when he returned to Sea Tower, they were having a serious conversation. He loved his wife, plain and simple. They had grown so close, were married, and were having a baby. She had said when the bad guys were in jail, when she was safe, she would give him a divorce. Those feelings, he knew, were because she felt he had forced himself to marry her.

Chase had *wanted* to marry Laura. He enjoyed being with her. Seeing her smile, hearing her laugh, holding her in his arms while they slept. He saw no reason why they couldn't have a real marriage, the life together, forever after, the whole shebang. Hell, the two aspects that his buddies whined they battled with their wives over, money and sex, Chase and Laura had covered. He had plenty of money, and they had great sex.

As the BMW cruised, Chase practiced the words "Laura, I love you," the manner, voice pitch, the perfect touch of emotion. Laura had to love him, he decided. He refused to believe her feelings for him were nothing more than gratitude.

He passed through the chain link gates and pulled his car into the cement lot adjacent to the Donovan warehouse. The lot was used for loading merchandise onto customer trucks, but right now it was empty. At three in the afternoon, the majority of workers had finished. Those who remained were foremen, security guards, and office workers.

An uneasiness crawled through Chase. Not sure why he felt the need, he opened the glove compartment, took out the handgun, and secured it in the back waistband of his jeans. His denim jacket hid the piece well. Despite having the permit for six years, the closest he had ever been to using the weapon had been the night he found Laura terrorized.

He climbed the stairs quickly and pushed open the glass door leading into the office. He was careful not to let it clang behind him. How strange seeing another woman sitting at Laura's desk, a willowy bleached blonde, her dark roots advertising a touchup was long overdue. Her fingers plugged at the keyboard.

"You must be the new bookkeeper," Chase said. The woman, several years younger than Laura, swirled from the monitor. "I'm Chase Donovan." He extended his hand.

Her stare crept over him, then she smiled. "Marla Baker." She shook Chase's hand, holding on a bit too long and squeezing a bit too hard. "Gee, I wish I had this job before her."

He took back his hand. "Excuse me?"

Her gray eyes had a sizzling glint, her smile an edge as her top lip curled higher on one side than the other. "If I had been the bookkeeper before Laura, I might be in her shoes today." The V-neck of her ruby red sweater plunged a bit too deeply for office wear. She leaned forward in her chair, giving Chase a view of her ample bosom.

"My wife's shoes?" His expression was stony.

"You know what I mean," she said with a wink.

He shook his head. "No, I'm afraid I don't."

Yes, Chase most certainly did get the meaning. And he wasn't interested. He had exactly what he wanted back in Sea Tower.

The woman pouted and eased back in her chair.

Chase nodded toward Dick's private office. "Is he in?"

"You didn't tell your father you were coming? He's in Florida."

A wave of relief washed over Chase. Breathing space. He had easy access to the files with his father gone. And their conversation would wait.

Again, Marla leaned forward. "I don't know when he'll be back." The tip of her tongue darted out and circled her lips. "You might have to stay a few days."

If nothing else, the woman was persistent. "I wasn't planning on staying more than a day," Chase said. "I'm still on my honeymoon. I have a wife who I miss, and I am anxious to get back to her."

"Chase Donovan!"

Chase and a glowering Marla turned to the doorway. Rachel, her streaked hair extra spikey, stood by the photocopier. She had a large white plastic bag, obviously having returned from a Rita's Diner snack run.

His smile was a simple one. "Hi, Rachel."

She placed the bag on Marla's desk and threw her arms around his neck. "I can't believe it! Are you really, truly married, or just pulling my leg? I'll tell you, I nearly fainted when I got the email." The day Laura had emailed Kate about missing a lunch date, Chase emailed Rachel requesting Laura's transfer from her own individual health care coverage to his.

He grinned. "Laura and I are married."

"Congratulations." Rachel pressed against Chase, a little too close for a congratulatory hug. He quickly backed away.

"Is she with you?" Rachel asked.

"No. Laura tires easily these days. You did take care of that health insurance business, right?" They had used his membership number with Dr. Silver's office.

Rachel nodded. "Is Laura sick?"

His father hadn't spread the news. "Laura's pregnant. We're having a baby," he said proudly. "My father didn't tell you?"

Rachel responded with a gaping mouth and a head shake. She was speechless. *Savor the moment.*

"Marla tells me my father's in Florida," he said, moving on.

"Meeting with a new orange broker. If you want to call him, I have contact information. He'll be home tomorrow night." She cocked her head to the side. "Laura's actually pregnant?"

"Sure is," Chase said. "I'll get Dad's number later. I want to use his office for some calls." He gave Marla a cordial smile. "Nice to meet you. Good luck with your new job." He turned toward his father's office.

As he closed the door behind him, Chase heard Marla say, "Damn! He's hotter than I heard."

Rachel snorted. "And I'll be a naked slut. In all the time Laura Roberts worked here, sitting right where you are, she barely spoke to Chase. It turns out, she was screwing him." Rachel's astonishment was clear; part shock, part envy. "She even managed to get herself knocked up."

"And married. Lucky bitch," Marla muttered.

Rachel's laugh was more like a snort. "More like smart bitch."

Chase scowled, having no patience for office gossip. And having gotten to know Laura, grow closer to her while they were docked during the storm, he understood why she and Rachel were civil office mates, but little else. Snippy chitchat wasn't his wife's style.

He didn't want to go directly to the file room and begin snooping around. So he snooped in his father's office. Nothing out of the ordinary caught Chase's attention. Dick's golf trophies on the top shelf of a mahogany bookcase needed a polishing. The bookcase held a backlog of farmer's almanacs. Chase never quite understood why the old man had them. He certainly didn't read them. Photographs hung on the wall, Dick with mediocre politicians and local sports celebrities.

He flipped through the day planner. Nothing unusual regarding the broker in Florida, a dealer that other area proprietors used. It appeared the trip had been planned for several weeks. Dick may have mentioned the jaunt to Chase. Many times, perhaps too many, he simply ignored his father's conversations.

After skimming the computer printouts, he pulled on each of the four desk drawers. He yanked harder on the last one and muttered a curse. He wasn't aware the drawers locked, let alone knew where a spare key was kept. Asking Rachel would arouse her suspicions.

He strolled back into the general office area. Both women were busy at their computers. He walked into the file room, a spare room with three four-drawer black metal file cabinets. His eyes grazed the cabinet's white labels. He was certain he'd never even been in this room, let alone looked in the file drawers. He hadn't a clue where to start his search.

Drawer one, cabinet one . . .

Chase thumbed through folders. The phones rang regularly with either woman answering and conversing, their tones either business or recreation. He looked for invoices to Daniels' produce business, or payables to Leisure Limo. He hoped to find an irregularity, something suspicious; anything questionable to challenge his father, a clue why the FBI harassed Laura. He pulled out Daniels' current folder when he heard Rachel's shout.

"Mr. Donovan! Chase is here!" she announced. "He's in the file room. Want me to get him?"

Damn it! Chase didn't want his father to know where he spent his time. Before the secretary caught him rummaging through Daniels' file, Chase shoved the folder into its proper place, closed the drawer, and exited.

Pressing the hold button, Rachel replaced the phone's receiver. "Your father's on three," she said with a full grin, expecting Chase to be happy about the call.

"Thanks." Chase walked to the desk next to Marla's, his desk whenever he decided to show up. He lifted the receiver and pressed the red button.

"Hi, Dad."

"Why are you in the file room?" Dick inquired edgily.

Chase's deceit came quick. "Can't remember if I submitted an invoice." He changed topics. "How's Florida?"

Dick wasn't deterred. "You don't need to poke through paper," he said, clearly not believing his son. "Marla can check the computer."

"Thanks."

"And you can always ask your wife. Is she with you?"

"Laura's feeling fine." Chase was conscious of the two women who were openly watching and tuned into the conversation. "She sends her love," he added.

"Is she with you?" Dick asked again, his tone sharp.

Once more, Chase overlooked his father's inquiry. "Laura tires easily, sleeps a lot. That's normal. The doctor said she's in great condition."

"I asked, is she with you?" Dick snapped.

Again, Chase ignored his father. "Don't worry. Laura and the baby are fine." Chase added purposefully, "I intend to keep them that way."

"There's nothing I want more than a healthy grandchild," Dick said.

"Healthy child and mother."

"Where have you two been?"

Chase persisted, careening off his father's route. "Rachel tells me you'll be home tomorrow."

"My plane arrives at six in the evening."

Chase was eager to return to his wife, but having exchanged these words with his father, he resolved to get their altercation over with, even if having their conversation meant being stuck in Philadelphia an extra day.

"How about if I pick you up at the airport?" Chase offered.

"Laura isn't with you, is she?" Dick spat. "Where do you have her stashed?"

The man was incredible. Chase could almost see the veins bulging in his father's neck, a general response when he was angry. "Laura will understand if I stay an extra day," he said, keeping his voice even.

Dick's tone hardened. "You were a fool getting her pregnant. If she's even pregnant." He grunted. "Marrying her makes you a bigger fool. If only you knew the problem you created for me."

Chase kept his features even. "Dad, call me on my cell if you want that ride. Have a good flight back." He hung up, unable to trust any more of his words to be cordial.

"Chase, your father had me order a car from Leisure Limo," Rachel said.

"If Dad wants Leisure to pick him up, he'll let me know."

Proper detective work was impossible with people around. He would return later. His father's absence provided easy access once the staff had left for the day. After an amiable goodbye to the two women, Chase headed out the door.

The bistro in Laura's condominium lobby served take-out. Having had only a fast bagel and coffee that morning while the plane had been given the once-over, he was hungry.

Conversations on *Madre*, and gentle bantering over coffee with Laura popped into his head. Passing the time with a burger and a phone call to her was definitely appealing. Maybe he wouldn't wait to say he loved her. Absence made the heart grow fonder. He would tell her now. His lighthearted steps quickened. Maybe she would say "I love you" back.

He reached his car and pressed the key ring's black box. The single beep signaled the car alarm off.

"Chase Donovan?"

The voice came from behind. Chase said nothing. Didn't even breathe. He turned slowly, deliberately, his arms relaxed at his sides. Two men, unmoving and straight-faced stood, both wearing jeans and dark down jackets. There wasn't a soul in the vicinity. Tension gripped Chase. Had Daniels' men been watching the warehouse? Waiting for him, or Laura, to return? Or maybe as soon as he had hung up with his father, the old man called Daniels, tipping him off that Chase was back. Cockroaches, even the human variety, were common around a produce warehouse. Chase feared these two had been hanging around, trying to find out where Laura was staying. One man looked familiar. Lou Kent? Chase couldn't recall.

"Chase Donovan?" the familiar looking man repeated.

Chase kept his features and demeanor smooth despite his heart's rapid pounding. "Yeah?"

The man reached inside his jacket.

His stomach coiling, Chase made an instinctive reach inside his jacket, behind his back.

There was no time to grab his weapon. The second man twisted Chase's arm behind his back, wrestling him to the ground. Pain shot through his wrist, scampering up his shoulder. He was roughly patted down, the gun snatched.

"Bastard has a gun," the man barked.

Chase lay face down with a hard, unfamiliar knee between his shoulder blades, suppressing his movements.

"Chase Donovan, you're under arrest," the man huffed, pausing as if waiting for a response. "Carrying a concealed weapon and threatening federal agents. You have the right to remain silent . . . "

Chapter Fourteen

The cell phone vibrated in Chase's jacket pocket. Face down on the ground and handcuffed, he wasn't exactly in the position to answer. By the time the phone joined his handgun in Special Agent Ross Saunders' pocket, the caller had given up.

At FBI headquarters, Saunders also confiscated Chase's wallet, watch, keys, and wedding band. Chase, anger seeping through him, dithered before removing the gold band. The metal slipping from his finger pissed him off the most. After fingerprinting and a photo op, he then exchanged his denim jacket, jeans and beige crewneck sweater for an orange jumpsuit.

Now he sat alone in a tight interrogation room, smaller than the warehouse's file room and even more oppressive. He leaned back in one of the hard, metal chairs, stretching his legs beneath the rectangular table. Irritation mixed with fatigue as Chase waited for that joke of an FBI agent to make an appearance. He hadn't seen Saunders since the man had dumped him in this room. They had taken his watch, there was no clock on the wall, but if he had to guess he would estimate he'd been sitting alone for about two hours.

Too late, Chase recalled at the slap of the cuffs where he had seen Saunders previously. He shook his head and sighed. An arrest for carrying a concealed weapon. More of Saunders' game playing.

Chase had the gun to defend himself if accosted, since he had always taken his Atlantic City winnings in cash. Of course, Chase kept the gun hidden. Five freaking minutes on a computer would give these dolts Chase's permit information.

He kept quiet. He would advise a client to do the same. Lucky enough to catch Ned Stahl before his friend had left his office, the only details Chase had given were to say he had been arrested and the name of the arresting agent.

Chase let out a deep sigh and ran weary fingers through his hair. His thoughts went to Laura. He was certain she had been calling his cell. When he didn't answer, he hoped she assumed his phone was out of range. He didn't want his pregnant wife to worry.

The door swung open, and a breathless Ned Stahl rushed in. Dressed in a brown Dick-Donovan-like suit, and not nearly as tall as Chase or athletically built, the dark-haired attorney slapped his briefcase on the table and scratched at his bristly beard.

"Chase, what the hell? They tell me you pulled a gun on two feds?"

"I didn't know they were agents. I thought they were looking to harm my wife."

"Your wife!" Ned's mouth dropped, his stare more horror-struck than amazed. "You? Married? When? Who?"

"I eloped two weeks ago. With Laura."

"Who's Laura?"

"My wife."

Ned's brows arched, then he frowned. "Suppose you tell me what's going on?"

"Suppose you tell me what those two jackasses told you?"

The agents, Ned repeated, claimed they had approached Chase outside the warehouse. They had questions regarding the disappearance of a woman, Laura Roberts. When Special Agent Saunders reached for his identification, Chase went for a weapon.

"The idiot didn't identify himself," Chase snapped. "I thought he was reaching for a gun."

"Saunders said you knew he was an agent. You two had met a couple weeks ago. In a diner."

Chase's eyes widened. "I saw him once. For two minutes," he said, his tone incredulous. "And he had on a suit, all G-man like. I'm expected to be carrying his face in my head like a twenty-five grand blackjack hand?"

"Was there anyone around to witness Saunders not identifying himself today?"

Chase shrugged. "I didn't see anyone, but that doesn't mean someone wasn't hanging out, grabbing a smoke." He explained where his BMW had been parked. "Who reported Laura missing? People knew we got married, my father, his secretary. Laura even emailed a girlfriend."

"Saunders said Laura had been under surveillance," Ned said. "About two weeks ago they saw her get into a dark car at the warehouse, but lost her. An agent saw her later with you, on your boat in Beach Bay. You returned to Philly without her."

Ned absentmindedly rubbed the back of a hand against his beard, which he generally did when bewildered. "Chase, what the hell's going on?"

Chase's brain cells shifted into overdrive. So someone had been watching *Madre*, but not one of Daniels' cronies. The FBI was watching Laura? If they lost her once she had gotten into the Leisure Limo car, how did they find her in Beach Bay?

His blood pressure spiked, a vessel near ready to burst. He clenched his fists. If Saunders had eyes on Laura, how the hell did he lose her? Why didn't he follow Ron Caldwell's car?

Chase jumped from the chair. The force and his anger so strong, the wooden chair crashed to the floor. "Laura was under surveillance? Where were these assholes when she got dragged on my boat to be raped and murdered?"

"W—What?"

The law prohibited the listening device to be in operation while Chase and Ned spoke, but Chase knew Saunders was watching. He stomped over to the glass and pounded his fist on the pane.

Fury and frustration overwhelmed him. "If you were watching her, you should have protected her!" Chase shouted. "You left her defenseless with those bastards! Where were you when she feared for her life? Why aren't you out there looking for those low lifes? No, you'd rather pester me!"

His final bang shook the glass pane. Ned clutched Chase's arm, breaking off his repeated efforts.

Ned put Chase's chair upright. "Chase, sit down." He took a sharp breath and shook his head. "Start talking. I want to hear everything. From the start."

"I want to call Laura," Chase stated firmly. "We haven't talked all day. She's pregnant. I have to call her." His final words were a steadfast plea.

Ned, reacting more as Chase's attorney than friend, was just as firm. "We'll talk first, and go on from there."

Disgusted, worried, exhaustion overwhelming him, Chase relented and sat down. This was all so insane. Ned settled across from his client and heard everything starting from when Laura had been escorted out of the diner.

Ned shook his head, amazed. "I always told my wife something crazy would get you hitched, but never did I envision this scenario," he said when Chase had finally finished.

Chase leaned forward. "What time is it?"

Ned glanced at his watch. "Almost nine o'clock."

Again Chase appealed to call his wife.

Ned frowned. "Let me see what I can do."

The attorney left the room, and returned a few minutes later with Special Agent Saunders.

"My client has a permit to carry the weapon you found on him," Ned stated. "Not only in this state, but New Jersey and New York. I'm sure you'll find that information if you check your computers."

"Computers are down," Saunders said indifferently.

"My client also tells me you failed to identify yourself," Ned said.

Saunders shrugged before speaking. "Didn't think it was necessary. Your client and I met before, but as a courtesy, I was reaching for my ID."

"I wasn't paying attention to you in the diner," Chase said, his tone tight. "I was concentrating on the woman you were intimidating. If I'm not mistaken, I believe your rule book requires you to have your identification out and in my face as you approach me."

Saunders expelled a breath as if bored. "Tell me something, Donovan. What is it you do at the warehouse?"

"Tell me something, Saunders. Why are you stalking my father's business?"

"Chase, let me talk," Ned chided.

Chase ignored his friend. "Why are you harassing my wife?"

"Where's Laura Roberts?" Saunders asked straightforwardly.

"Her name is Laura Donovan," Chase replied sharply.

Saunders tightened his lips. He didn't appear surprised or impressed. "What have you done with her?"

"Done with her?" Chase's groan was a caustic laugh. "Laura is with my aunt."

"Where? I need to speak with her," Saunders said.

Chase hesitated. If he told Saunders Laura was in Sea Tower, and how she had gotten there, an agent from the Baltimore office would be dispatched to Lonnie's. Maybe with a warrant to search the boat. They would find the remnants of Laura's encounter with Ron and Lou, and bombard her with questions. Chase was convinced she remained too distressed, her wounds still too fresh, to discuss the incident with the likes of Saunders.

"My wife is pregnant, and you stress her out." Chase sat back in his chair and folded his arms across his chest. "I'd rather you not bother her."

"I'd rather not believe she was fool enough to marry you," Saunders retorted.

Chase jerked out of his chair, fists clenched at his sides. "Look, you rotten—"

"Chase!" Ned cautioned, silencing his client. He grabbed Chase's forearm and pulled him back down. "My client and Laura Roberts are married." Ned relayed the date and place where Chase and Laura had married, and advised Saunders to check the courthouse records.

"Can't do until morning," Saunders said, almost as if annoyed the marriage was an honest-to-God possibility. "Sorry, Donovan, until we can get this permit thing straightened out and check the records in Beach wherever, you're a guest of the federal government."

Chase threw his hands in the air. "This is ridiculous!"

"So is you being married to Laura," Saunders said.

Chase felt smug. "It's a fact, Special Agent Saunders. Laura and I are married. We're expecting a child. We'll send you an invitation to the christening."

"Oh, I'll see her before then," Saunders said, stroking a clean-shaven chin with the back of a hand. "Your pregnant wife will have to show her pregnant self here, in my office."

Chase glared at Ned. "I see a pattern of harassment toward both Laura and me, don't you?"

Saunders sat easily on the table's edge. "This turned out nicely for you, Donovan," he said, his tone a sanctimonious one.

"What turned out nicely?" Chase asked, unable to hold back the bite in his own voice.

A wry smirk twisted Saunders features. "You marry the bookkeeper, get her pregnant, and then she can't testify against you. We bring her in for a few questions, and you take her on a boat ride. Out of our reach."

Before Chase snapped a retort, Ned interjected. "We're here because you arrested my client for having a firearm. Which he has a permit to carry."

"Permit or not, it's never a good idea to draw on two federal agents," Saunders said.

Ned wore his best courtroom demeanor. "And explain to me how we got from the insane charge you're holding my client on, to an insinuation he married his wife to keep her from testifying against him?" he asked. "Testify against him for what? If you're prepared to charge my client with another crime, do it. If not, keep the goading comments to yourself before I find something to add to the false arrest charge I'm filing once Mr. Donovan is released."

Saunders stood and set his hard features on Chase. "Look, Donovan, I've dealt with plenty of rich, spoiled brats like you over the years. Too much with your old man and you doesn't add up. We decide your bookkeeper has a tale to tell, she disappears, shows up with you on your boat in some hick town, then you show up back here. Without her and claiming to be married. What is it you don't want your bookkeeper telling me?"

Ned answered for Chase. "My client took his wife to meet his aunt. He returned to Philly for the day, and Mrs. Donovan chose to remain behind. When you interviewed Mrs. Donovan previously, did you advise her not to leave Philly?"

Saunders' lips remained tight.

Ned's easy smile was pompous. "In that case, Mrs. Donovan is free to go wherever she pleases."

"Why did you have Laura under surveillance?" Chase asked.

Saunders clamped his lips as if he had been provoked into saying more than he intended. After a pause, he spoke directly to Ned. "Laura Roberts, Laura Donovan or whatever she calls herself, needs to answer more questions. Your client, counselor, will be released when she walks into this building to do so."

Before giving Ned a chance to comment, Saunders stormed out.

Chase turned to Ned. "He does have a certain charm, doesn't he?" he asked with a sarcastic bite.

Ned disregarded his friend's familiar cutting wit. "Chase, what the hell is going on around here?"

Chase frowned. "I have no idea, counselor. Isn't it your job to find out?"

"How well do you know Laura? How much of her background do you know?"

Chase almost replied the truth; not much. "Why?"

Ned answered Chase with more questions. "Are you sure she told you the truth about her meeting with Saunders? That he kept her waiting? Asked a few crummy questions about merchandise? How do you know that she's not involved in anything criminal?"

Chase laughed. The suggestion was an asinine one. "Criminal? Laura? No way."

"Why? Because she's a pretty woman? Who was quiet? Because she came to work and did her job?"

"Because of how I found her on my boat. My father's behavior on the telephone," Chase snapped.

"All he told you was to not get involved with her," Ned reminded him. "To stay out of the situation. Your father's words are open to many interpretations."

Chase's response was a contemptuous scowl.

Ned leaned closer. "I'm not saying those actions on your boat weren't deplorable, or your father and this Daniels aren't involved in illegal activities."

Apprehension crawled through Chase. He wasn't clueless to Ned's implication.

Ned continued. "Suppose whatever's going down, Laura is a major player. So major she has the FBI watching her."

He waited for Chase's reaction. When all he got was a fixed stare, Ned went on. "Laura's role is so key the fed's interest makes somebody decide she needs to be disposed of. Your father, Oliver Daniels, whoever. They're afraid she'll cut a deal for herself and start talking.

"That's crazy," Chase muttered.

"You think?" Ned raised an eyebrow. "So involved is Laura that when you suggested you both get married and pregnant, she agrees. She knows you'll do everything possible to keep your wife, your child's mother, out of jail. You're an attorney. Plus, you got money, lots of it."

"No way," Chase said, shaking his head. Ned's theory was incredible. "Not Laura."

The attorney refused to give up. "From what you told me, it took you two minutes to convince her to marry you and have your child,"

Ned said. "I've seen firsthand your way with the ladies, buddy. Sure, you attract women like ants to a picnic. But be realistic. You said yourself that you and Laura hardly spoke in the office."

"I said we made general conversation," Chase corrected, aware the slight modification wouldn't deter his friend.

Ned continued honing his point. "You say let's get married and have a baby ASAP, and she agrees." Snapping his fingers, he added, "just like that."

Laura had been so excited to be pregnant. Chase had been relieved, although her reaction had puzzled him. He hadn't dwelled on her enthusiasm, but rather reveled in his own.

She had been putting on an act? No, it couldn't be. He didn't want to believe his sweet Laura, who he had fallen in love with—he, Chase Donovan, who never imagined wanting only one woman—was pure and simply playing him for a sucker.

Ned went on. "When you found her on the boat, she said no hospital. No calling the authorities. Maybe she didn't want to explain her own dirty deeds."

Chase quickly defended her. "After I talked to my father, Laura did suggest we contact Saunders. I nixed the idea."

"She suggested because she knew you'd refuse." Ned pursed his lips. "She gambled on you protecting your father."

This was nonsense. But unease nagged at Chase like those buzzing green-headed flies on Magic Lake Island.

There was Laura's rainy-day money. Was it really from a trust fund? Or was the money her share of a corrupt business arrangement with Dick Donovan and Oliver Daniels?

"You still want me to see if you call her?"

Silence hung for what seemed like eternity. Feeling a tightness in his chest, Chase thought the ache might be his heart breaking.

"Let's wait until tomorrow."

Chapter Fifteen

Laura recognized the name, Ned Stahl. Cooped up on *Madre* during the storm, Chase had amused Laura with college stories of pranks with his friends, Ned and Tom. Lonnie gripped the phone's receiver, and the color drained from her face. Laura clutched her stomach. Chase was injured. That was his reason for not answering his cell phone, and for not calling last night.

Oh, God, an accident had never occurred to her. She had assumed Chase was apathetic about speaking with her. Her mind ran with speculation. Ron and Lou had caught him. The man on the pier watching *Madre* had returned. Or Daniels or whomever—they couldn't get Laura so they hurt Chase.

Lonnie replaced the receiver. "Laura, Chase has been arrested," she murmured, her tone incredulous.

Laura felt her insides tighten. "What?"

Lonnie explained the events that had Chase in a federal jail cell. Laura needed to return to Philadelphia and secure his release.

Relief that Chase was physically intact, evolved into a simmering anger. Any thoughts of the man on the pier disappeared, and she targeted her ire at Special Agent Ross Saunders. Laura was convinced the man hassled Chase to spite her. If she remembered whatever the agent was so certain she knew, she would surely tell him. Saunders wasn't as terrorizing as the men who had dragged her on *Madre,* but his constant threatening presence was as disturbing.

Lonnie drove the Toyota into Baltimore, and the two women caught a late morning train. Laura caressed her cell phone, smiling, remembering the evening Chase had given it to her. He had been so thoughtful. Perhaps he didn't love her, but he did care about her. That he was locked away like a two-bit thug tore Laura's heart.

She dialed the phone number Ned had given Lonnie.

"Ned Stahl," the voice answered.

After introducing herself and inquiring about her husband's welfare, Laura gave the attorney the time their train was due.

Clipping her phone to her jeans, Laura thought Ned sounded aloof. She shrugged off her qualms. Not only was he Chase's attorney, but his friend, and the detached manner Laura had heard was preoccupation with Chase's circumstances.

Scarcely two hours, the train ride felt like two long, tedious days. Tears stung Laura's eyes. The minutes must have hung for Chase as he sat in a jail cell. She bit back her fury toward Saunders. Why wasn't he looking for the men who had abducted her? Who Chase was convinced were still after her?

Unless Chase hadn't given up Ron and Lou? Hadn't told what had occurred on *Madre*? Why not? Was he sacrificing himself to protect his father?

The women stepped from the train car and onto the cement platform. Lonnie pointed to the stocky, bearded, dark-haired man standing by the escalators.

"Laura," Ned said, with a fast nod after Lonnie had made the introductions.

Anxiety coursed through her. "How's Chase?"

"Jail's not fun," he replied, his tone curt.

As the group walked from the train station, through the parking lot to Ned's maroon Ford sedan, he explained Chase's situation. He directed his comments to Lonnie. Laura speculated Ned spoke to Chase's aunt because they were familiar. He offered Lonnie the front passenger seat while seating Laura in the back. He conversed with Lonnie, telling her Chase had conveyed the details of the past two weeks. To Laura's knowledge, Chase's aunt wasn't aware of what had led the couple to Sea Tower. Nevertheless, Ned continued his dialogue with the older woman, overlooking Laura completely.

By the time Ned drove the sedan into the parking lot across from the federal office building, Laura's suspicions had been confirmed. Either as Chase's attorney or Chase's friend, Ned Stahl did not like Chase's wife.

Ned marched the women through the revolving door, stopping for the portly navy-uniformed security guard. The attorney then led the way to the bank of elevators where an available one, doors spread, waited. He pressed the floor button and the elevator ascended upwards. They were the only three people in the car.

"When can I see Chase?" Laura asked.

Ned looked at her briefly, before turning back to the panel of floor numbers. "You'll have to see Saunders first."

"Laura, are you feeling okay?" Lonnie asked, putting a protective arm around the younger woman's shoulders.

The baby demanded a nap. "I'm a little tired," Laura sighed. "I want to pacify these people, get my husband, and get out of this city."

The elevator doors opened. A man leaned casually against the wall. Tall, light-haired, California surfer type, in his early thirties, he straightened when he saw them.

"This is Kevin Woolfe." Ned made the introductions all around. "Laura, Chase wanted me to sit in while you spoke with Saunders, but one attorney representing you both might be perceived as a conflict of interest. Kevin is a former associate. You're in good hands."

Kevin smiled. "That's a sincere compliment coming from you," he said to Ned.

Fear gripped Laura. "Chase wants me to have an attorney. Am I being arrested?"

"No, not at all," Kevin said. Exchanging some legalisms with Ned, Kevin appeared up to snuff on events. "It's never a good idea to speak to a federal badge without an attorney."

From that very first day, when Chase had intervened, he had wanted Laura to have an attorney. She had refused, convinced everything was a misunderstanding. Misunderstanding or not, the situation grew worse with each passing day. She wished she had listened to Chase that day in the diner and allowed him to accompany her.

"I'll show you where you can wait," Ned said to Lonnie, taking her elbow. "Laura, Kevin will take you to Saunders."

Kevin lightly touched Laura's back and guided her down the corridor. "When will I be able to see my husband?"

"Let's go talk to Saunders," the attorney replied.

The agent's office was simple and efficient. Desk with computer. A beige four-drawer file cabinet. There was nothing to personalize the room. No family pictures on his desk. No paintings on the wall. Not even an accommodation plaque.

All day Laura had been piloting on a combination of fear, annoyance, and despair. Upon seeing Saunders, the man who had turned her life upside down, she seethed. Breaking her stride with Kevin, she headed straight for the agent sitting behind the desk and studying a computer monitor.

"Tell me, Special Agent Saunders," she blew up. "Have I done something to personally offend you? Have you and I met before? We were reincarnated, and in a past life I rejected you? Got ahead of you in line at the grocery store? Dropped a frog down your pants as kids? What? Because whenever some grievance befalls me, you're at the center. Now you're picking on my husband."

Saunders, taken aback, rose from his chair. Laura stood before him not as the timid, anxious woman he had ushered from the diner. She displayed her personality's feisty, fighting side that appeared whenever she was pushed to her limit.

Kevin, having caught up, stood beside his client. "Laura, I'm your attorney. Let me talk."

"Yes, Miss Roberts. If you have an attorney, I advise you to listen to him," Saunders said.

"It's Donovan!" she snapped. "Laura Donovan. Mrs. Chase Donovan." She took a deep breath, considering the baby. After a calm exhale, she continued. "I'm told you want proof of my wedding to Chase." She took a paper from her purse along with two snapshots. "Our marriage certificate and two pictures."

Saunders took the items. The official document stated Laura and Chase's names, date and place of marriage, appropriate signatures, including officiator and witnesses. Of the snapshots, one showed a black-robed, balding judge pronouncing the couple husband and wife; and the other was a simple photo taken afterwards. The newlyweds smiled, facing one another, arms wrapped around each other. They had held each other so tightly, she remembered. As if each had been afraid of losing the other. This picture was her favorite.

Saunders glanced at the objects and handed them back. "No picture of Donovan kissing his bride?"

Kevin spoke quickly, cutting off Laura's hostile remark. "My client has provided documentation proving she and Chase Donovan are married," he said. "You stated you have follow-up questions from your prior meeting. In everyone's best interest, Special Agent Saunders, I suggest you ask your questions, release Mr. Donovan, and allow my client and her husband to return to their honeymoon."

There was a long pause before Saunders nodded, indicating the room with the opened door. "In there."

Laura and Kevin followed the agent into the room, a small dreary, windowless area with a square table and four chairs. Kevin pulled out a chair for Laura. Once she was settled, the two men each took a chair. Kevin sat next to her; Saunders across from them.

"Where have you been, Mrs. Donovan?" the agent asked.

Laura hesitated, guarded more over his reason for the question, than the actual question. "Why?"

Saunders shrugged. "It's a normal question."

She glared at the man. "Nothing is normal where you're involved."

Kevin cut in. "When you interviewed my client, did you charge her with anything? Advise her not to leave the area?"

"No," Saunders replied grudgingly.

"In that case, my client has the right to go anywhere she pleases," Kevin said. To Laura, he whispered, "Tell him where you've been."

Laura lingered with an answer, hoping the pause annoyed Saunders. "Honeymooning on my husband's boat. We stopped in Sea Tower. It's a town in Maryland along the Chesapeake Bay. His aunt lives there." Didn't Chase tell Saunders? Or had he? And the agent checked to see if their stories matched?

Saunders leaned back. "Laura, I have nothing against you. Honestly. It's not your life I want to make miserable."

Her expression twisted in a sneer. "Could have fooled me."

He ignored the comment. "I suspect some questionable activity at the Donovan warehouse, and I believe you can provide information."

"What kind of—questionable—activity?" Kevin asked.

Saunders paused. "I'm not at liberty to say. Our investigation remains ongoing."

"Last time we met, I answered all of your questions truthfully," Laura said.

However, Saunders asked her the same questions as before, regarding the company's merchandise and invoices, and Laura gave him the exact same answers. Her temples started pounding.

"How much of our conversation did you tell Chase Donovan?" he asked.

She looked at Kevin, and he nodded for her to answer. "Everything. Chase was as confused as I was. He was concerned over your inquiries, why you were bothering me."

"Laura, do you know who owns the produce company?"

"Dick Donovan."

"And his son," Saunders informed her.

"The corporation papers are only in Dick Donovan's name," she said. Both Donovan names were on the warehouse lease, Laura knew, to allow Chase to make maintenance and tenant voting decisions in his father's absence.

Kevin looked directly at her. "Doesn't matter, Laura. The business can still be in both names, father and son."

Laura shot him a stinging glance. "Whose side are you on?"

"This isn't about sides," Kevin said. "My job is to represent you. Advise you and look out for your interest. Not your husband's. He has his own attorney."

"Listen to your attorney, Laura," Saunders said with a triumphant chin tilt. "Everything the Donovans have, they own together. The business. The fancy house in the suburbs. Their bank accounts. Their cars. Everything is in both Donovan names. Even Chase's boat."

"You have evidence?" Kevin asked.

A phone sat on the table. Saunders pushed a button and spoke into the speaker. "Bring me the Donovan File B."

Laura felt dizzy. She had been too anxious to eat lunch, and her stomach was queasy. *Donovan File B* indicated more than one Donovan file. Was there a separate file entirely on Chase? Kevin seemed to surmise where Saunders' implications were leading. The fact Laura was clueless frightened and unnerved her.

A dark haired woman in her late fifties, wearing a black tailored skirt and jacket, brought in a manila folder. She handed it to the agent. Saunders looked through the contents before sliding the opened folder across the table. Both Laura and Kevin examined the papers together. Tax returns for The Produce Market, bank statements, deeds, and titles, including the title for *Madre*, all in the names of Richard Chase Donovan, Jr. and Richard Chase Donovan, III—Dick and Chase Donovan.

Saunders leaned forward and rested his folded arms on the table. "Your husband doesn't own a thing by himself, doesn't have a personal pot to piss in. If the Donovan business went down the tubes today and all the assets seized, your husband would be flat broke. Left without a cent." The thought of Chase being penniless seemed to make the agent happy.

Despite the churning in her stomach, Laura held her own with Saunders. "Are you saying my husband married me for my money?" she asked caustically. "I'm not exactly an heiress."

Saunders pursed his lips, then spoke. "What I'm trying to tell you is we've launched an investigation into Donovan business dealings. And your husband may have his hand in the cookie jar, so to speak. Isn't it rather advantageous to suddenly marry a woman we bring in to help us gather evidence?"

Kevin's tone was even. "How about bringing evidence against Chase Donovan, rather than your speculation, to the table?"

Saunders paid the attorney no mind, and continued. "Laura, how did you and Chase come to marry? Did you have some dates? Where did he take you? How long were you seeing each other? Whose idea was it to marry?"

Laura remained quiet. Her brain beat against her temples.

Saunders persisted. "You and Chase are both Catholic, right? No church. No priest. No fancy gown. Why not, Laura? Who put together your wedding?"

Laura wasn't surprised to know Saunders was aware of Chase's religion, but hers? What else did the agent know about her? The sudden wedding? Did he know the idea belonged to Chase?

She clutched her stomach.

"Every woman wants the long walk up the aisle, her girlfriends as bridesmaids, right, Laura?" Saunders prodded.

Her fingertips brushed her throbbing temples. "That never mattered to me," she whispered.

The agent went on. "You're wearing jeans at your wedding, not even a dress."

Laura remained silent, feeling her insides knot. A cold sweat tickled her brow.

Saunders snickered. "To top it off, you went and got yourself pregnant."

"You're out of line," Kevin said in the same tone of voice a television district attorney would call out, "objection."

Saunders ignored Kevin. "Laura, what do you intend to tell your kid about Mommy and Daddy's wedding day?"

She stared at the agent, the knot in her stomach crawling upwards. He made her relationship with Chase sound sneaky, dirty, and underhanded. "I need to use the ladies room. I feel sick."

She thought Saunders' face held genuine concern as he spoke into the telephone speaker, calling for a woman named Judy. Judy, the woman who had brought in the folder, escorted Laura.

The facilities were across the corridor from Saunders' office. Laura declined Judy's offer to stay, insisting she only needed a short break. The woman hesitated, but eventually left.

Laura stood over the toilet, and eventually, the urge to vomit passed. She washed her hands and patted her face with cold water, the icy wetness a cooling relief.

She understood Saunders' insinuation. Whatever criminal Dick Donovan was a party to, Chase was also.

Laura cringed. She hadn't heard Dick's end of the telephone conversation with Chase on *Madre*. That exchange had led to a marriage proposal.

Being their bookkeeper, Laura hadn't paid much attention to the relationship between Chase and his father. Not until her current state of affairs did she became aware of tension between them. That animosity apparently bore no interference where money was concerned. Or was their dissension a ploy for her benefit?

If whatever criminal activity the Donovans were involved in was ready to surface, what better way for Chase to keep track of Laura's visits to the FBI than by marrying her? Better yet, keep her away altogether with a boat ride down the Atlantic. The law stated a wife couldn't testify against her husband, and Laura would never send her child's father to prison.

Chase was an attorney, a non-practicing one, but one nonetheless. He was aware of loopholes. What better insurance to keep Laura quiet than to be her child's father? Hadn't he continuously insisted she was aware of what the FBI wanted, but just couldn't recall? He had been trying to get her to remember. She assumed to help her, but perhaps to help himself. She recalled Saunders prodding her into the back of a car. *That was the kid*, he had said referring to Chase. While Saunders had been watching Dick Donovan, had he kept his eyes on Chase, too?

Perhaps Chase's kindness was no coincidence. He was smart where women mattered, conscious of pushing their appropriate buttons. Laura had been vulnerable, and he pushed hers, making her depend on him. To even fall in love with him.

Perhaps it wasn't fate that had Chase showing up to save her. He had devised a way to silence her without killing her.

Chapter Sixteen

Chase tossed his long legs over the side of the bunk. He hadn't slept during the night, but merely switched his stares from ceiling to wall. He was accustomed to a thicker, firmer mattress, and the narrow cot was missing the luscious body he had enjoyed holding against him. Until his wife, it had never occurred to Chase that a woman curled around him in sleep was so pleasant. He closed his eyes, feeling Laura's soft, silky breast brush up against his arm, wishing she were real and not just a memory. Chase didn't need to make love to his wife to be satisfied; feeling her sleeping pressed against him was just as gratifying.

Ned's accusations popped into his head. Disgusted and angry—additional reasons sleep had eluded him—he remembered why he had given up the law. One became suspicious of everything and everyone, even a wife he loved.

Being the only prisoner in the cellblock did have some advantages. Hearing the clang of the steel door opening, Chase knew he was getting a visitor.

Ned peered through the bars. "You gotta admit this sure ain't the Four Seasons."

Chase stood up, stretched his arms overhead and eased out the kinks. He walked to the cell door. "Welcome to my humble abode."

"You're mighty comfortable," Ned said with a dry grin. "Such a shame. They're doing the paperwork to spring you."

"Laura?" Chase asked anxiously.

Ned nodded. "She was here. Kevin Woolfe, the attorney I got her, told me she showed up with your marriage certificate, and a couple of photos."

"She met with Saunders? How'd it go?"

"I wasn't asked to sit in, and you know Kevin can't discuss anything with me. You'll have to talk to your wife. Your Aunt Lonnie's with her," Ned added.

Relief flooded Chase; thank God for his aunt. "I hoped Laura wouldn't travel alone."

"Listen, they couldn't wait for you," Ned said. "Laura felt sick with Saunders. Kevin said she was as white as a sheet."

Chase muttered a curse aimed at Saunders. "Did Aunt Lonnie take her to the hospital?"

Ned waved the concern away. "Chase, I got kids, been through this three times. When women get pregnant, they eat, sleep, puke, and cry about their hormones. Laura's fine."

Chase's spirits perked. Yeah, Ned had been through this pregnant thing multiple times and with happy, healthy babies and a healthy wife being the result. What better person to ask for advice on mood swings, hormones, pregnancy sex . . . inquire delicately, of course. But this didn't seem like the time or place. The conversation could wait until Chase was out of here and assured Laura was okay.

"By the way, they're at Laura's condo," Ned said. "You married a woman you're barely acquainted with. Do you know where her condo is?"

"The Square." Laura had a condominium in the stylish Rittenhouse Square section of the city. "She gave me her key in case I planned to stay in Philly overnight. But Saunders took care of my lodgings."

"Detaining you, the interrogation, Saunders and his pompous routine was bull." Ned's lips twisted in a sneer. "Let me know if you want to file anything against the creep."

"This was more Saunders' game playing, another fishing expedition." Chase ached to put his arms around his wife. He never realized missing another human being hurt so much. "I'm too tired and hungry to figure out what's going on at the warehouse, and I'm not putting Laura through any more stress."

Chase also wanted to get Laura back to Sea Tower before his father realized she was in Philadelphia.

"Which by the way," he began.

"What?"

"That bullshit last night about Laura being involved in my father's nonsense, you're wrong." Chase stared without a flinch. "I know you were doing your job as my attorney, but I don't want to hear that crap from my friend."

"I was looking out for your best interest. As your attorney and friend," Ned added. "You seemed to consider my suggestions."

"I know my wife." Laura involved in anything unlawful, that she had brought on her own violent attack, was outrageous. "It's this damn, crazy place. Puts extreme thoughts in a person's head."

"Regard the subject closed," Ned said.

"What time is it?"

Ned glanced at his watch. "A little after six. You've been here almost twenty-four hours."

Chase considered another dilemma. His father, who was aware of his son's file search, had returned to Philadelphia. If anyone had caught the scene with the two agents, and surely if Rachel knew, Dick was bound to get wind of his son's arrest. Chase was certain that whatever he had hoped to find among the invoices was no longer there.

*

Lonnie stood at the foot of the bed holding a pack of crackers. "Try some of these."

Laura, her body curled in a spoon position on her mauve chenille bedspread, shook her head. Of all the ills she experienced so far with being pregnant, nausea hadn't been one of them.

Until Saunders.

The overwhelming urge to heave lingered. Although she wasn't quite sure Saunders was entirely to blame. She tried to shake the feeling, the nagging instinct refused to go away. Could Chase be involved in criminal activities? And his attention and concern for her a ploy?

"Are you sure I can't bring you tea?" Lonnie asked. "I noticed you have blueberry in the cabinet."

Laura shook her head at the woman's umpteenth offering. Nothing Lonnie suggested made her feel better, leaving Lonnie feeling helpless and Laura feeling guilt-ridden.

"Thanks, Aunt Lonnie. You're the greatest." Laura managed a tender smile. "I can see why Chase loves you so much."

"When it comes to my nephew, the feeling is mutual."

Laura relaxed back into the pillow. "Sit with me?"

Lonnie sat on the bed's edge and took Laura's hand. "Do you want to tell me what that agent man said to upset you?"

Laura let out an exhausted breath. "Where should I start?"

"You pay these people no mind. They play head games."

"Chase said something to that affect."

"Whenever Chase has something intelligent to say, he takes after his mother's family. Remember that." She patted Laura's hand.

"Aunt Lonnie, Saunders implied Chase is involved in something illegal with his father," Laura said softly. "That he married me to keep me from testifying against him."

The words poured out. How Laura and Chase came together, their decision to be husband and wife. Relief gushed through Laura as she detailed her initial meeting with the FBI, her resignation from The Produce Market and all that had followed. Lonnie listened with quiet patience, alternating between patting and rubbing the back of Laura's hand tenderly.

"Chase told me while we shared my whiskey. I didn't let on because I wanted you to tell me when you were ready." Lonnie's features echoed sympathy. "Laura, I can't even begin to imagine how terrified you were on that boat."

"If not for Chase," Laura took a deep breath and choked back tears. "I can't believe he was all an act." She paused. "Or maybe I don't want to believe."

"What exactly did Saunders say?" Lonnie asked.

Laura repeated her earlier conversation with the agent. When finished, she felt drained. "Kevin Woolfe seemed to agree," she said. "His face gave him away. He and Sanders. They're both suspicious of Chase's motives for our marriage."

Lonnie clutched Laura's hand. "They don't know the whole story. When Saunders asked how you and Chase came to be married, what did you tell him?"

"I felt sick and asked to leave. I didn't want to tell him about Mr. Donovan arranging my ride from the warehouse, what happened on the boat." Apprehension returned. "They already had Chase locked up. I didn't want to add fuel to Saunders' fire."

Lonnie's voice was strong. "The idea that my nephew is doing anything criminal, I can guarantee, is the most absurd thing ever suggested."

"But why is Chase protecting his father? I don't understand their relationship. They're not like any father and son I know."

"Chase reacts to his own guilt," Lonnie said. "He feels guilty because he doesn't like his father. One minute he'll call Dick all kinds of vile names, deservingly so. The next minute Chase feels remorse, and he goes out of his way to make it up to the old coot."

"What about all the assets being in both names?" Laura asked. "Everything is either in the name of the business or owned jointly by Chase and his father."

"Probably so if one of them dies, and my preference is Dick go sooner than later, the survivor doesn't have to pay an inheritance tax."

Laura was a bookkeeper with a shrewd proprietor for a boss. She should have deduced his motives.

"I wonder if Chase knows this, that his father owns the boat with him," Laura mused aloud.

"Maybe not." Lonnie's expression was half smile, half frown. "I love my nephew but his comprehension of anything having to do with money, is that it should be there when he wants it."

Laura silently recalled Chase on their wedding day. He had been determined they would marry that day. With everyone, from the lab tech who drew their blood to the jeweler who sized their rings, Chase had generously tossed whatever cash had been needed to ensure he got what he wanted.

"Chase sometimes pretends his father is a nice man," Lonnie added. "Then an incident occurs like what happened to you, and he struggles to admit Dick Donovan is plain no good."

"Saunders was so convincing."

"That's his job." Lonnie's voice was warm. "Laura, any difficulties you and Chase have, I know you can work out for yourselves." Her eyes twinkled like Chase's when he was in high spirits. "I have to tell you. You bring out a side of my nephew that warms my heart."

Lonnie paused. When she started to speak again, her voice held a twinge of sadness. "Sometimes watching Chase grow up was heartbreaking. He so much wanted a real father, a father who was patient, loving, a man he could be proud of and who would be proud of him."

Her tone grew bitter. "Instead Chase got Dick Donovan, who is intolerant, indifferent, and all-around narcissistic. When Chase was about ten, he started bringing home stray dogs. Dogs that were malnourished, a couple were notably abused. Chase was so gentle and tender with each dog. Feeding it, promising that everything was going to be all right. The dog had a home now. Chase was so happy he was saving the dog."

Lonnie was quiet, no doubt remembering the past, then pursed her lips. "Dick would come home from who knows where. The warehouse. Some business trip that I sometimes wondered if the trip was really about business. Not even noticing or caring that Chase had love invested in the dog. That bastard would grab the dog, insist there was no place in their lives for a filthy mutt, and cart the dog away. Chase would cry for days."

Laura felt compassion for the sensitive child who'd become attached to another living creature only to have the dog taken from him.

"Then Chase would find another dog," Lonnie went on. "Take it home as if his father's reaction to the previous one hadn't happened. Dick would take that one, too. Dick had taken three dogs before Chase realized his father's actions weren't going to change."

Lonnie shook her head as if the motion would shake away the dreadful memories. "Chase would sometimes idealize his father, almost in total denial of Dick's lousy character. Watching that boy deceive himself . . . " She paused then smiled. "When Chase is with you, Laura, he doesn't pretend he's happy. He is."

Laura was afraid . . . for herself and for Chase. Was he so desperate for his father's affection that he would cover up Dick Donovan's crimes or even be a part of them?

"Aunt Lonnie, I have so much to sort out. When Chase gets here, please tell him I'm asleep. I don't know what to say. Or what I'm feeling. Until I do, I'm afraid to see him."

*

Chase's BMW had been seized as evidence. He suspected Saunders' cockamamie arrest had actually been a ploy from the beginning, just an excuse to search the car. Chase smiled as visions of an angry and frustrated Saunders, discovering the car was clean, pranced before his eyes. Once the charges against Chase had been dropped, the car was released to him.

Darkness had fallen long ago, and he noted the time on the dashboard clock. His first stop was the condo, to check on Laura, and give her a gigantic hug, then head to the warehouse for a showdown with his father. A perturbed feeling inched through

Chase. Recent events had him anxious for that go-around. Dick Donovan's plane had landed about an hour ago, and Chase knew the first stop would be the warehouse. Dick lived for the place.

He drove the BMW downward into the condominium complex's underground garage. Laura had an assigned parking spot, B17, her unit's number. Since she didn't have a car, she had told him to finally put the long-vacant spot to use. He introduced himself to the attendant at the garage window, and pointed out the BMW. The elderly man, with sparse white hair and thick black-rimmed glasses, congratulated Chase on his marriage. Laura was a sweetheart, the man insisted, and Chase was a lucky man.

The middle-aged, frizzy-haired woman who worked the reception desk passed on the same sentiments. Laura was a living doll. Chase agreed wholeheartedly.

He took the elevator to the second floor and searched the oak-paneled doors for the gold-plated, B17. Using the key, Chase let himself into the unit. Decorated in ivory and green with mahogany furniture, Laura had told him the unit was small, but cozy. The condo was quiet, so quiet that Chase wondered if the women were out.

"Laura. Aunt Lonnie," he called.

Lonnie emerged from behind an ivory painted wall, a dishtowel in her hand.

"Oh, Chase! Chase." Her arms went around him, and they bear-hugged one another.

"Interesting couple of days I had," he said with a light laugh. He was determined to put the lousy disposition aside while with his wife.

"What a mess, such a mess." Lonnie drew back from Chase. "Your father." She shook her head, distain apparent. Dick had that effect on her. "You know how I've felt about that louse all these years. I don't even want to discuss him."

Neither did Chase.

He needed to see Laura, to hold her. Perhaps because of the

negative thoughts Ned had planted in his head about her, or perhaps because Chase had even considered them, he needed to feel Laura in his arms. To reassure her, and himself, that they were in this mess together and everything would work out.

"Laura's sleeping. Don't tell me," he said with a good-natured chuckle. "Which way's the bedroom in this joint? Ned said she wasn't feeling well. She's better, right? Probably just tired, I bet."

He waited for an answer. Lonnie's fingers, wrapped around his forearm and held him in place.

"She's fine. Chase, let her sleep."

Last night he had gazed upon Laura in his dreams. His heart beat rapidly, eager to look at the real deal.

"Point to the bedroom. I won't wake her. I'll sneak in, give her a quick kiss, and sneak back out."

"Chase, let her sleep. Come into the kitchen," Lonnie coaxed. "You must be starving. I'll fix you something."

Panic gripped Chase. "The baby? She's in the hospital, isn't she?"

"No. Laura's fine. The baby's fine." Lonnie took him in her arms, hugging him and rubbing a consoling palm over his back as she had done whenever his father had taken one of his beloved strays to the shelter. "Let her sleep. It's been difficult for her."

Chase pulled away from his aunt. "She can join the club." His miserable nature returned, overtaking his brief previous panic. "I want to see my wife."

Lonnie held firm. "Chase, listen to me."

He gritted his teeth. *Why was his aunt keeping him from his wife?* "What the hell? Laura," he called.

"Chase, leave her alone. She doesn't want to speak to you."

Clenching his fist at his sides, his agitation rose. "She doesn't want to speak to me?" His voice was a growl. "What's that mean? I spent the damn night in a jail cell for her."

Lonnie kept her tone and demeanor even. "Chase, Special Agent Saunders said some awful things regarding you, and Laura needs to sort them out."

"Me? Like what?"

Lonnie shook her head. "It doesn't matter. He confused her, and she needs some time alone."

Chase pursed his lips. "What did that bastard say?"

She paused. "Laura's afraid you married her to keep her from testifying against you."

Chase's blood boiled. "That's crazy. Testify against what?" he barked. "I didn't do anything." His lips compressed, forming a single line, then he sighed. "Saunders is blowing smoke. Laura believed him?"

"She needs to rest and think."

"I'll take that answer as a yes. Laura!" he shouted, taking a step toward the first closed door he saw.

Once more, Lonnie grabbed his arm. "Leave Laura be, Chase."

Chase roughly shook off his aunt's grip. Clasping the door handle, he rattled it hard.

The door was locked. "Shit!" His fist banged hard. "Laura, open the damn door!"

No answer, and the door didn't open.

His heart crumbled. Seeing Laura, putting his arms around her had kept him afloat these last miserable hours. Pain knifed through him. He was tired, angry, hungry, and fighting like hell to keep the wretchedness in check. Since leaving Sea Tower, he had been dying to tell her he loved her. He prayed that she loved him. He had married her to help her. He had feelings for her. Damn it, she truly thought some selfish, devious plot motivated his actions.

"Laura!" He pounded on the door again.

The voice on the other side was muffled. "Go away."

He was long past exhaustion, and the last ounce of his resolve disintegrated.

"Laura! Open the door!"

No sound, not even tears.

He banged so hard the door shook. "Open the damn door! Now, Laura!"

"Go away," she said, her tone warning. "Or—or I'll call Saunders."

Chase spun around to his aunt. Fury masked his hurt and whatever words popped into his head exploded out of his mouth. "The woman's nuts. I'm married to a head case."

"Chase!" Lonnie scolded.

He decided he was a fool. "I spent the night in a jail cell, on a cot that was harder than a linoleum floor. I couldn't sleep, wrestling with Ned's suspicions that maybe Laura wasn't the innocent victim she pretended to be. Maybe she was a partner in my father's bullshit and what I walked into on my boat . . . " He smiled cunningly. "What do they say? You reap what you sow, and she was getting what she deserved."

Lonnie gasped. "Chase Donovan, Laura—"

Chase was drained, wounded, insulted, and most of all, defeated. His heart had been ripped and stomped on.

"Aunt Lonnie, I'm worn out. I'm sick. Sick of my father. Of his deceit. His schemes. All I've done for Laura," he said, his temper hitting its peak. "First, she believed I was part of the scheme to kill her. Now, she thinks I married her and got her pregnant to save myself?"

"Chase," Lonnie pleaded.

His eyes narrowed. "Everywhere I turn, there's hysterics for me to deal with. I'm tired. I'm tired of her, her lack of trust, her moods, her hormones . . . " His heart beat hard. Laura didn't believe in him. The thought stuck in his craw. "I'm sick and tired of everything."

He tossed the key on the coffee table, pulled open the front door, and stepped into the hallway. Lonnie ran after him. She stood by the unit's door as Chase strode to the elevator.

"Chase Donovan, you be a man and listen to me," Lonnie called sharply. "I always prayed the day wouldn't come when I'd see your disgusting father in you, but I obviously haven't been praying hard enough."

A comparison to his father halted Chase, and he turned back toward his aunt.

"All you did for Laura? You did what you did for you." Lonnie's eyes, vibrant blue like Chase's, blazed a wrath he had never before seen. "You didn't want to admit Dick was capable of doing such a horrendous thing to Laura. You didn't want to send him to jail, which is where he belongs, then have to live with your regret. No amount of looking the other way will ever alter what your father is. He's a selfish, devious bastard."

Chase was unmoved and his aunt continued, her anger uncompromising. "If you wanted what was best for Laura, you would have taken her to the nearest hospital and called the police. Sent them straight to your father's doorstep," she hissed. "Gotten Laura the professional care she needed. Not taken her down the Atlantic like Huckleberry Finn. Or talked her into a marriage when she was too disorientated to make a coherent decision. To top everything, you bring a baby into this mess."

Chase stood, taking in words he didn't want to hear.

"Laura was traumatized." Lonnie unleashed her fury in full force. "You didn't help her cope. You helped her pretend it didn't happen, just like you pretend your father isn't a poor excuse for a man, like you pretend he didn't hit your mother, my sister. I'm so grateful Michelle's not alive to see the Dick Donovan stunt you pulled. You didn't make this about Laura. Like your father, it's all about you," she finished, her angry eyes dueling hard with his.

Chase waved away his aunt's comments and her asinine thoughts. The elevator doors opened and he stepped inside the empty car, riding alone. There were no polite words to the staff he had greeted warmly mere minutes ago. Chase got behind the BMW's wheel and sped away.

Chapter Seventeen

"Chase, it's Aunt Lonnie. Laura's with me in Sea Tower. Please call the house," she pleaded.

Taking a long swallow from his beer bottle and stretching out on the hotel's king-size bed, Chase listened to his cell phone's voicemail again. For the past three days, his aunt had left similar messages. After storming out of Laura's condo a week ago, he had headed straight for Atlantic City. He was grateful Laura was safe in Sea Tower, but quite frankly he didn't want to deal with either woman. Aunt Lonnie's calls weren't returned.

"Damn it, Chase!" his father barked into the voicemail. "Where the hell are you?" His tone had the same stern pitch as messages left during the journey on *Madre*. "Call me!"

Chase didn't want to speak with Dick either, but for a different reason. Once the hostile words poured out, Chase knew there was no taking them back. He ignored those calls, too.

His emotions see-sawed between hurt and bitterness. Hurt, because he had fallen in love with Laura. If she didn't believe in him, then obviously her feelings didn't mirror his. In his dealings with women, Chase had always been ready to give a woman his body. But, with Laura, he had also given her his heart.

Which brought about Chase's bitterness. He had put her back together physically and emotionally. His care had meant nothing to her. She had chosen Saunders' words over Chase's actions.

At times, he wondered if Aunt Lonnie's sentiments held an iota of truth. That he had come to Laura's aid to ease his own conscience and his own guilt for the torment his father had caused.

On top of everything else, he felt like a putz, the biggest bastard on God's green earth. He had a baby on the way. A baby whose conception had been his idea. A baby he had promised to take care of. Only he didn't know how to deal with the child's mother and so he stayed away.

Add helplessness to Chase's list of emotions. He didn't deal well with the struggle between his feelings and his conscience.

Whiling away in Atlantic City, Chase drank, gambled, and hung out with whatever acquaintances he met. Days turned into weeks, his activities a feeble attempt to pretend he didn't have a wife with a child on the way. And that he didn't miss them so much the ache hurt like hell.

*

Today was July 4th, yet the air held an autumn nip. Her belly rounded by her fourth month of pregnancy, Laura pulled on the too-snug denim jeans. She needed to add maternity jeans to the shopping list. After running a brush through her long, loose hair, she slipped a white cardigan sweater over her blue cotton T-shirt.

"Aunt Lonnie, I'm heading out for my walk," Laura called.

Lonnie was in the kitchen baking her famous apple/blueberry muffins. "Enjoy," she shouted over the hand mixer's buzz. "We'll leave for the park around eleven." They planned on attending the county's holiday picnic.

Laura stepped outside and inhaled the briny sea air. Despite the chill, the sky was clear with the sun shining. She enjoyed her daily walks, benefiting for another reason other than the exercise was good for her pregnancy. She always found herself walking to the marina. She relished sitting on *Madre's* deck and watching the boats sailing along the Chesapeake, seagulls soaring overhead. Being on *Madre* reminded her of happier times with Chase, and calm, happy thoughts made for a calm, happy baby.

Weeks apart had turned into months. No phone call, no letter, not even an email on Aunt Lonnie's computer. Chase had no intention of discussing Saunders' insinuations with her. Or listening to her concerns. When their relationship had gotten tough, when Chase realized he had better things to do than deal with her, he bailed.

She felt safe in Sea Tower. Despite Chase's indifference toward her, she doubted he'd tell anyone where she was staying. Even Aunt Lonnie agreed. Chase had a lot in his head to sort out, she insisted to Laura. But he wouldn't do anything to jeopardize her safety.

Probably so. But what the heck had she been thinking marrying Chase? Maybe she had been feeling the loneliness. It hadn't even been a year since her mother had passed away. Then Jack left. And her best friend, Kate, had gotten married.

An image of Chase's smile flashed before her eyes and how she had enjoyed being with him, how he had made her laugh with his self-deprecating sense of humor. She thought of how captivating he was, how he cared for her at the lowest point in her life.

Having a baby? It wasn't as if Chase had twisted her arm. She liked the idea of a baby. Laura had never actively wanted or pursued a career in business. Before working as Dick Donovan's bookkeeper, she had been the business manager of a gift shop that had closed when the economy hit a snag. While collecting unemployment, she saw the ad for The Produce Market online. The warehouse environment was far from fancy. But after three weeks of being without a job, she was bored staying home and bothered by collecting a check for doing nothing. She was grateful when Dick Donovan made his decision quickly to hire her. All in all, her job was just that, employment to pay the bills and keep her busy.

Besides her dream of an antique shop, what she really wanted was a home, a family, the PTA. Perhaps being on the boat with Chase, the romantic ambiance of their situation, she saw herself on the road to her dream. Instead, what she got was a quick dose of reality.

And a baby.

As she strolled along the green tree-lined streets, Laura placed a hand on her rounded tummy. She loved this tiny person growing within her. At night, she lay in bed, her arms wrapped around her belly. She embraced the baby inside her, soothed by its presence. She cared for and nurtured this being. This child was her life.

Her eyes narrowed as her blood pressure rose. For her baby, she was angry at Chase. No matter how he had felt about her, he had a responsibility to his baby. What had he said about not walking away from his child? Those words spoken, right now to Laura, seemed like empty ones.

As she started up the pier's steps, she got a whiff of the fishy breeze blowing from the bay. The water was bathed in sunlight. Today was the holiday. Boats crowded the marina, but Laura was surprisingly alone as she strolled the concrete and wood pier.

Her eyes caught an empty space in the water along the dock's edge. One sole, lonely, vacant space looked out of place. She continued on at a casual pace, then stopped horror-struck. *Madre* was missing. Someone had stolen Chase's boat. Her throat went dry, her heart raced. She half walked, half ran to the office.

She pulled open the glass door and ran in, breathless. Tammy, the college student who did clerical duties, was alone at her desk. Stirring her coffee, she looked up with a smile, then went back to stirring. She was oblivious to a pregnant woman's red face and agitation.

"*Madre*, my husband's boat," Laura gasped. She paused for a deep breath. "It's missing. Our boat's been stolen."

Still stirring, Tammy shook her head, her long, cascading, sun-streaked hair swaying with each movement. "It's not stolen. When I got in this morning, I saw your husband. He said he was sailing to Magic Lake Island. Didn't he tell you?"

Laura stared incredulously. Chase had been to Sea Tower? He had taken the boat. The boat she loved, where she quietly sat, gazing out onto the bay. Where she found heavenly peace.

Mumbling a thank you, Laura slowly walked back to where *Madre* had stood. The letdown coursed through her, and she gaped at the swishing blue water. Chase hadn't come to see her. Tears stung her eyes. All these weeks, she had been telling the baby his daddy loved him. Only Chase had returned to Sea Tower, but not for Laura or their child.

Her emotions rollercoastered. Laura realized that within her heart she had been hoping he would return, and they would work out their difficulties. If not for her, for the baby. But he hadn't and was truly gone from their lives.

She began crying, silent, gentle tears. Her knees unsteady, she sank to the ground. The boat was gone. Chase was gone. She felt cold, then numb. The sun blazed. It was July. Why was she freezing? Her quiet tears evolved into gut-wrenching sobs.

She gasped, feeling as if a hand clasped her throat, squeezing. Air. She needed air. Her stomach hurt and the pieces of her broken heart pounded rapidly. She struggled to get air into her lungs. Terror sprinted through her. The baby . . . her baby . . . her baby needed air.

She dug into her sweater pocket, pulled out her cell phone and pressed two numbers. She couldn't remember. What was Aunt Lonnie's phone number? If her tears stopped, she could breathe, the baby could breathe, but Laura's sobs only increased. Her body shook and a pressure crushed her chest. She gasped.

One single digit. On speed dial. One.

*

Chase sat on *Madre's* deck, barefoot, dressed in red sweatpants and a white crewneck sweater, and leisurely watched the sunbathers lounging on shore. He twisted the cap off his second beer and took a long swallow. Nippy for a beach day, but the sun stood out clearly in the blue sky. Bored with cavorting in Atlantic City, Chase had wanted his boat and charted a plane to Sea Tower. After taking care of business in the office, he began sailing up the Chesapeake toward New Jersey. One hour later, he docked at the marina in St. Martin, coming up with some fancy words to get a spot for the weekend.

His cell phone chime jolted him out of his thoughts. The sound was an unfamiliar one. He had been keeping the phone off, but Mac had promised to call if the Magic Lake marina got a summer cancellation.

Chase flipped up the cell's lid. A tension crawled through him. Laura's number. After months of not speaking, his heart skipped a beat simply seeing her cell phone number. What did she want? How the hell should he behave? What should he say? He had been proud, getting in and out of Sea Tower undetected. Maybe his self-congratulatory pat-on-the-back had been premature.

The phone continued ringing. He relented and answered.

"Laura," he said evenly.

She half screamed, half cried, and he barely understood her words. Until Laura's anguished voice had paralyzed him, Chase had forgotten a promise he had made to her. To keep her safe from his father and Oliver Daniels. Fear tightened his chest, his initial reaction that Ron, Lou, Oliver Daniels himself had gotten her.

Her sobs were heavy. She was at the marina . . . he took the boat . . . she couldn't breathe. *She couldn't breathe.* Her distress sliced through him.

Chase willed his voice to sound calm. "Laura, listen to me." This was a holiday weekend! Wasn't someone around to help her? "I'll get you help. Laura, I—"

Her phone went dead.

Chapter Eighteen

She was pale and her eyes fluttered occasionally, but Laura slept without incident. An IV contraption was taped to her left arm. What had he been thinking, staying away? He had kept his distance because he hadn't known what to say. He hadn't known how to apologize and didn't want to feel the pain if she refused to forgive him. What if she still wouldn't forgive him?

Well, he was certainly starting out to be one helluva marvelous father, he chastised himself. His child didn't ask to be brought into the world. Laura didn't even ask for his child to be brought into the world. Conceiving a child had been Chase's idea. With good reason—he believed—to protect her. Along with his own desperate reason, to forever be a part of her.

And what did he do? He walked out on them both, forgetting what he had promised the baby, and Laura. Aunt Lonnie's words ate at him. Chase had turned into his father's son.

Perched on the edge of the tapered hospital bed, Chase gazed at his wife's tired, pallid, but beautiful face. He had been staring at her as day turned into dusk and now night, refusing Aunt Lonnie's insistence he take a break. He feared Laura would wake up and believe he deserted her again.

Her eyes flickered, then slowly opened.

"Laura? Can you hear me?"

"My baby?" she whispered, a hand clasping her stomach.

"The baby's fine," Chase assured her, patting the delicate limb cradling her stomach. "You're fine. You had an anxiety attack. You and the baby are both okay."

"Are you sure?" Her voice was no more than a croak.

"Yes. They did some tests, an ultrasound. Baby's fine."

"Thank God," she murmured, closing her eyes.

Chase had already done that a dozen times. "You need rest."

She opened her eyes again. Husband and wife were silent, each looking intently at the other.

"You took the boat," she accused.

"It's my boat."

"My baby was conceived on that boat."

"The child gets bragging rights," he teased. "Nothing else." His smile, he hoped, eased the tension.

"I can't believe I called you," she muttered, her tone seemed laced with regret.

"I'm glad you did."

The few-second pause seemed like hours to Chase. Laura merely stared at him as if trying to decide if she should tell him to leave. He hadn't removed his hand, both their hands caressing her abdomen and their baby.

Silence again before tears welled in her eyes. "My baby. Chase, I was so scared."

"I know, honey. Me, too."

"Why do I have these attacks? It's so strange," she said, her voice shaken.

"You've had a lot of strange stuff happen lately." Idiot that he was, he had forgotten any lingering emotional concerns from her trauma on the boat. Those feelings could have influenced any interaction she had with Saunders.

He looked at her for a long moment. "We'll get through this."

She glanced down and saw his wedding ring. Her head jerked up, her green eyes incredibly wide. "You're wearing your ring."

"I'm a married man." During these weeks, he had attempted several times, clasping and pulling, but couldn't bear sliding the ring from his third finger.

"Unless you're planning on changing my status anytime soon," he added. Not giving her a chance to mull over his offer, he took her ring from his sweater's chest pocket. "You were still wearing yours. The nurse gave your things to Aunt Lonnie." That she had been wearing her own ring all this time gave him hope.

Holding her appropriate hand, he slipped the ring on her dainty third finger.

"I'm a bit old-fashioned. A pregnant woman should have a wedding ring," she said softly.

Chase felt the letdown. So much for hope. "How about some water?" He wasn't giving up.

She nodded eagerly.

Chase propped the pillows, enabling her to sit up comfortably. A white plastic pitcher and cup sat on the nightstand. After filling the cup halfway, Chase slid his arm around her shoulders, holding her against his chest. He held the cup to her lips. Laura was where she belonged, in his arms.

"Thank you." After drinking her fill, she relaxed back into the pillow. "I'm kind of hungry. Where's my dinner?"

"Running through your veins."

Seeing the plastic bag hanging on the pole, Laura screwed her face into the adorable frown Chase had missed.

"I'd rather have a granola bar," she said.

"Dr. Silver wants you to stay tonight. For observation." He returned the cup to the nightstand. "Tomorrow, we'll get you better food."

"What time is it?"

"After eleven."

Her eyes widened. "In the evening?"

He melted in those bright green glitters staring back at him. "In the evening. Whatever they gave you knocked you for a loop."

"Where's Aunt Lonnie?"

"Once Dr. Silver told us you and the baby were fine, I convinced Aunt Lonnie to go home."

"How did I get to the hospital?"

"I called Sea Tower's emergency station," he said. "By the time the paramedics arrived, the couple on the boat next to *Madre* had found you. They rode with you to the hospital."

"That was nice of them. To ride with me," she murmured. "They don't know me. Except for seeing me on the boat."

"On the boat?"

Laura explained her walks. "I sit on *Madre's* deck and rest, then head back. When I saw the boat wasn't there, I guess I overreacted." She spied the cot in the corner. "What's that?"

"For me. I rushed from St. Martin. You don't expect me to sleep on the floor, do you?"

"You're staying?" she asked, her eyes wide.

"That's my plan."

"For how long?"

"As long as you want me to." He added a silent prayer that she not ask him to leave.

She leaned back into the pillows. "Chase, what you said to Aunt Lonnie at my condo. I told the baby you didn't mean those harsh words. You were angry with me, but you love him."

Chase arched an eyebrow. "Him?" After the ultrasound, Dr. Silver hadn't said anything about the sex of the baby. Had Laura had a previous ultrasound and knew they were having a son?

"The baby's a boy. A mother knows these things."

"Boy or girl, whatever . . . I love this baby."

"Then how could you just walk out on him?" Her eyes narrowed. "Not call all these months?" She made no attempt at hiding her disgust. "You didn't have to talk to me if you didn't want to. You could have spoken to Aunt Lonnie. You came to Sea Tower and left with your boat, but didn't bother to call and ask how your child is doing?"

"I'm not going to try and defend my actions." He paused, trying to find the words to explain his juvenile behavior. "When I walked out that day, I was angry. But you're right. There's no defense. I made a promise to you and the baby."

Chase's own eyes welled as the overwhelming realization hit him. The baby inside Laura, *his baby*, was a real human being. Chase had been given a gift, entrusted with the sacred responsibility of helping a child become everything he was capable of becoming. He would love their baby unconditionally, regardless of the child's talents, or feats. He would encourage his son's hopes, and ease his fears, respect the child's personality and individuality. He would be a much better father than the one he had.

His assurance came without hesitation. "You don't need to worry. I plan on being a good father to our baby."

She frowned. Then with a sigh, she closed her eyes and drifted back to sleep.

"And I'll be an even better husband to our baby's mother," he whispered.

*

After a meticulous examination from Dr. Silver the following morning, Laura was released. She was starving, having only picked at the slushy eggs and floppy toast the hospital called breakfast. Chase heated canned New England clam chowder and made grilled cheese sandwiches. The couple ate on the patio while Aunt Lonnie went food shopping, probably for items she didn't need, but wanted to give the couple alone time.

Laura listened politely, while Chase talked of how Sea Tower had grown over the last few years. She had spent the last several weeks, hoping he'd come back into her life. Now, he was here. And she didn't know how to feel.

Perhaps she had only thought herself in love with Chase. Working in the office, she had been fascinated by his good looks, polite manners and disarming casualness with everyone. Then, a trauma brought them together, a nightmare from which he had rescued her. He had showered her with attention, charm, and his self-depreciating sense of humor. He laid next to her, pressed his hot, sexy body to hers . . . and she couldn't cast sole blame on him . . . she had wanted a child.

Either way, whether she was in love with the man or not, he was here. And intended to stay. Or so he said. Laura needed to believe him for the baby's sake. She also needed to be cordial to him. Again, for the baby's sake. Sniping was juvenile and counterproductive to good parenting. So Laura would be easygoing with her baby's father. Probably was also a good idea for her to guard her heart.

Chase's main duty within his father's business had been schmoozing new customers. As they sipped their iced tea, Laura suddenly understood why. Obviously, he also feared circumstances and their time apart would make being together awkward and worked quickly at putting those qualms to rest. As he undoubtedly did with a new business prospect, Chase kept the dialogue easy and relaxed, as if they were having a meet-and-greet lunch.

Later that evening, with Aunt Lonnie, they sat on the front porch and enjoyed the evening's fireworks display. Sea Tower had a tradition of getting carried away when it came to celebrating the nation's independence. The town's fireworks festivities lasted three evenings.

Now, after having showered and changed into her yellow nightshirt, Laura slid between the cool, white, cotton sheets in the comfortable queen-size bed.

"I came to say goodnight."

Laura looked up from propping the two bed pillows behind her to see Chase leaning against the doorjamb. A light glimmered in his eyes, then his mouth curled a little higher on one side.

Why did he have to be so damn handsome? As he strolled into the bedroom, she ignored his grin and pulled the sheet up over her chest.

"You heading back to the boat?"

He shook his head. "No, I'm sleeping in the room across the hall."

"Oh." She couldn't think of another response and hesitated telling him she was glad he was staying.

"Are you sure you didn't overdo it today?" he asked and sat on the edge of the bed. "Too much activity?"

"Chase, I moved from the back patio to the front porch," she replied with a frown. "You wouldn't even let me walk upstairs. You didn't have to carry me."

"Just being careful."

"Chase, did you know your father owns *Madre* with you?" She needed to say something, anything to keep her mind off his warmth so close to her. Saunders popped into her head first, followed by Dick Donovan.

"Tax purposes. How did you know?"

"Special Agent Saunders." She relayed Saunders knowledge regarding the Donovan financial situation. "Aunt Lonnie told me how your father came into the business."

"I'm sorry I missed her colorful version." He chuckled. "Aunt Lonnie hates my father."

Chase's maternal grandfather, John Lambert, had founded The Produce Market. Chase's father had been warehouse foreman when he met the boss's daughter on her college spring break. Once Michelle Lambert had become Michelle Donovan, Dick became more a part of the business. He inherited the entire production when Lambert passed away shortly before Chase's tenth birthday.

"Aunt Lonnie was kind," Laura said. "She said her father had only carried local produce in season, but she credited your father with bringing in fruit from around the world."

"Aunt Lonnie, kind, and my father in the same breath? Was she drinking Irish whiskey when you had this conversation?"

Laura thought, then smiled. "As a matter of fact, she did put a shot or two in her tea."

They laughed, then Chase grew serious.

"So Saunders looked into the bank records," he mused aloud

with a frown. "And came up with this idea I married you to keep my money and stay out of prison." He paused. "Well, first, Saunders has to prove whatever illegal crap he suspects my father's into, then he has to prove I'm involved. He also has to prove I'm totally broke without my father's assets. Which I'm not, and I'll have a good laugh when that suit ends up with egg on his face."

Laura wished she had kept her mouth shut, hoping she hadn't torched their peaceful harmony by bringing up Special Agent Saunders, the FBI, and what had torn Chase and her apart.

"Your finances aren't my business," she said in an effort to end the discussion.

"You're my wife. My money is too your business," he stated firmly. "I'll tell you something that nobody else knows—not even the almighty Saunders."

She was curious. "What?"

"I have two private bank accounts, a checking and a savings where I deposit my gambling winnings. I have a credit card only in my name. All the statements come online," he confided. "My father's convinced I'm totally dependent on Dick Donovan's money. Saunders is convinced I'm totally dependent on Dick Donovan's money." Cheerfulness clipped his voice. "I would just rather *spend* Dick Donovan's money."

"Why did Saunders say what he did? Why you married me?"

"He believes it. Hoped to play us against each other," Chase suggested. "Or he hoped you'd give up information you were withholding if you thought I was using you."

Yes, she had been hurt that he walked out on her and the baby. But recalling what led up to his desertion, and her refusal to talk to him, reminded her of what had made him angry. He had been raked over the coals by Saunders. She, of all people, knew how that man could intimidate.

"Honey, listen to me," he said softly. "When you were with Saunders, you were scared, confused, pregnant . . . all of the above."

He swore softly at himself. "I shouldn't have run out on you."

"I should have talked to you. Been mindful that you had spent a night in jail." Her eyes filled with tears. "Oh, these damn hormones."

His hand tenderly touched her silky hair. "Laura . . . "

"On the boat, those days were the best in my life," she whispered, sniffing back tears. She spoke the truth. "I forgot why we were sailing to Aunt Lonnie's. Those men who attacked me, the danger." She paused a thoughtful minute, then continued. "Sitting at the table across from Saunders, looking at him, listening to him . . . it all came rushing back." Her throat felt thick and she remembered how scared she had been that first night on the boat until Chase had held her, convincing her everything would be all right.

As if reading her mind, he took her hand and squeezed gently. "At the condo, I should have stopped to consider your condition, how Saunders operates . . . instead of reacting to my own frustration," he said.

"I was wrong for locking you out. Telling you to go away," she said. "What kind of wife does that?"

"I was wrong for stomping out, acting like a toddler who couldn't have his favorite toy," he said. "I should have gone for a walk, gone to a bar for a beer or something, cooled down. Then came back."

"It was as if *Madre* had been a pleasant dream. Seeing Saunders brought back the nightmare reality."

The back of his hand, that had been stroking her hair, now wiped the tears from her cheek. "I don't know where we go with Saunders and this nonsense my father's wrapped up in. I never got to finish looking through the warehouse files. Maybe I can hire a private detective."

Her heart pounded in her chest. "A detective will want to ask me questions," she said quickly. "About that night on the boat." Telling a stranger what those men had done to her, how they had put their hands on her and fondled her, was too embarrassing.

Chase took her hand in his, entwining their fingers, and squeezed gently. "Well, right now my priority is your health and the baby."

"Nothing's more important than the baby." She smiled. "I can't wait for him to get here."

"Me, too," he replied, returning her smile.

She grew serious. "Chase, we need to promise each other something. Right now."

"What?"

"If we have a dilemma, if one of us is upset, we have to talk. No hiding anything. Tell each other what we're feeling."

Chase frowned. "Laura, that's such a girlie-girl thing," he moaned, then a tiny grin pulled at his lips.

She knew he was teasing. "Chase!"

He chuckled. "Okay. Okay, we talk about everything."

"No hiding anything. Everything out on the table. It's the only way we're going to work."

"You want us to work?"

"We're having a baby, aren't we?"

"Yes, we are." He smiled. "May I kiss the baby goodnight?"

"He's your baby, too," she said, her voice low and tender.

Chase leaned over and his lips brushed her belly through her nightshirt. An indescribable emotion enveloped her, his gesture just so sweet. She recalled the first time he had kissed her there, the first time they had made love.

"What's that, fella?" He pressed an ear to her stomach.

Chase looked so comical with an ear pressed to her body. Laura couldn't help but laugh.

"Say that again," he said to the curved belly. "I didn't hear you. Your mother's laughing at me."

"Sorry," Laura whispered.

Chase remained with his ear against her, an intense expression covering his handsome face.

"Thanks, pal. Goodnight." He kissed her belly again.

"What did he say?" she asked as Chase lifted his head.

"Never you mind. That was a man-to-man conversation with my son."

Chapter Nineteen

Chase smiled whenever he thought of Laura's words. *Those days were the best in my life*, she had said regarding their time on *Madre*. That was how he had wanted her to feel because he felt exactly the same way. With a little work and a lot of effort, they could get to where they were before Special Asshole Saunders had resurfaced in their lives. The fact that Laura hadn't kicked Chase out on his ass when she found him in her hospital room gave him courage. That they were talking and enjoying this time together inspired him. He had hope for their future.

So what if they were an unconventional couple? Most people dated, married, and then got pregnant. Chase and Laura got pregnant, married, and now dated.

He continued sleeping in Lonnie's spare room. He had hurt Laura with his words, broken his promise to keep her safe, and walked out on her and their baby. He didn't want to insinuate himself too quickly into her life. Chase needed to work to win his wife back. His plan was to take it slow and woo her.

Last night he had taken her to dinner at the *Seafood Shack*; the night before, they had enjoyed a picnic concert in the park. Although this afternoon, pulling Lonnie's Toyota into Dr. Silver's parking lot, Chase and Laura had planned a rather atypical activity for a dating couple. Laura was scheduled for a follow-up ultrasound.

She flipped through the pages of a magazine in the white-painted waiting room. Chase sat in the chair beside her, nervously tapping a sneakered foot. When the technician called Laura's name, she tossed the periodical aside and stood. Chase remained seated.

"Aren't you coming?" she asked.

"Fathers allowed?"

"If they want. Please come." She held out her hand.

Chase wanted immensely. Laura went into a side room and changed into a white hospital gown. He waited in the examining room, investigating all the technological thingamajigs. When she joined him, he lifted her onto the table. Chase loved looking at his wife. Her hips curvier, her belly rounder, she carried their child inside her, and that was oh, so sexy. His hands lingered on her waist longer than necessary.

Her eyes twinkled, her grin enhancing her usual radiance. "We're about to see our baby," she whispered.

What an awesome experience!

"You want to put your ear to my stomach and talk to the baby, *now*?" Laura laughed, flat on her back, as the technician spread the sticky substance over a bulging belly.

She was still teasing Chase when Dr. Silver came in. In her late fifties, tall with salt-and-pepper hair knotted on the top of her head, she made a few pleasantries before passing the magic wand over her patient's saturated abdomen. Laura grabbed Chase's hand as the parents-to-be watched their baby on the gray monitor, rocking back and forth.

The baby's upper body was in full view. The head, mouth, eye sockets, the right shoulder leaning toward them, all perfectly formed. Chase laughed, unable to resist pointing out that the baby curled on its side, positioned just like Laura when she slept. Although undetectable on the screen, Laura was positive the baby had Chase's blue eyes.

"This is one healthy baby we're looking at," Dr. Silver said. "Heartbeat is strong."

"Thank God," Laura whispered.

Yes, siree, thank you, God, Chase silently echoed Laura's gratitude. No lingering effects from Laura's panic attack or a night spent in the hospital.

"Do you want to know the baby's sex?" Dr. Silver asked.

Laura spoke up. "We already know. We're having a boy," she said without a doubt.

Chase was quiet. Laura's heart had been set on a boy, and he had gone along. He hoped she wouldn't be too disappointed if the baby turned out a girl.

"Chase?" Dr. Silver asked, soliciting an opinion.

For the time being, a boy made Laura happy. "We're having a boy," he agreed.

Dr. Silver grinned. "If you two have a secret for predicting the sex of a baby, patent it," she advised. "You'll make a fortune. You're having a boy." She pointed to the monitor, emphasizing what made the child a boy.

Laura's head spun around to Chase, her expression smug. "See, I told you."

"You did." What had she said? *Mothers know these things.*

Laura smiled and returned her attention to the monitor.

Chase did his best to contain the excitement spreading through him. In front of his eyes, swaying with ease, was their fit and looking very happy—or so Chase was convinced—baby boy. He was mesmerized with the tiny being he had created with Laura.

Finished with Dr. Silver, Laura craved ice cream. Not just ice cream, she insisted as they walked into the diner.

"I'll have a hot fudge sundae with chocolate ice cream, extra hot fudge, and a double order of nuts," she told the youth in a white waiter's uniform. "Extra hot fudge," she repeated as he wrote down the order.

"I'll have a cup of coffee. Black, no sugar," Chase said.

She dug in deep. The huge sundae was drenched with an abundance of dark sauce. Chase had trouble seeing the ice cream.

"A tiny bite." She held the spoon out to him.

"No, thanks," he said, wincing at so much sugar. "Enjoy." She couldn't possibly finish it.

She did, savoring each mouthful. Chase tolerated his queasy

stomach, the least he could do for the woman who carried his baby.

Dr. Silver had given Laura pictures from the ultrasound. Chatting animatedly about the experience during the ride home, she couldn't tear her eyes from the photos.

Chase pulled the Toyota into the driveway.

"I can't wait to show Aunt Lonnie," she said excitedly. "Who do you think the baby looks like?"

He switched off the ignition. "In those pictures? A little space alien."

Her eyes widened and she broke into a huge grin. "Did you ever notice how cute space aliens are in movies? Not the big, lurking ones. But the little ones that waddle. I always want to take them all home!"

"It figures," he said with a laugh.

After walking around to her side, Chase opened the door. Caressing her hand, he helped her slide out of the car.

She swayed, grabbing the door handle. "I'm tired," she stated as if her exhaustion wasn't commonplace nowadays.

Chase closed the door. Without warning, he slipped his arm under her knees, scooping her up. Her arms encircled his neck.

"You don't have to carry me," she said, her resistance a weak one.

Chase valued any excuse. He relished having her in his arms. "Take advantage while you can. Keep it up with those sundaes, by next month I won't be able to lift you." He started up the walkway.

At the reference to ice cream, she licked her lips. "Chase, you should've eaten some. The fudge sauce was the sweetest I've ever tasted. It was the best!"

"I appreciated your offered spoonful, but I wouldn't dare take one tiny bite from you."

"Oh, I meant you should have gotten your own."

They laughed, reaching the porch. Laura pressed her head to his shoulder. She fit perfectly in his arms, and in his heart.

"Laura," he said softly.

Her eyes were closed, her body relaxed against him. A slight smile curled her lips. "Umm."

"Honey, look at me," he said, his voice gentle. He loved her. She and the baby were his world.

Opening her eyes, she lifted her head from his shoulder.

"I like when you call me 'honey'," she whispered.

Chase couldn't help himself. His mouth covered hers in a deep kiss. Laura's arms tightened around his neck, and she returned his kiss fervently.

When he drew away, she smiled and laid a hand against his cheek. "I like when you do that, too."

Chase didn't have a chance to respond. The door flung open. Laura securely in his arms, both their attention swung to the person in the doorway.

"I was beginning to worry about you. Laura, you need to be carried? Are you ill?"

The person speaking was Dick Donovan.

Chapter Twenty

"I'm fine," Laura said, as Chase lowered her to the floor.

Dressed in an untarnished, well-tailored tan suit, Dick looked as if he had stopped in Sea Tower on his way to the office. His eyes appraised his daughter-in-law, then his lips distorted in a daunting smile. "I'm excited about my first grandchild."

His hand reached out to pat Laura's abdomen, and Chase grabbed his father's wrist. "Don't," he warned, his voice hard. After the hell this man had put Laura through, he wasn't touching her or their child.

A piqued expression passed over Dick's face, and he eased his limb from Chase's grip.

"Chase, I'm sorry," Aunt Lonnie said, stepping into the foyer. "This man's not welcome in my home." She sneered at her brother-in-law. "I asked him to leave several times, but he refused. I didn't want to call the police and have a scene."

Undoubtedly, Lonnie was adverse to making such a move where Dick was concerned. She had considered how the police showing up at her door would affect Laura. A slow simmer crawled through Chase for the uncomfortable position his father had imposed upon his aunt.

"Don't worry, Aunt Lonnie," he said. "My father and I do need to talk."

"Your father needs to learn some manners and not barge into homes where he's not welcome," Lonnie said, her sarcasm hard.

Chase slipped his arm around Laura. "Honey, would you join Aunt Lonnie in the kitchen? Leave me to talk with my father?"

Laura smiled adoringly at Chase. "If that's what you want."

"Thanks." He bent his head and kissed her.

Laura returned Chase's kiss, caressing his cheek.

As she moved from Chase, Laura's eyes burrowed into the older man. "Good day, Mr. Donovan." She started after Lonnie.

"Laura, there's no need for formality," Dick called over his shoulder. "You're my daughter-in-law. You're carrying my grandchild. Won't you call me 'Dad'?"

Laura halted. Turning to face Dick, her features taut. "My father died when I was a little girl," she said. "He's the only man I would ever honor with 'Dad'. If you don't want me to address you as 'Mr. Donovan,' I'll just call you—" she paused for the appropriate affect—"'Dick'."

Lonnie gave in to the impulse and laughed. Chase managed to stifle his grin. If his father was offended by Laura's acidic remark, he concealed the insult well.

Dick waited until the women were in the kitchen. "Laura got pregnant, what? February, beginning of March," he pointed out. "We're in July. She should be bigger."

Chase arched an eyebrow. His wife had been correct in speculating her father-in-law was counting months.

"Laura's doctor emphasizes healthy eating and exercise. Laura does both." Chase pondered Dr. Silver's opinion regarding the massive sundae his wife had packed away earlier.

"Are you sure the child is yours?"

"That doesn't even dignify an answer," Chase replied, growing impatient. "Why are you in Sea Tower?"

The lines around Dick's lips twitched. "It should have dawned on me sooner. You seeking refuge with your aunt." His voice tightened. "You always ran to Lonnie when in one of your sulking moods."

Chase stood firm, ignoring the comment, but grateful that a visit with Lonnie hadn't crossed Dick's mind earlier. For instance, when Chase hadn't been in Sea Tower.

Dick continued. "You haven't returned my phone calls."

Chase shrugged. "Maybe I don't want to talk to you."

Leaning against the door jamb, Dick folded his arms across his chest. "Your wife's orders? Avoid me? Your own father?"

"Laura and I don't discuss you. Your name reminds her you arranged to have her kidnapped, raped, and murdered," Chase said, his tone hard.

"Chase, I'm sorry you found out."

Chase lifted an eyebrow. "Oh, but you're not sorry you attempted murder?"

"I'm involved in something you can't possibly understand."

"I'll tell you what you were involved in." In vivid detail, he described the horrific scene he had witnessed on his boat. "Dad, I want to believe it's all crap. Tell me Ron was lying when he said you gave permission to hurt Laura."

There was a long silence before Dick exhaled a long breath. "You won't understand."

"Ah, Dad," Chase groaned. "I want to know everything. From the start. What's the game? Why Laura?"

"She happened to be in the wrong place at the wrong time."

"Wrong place, wrong time. For that she deserved to die?"

"There was nothing I could do. I had no say."

"But you felt free to offer my boat." Chase's voice dripped with bitterness. A conjecture had nagged him. "That's why you wanted us to have dinner that night. To keep me from the boat."

"Chase, you don't understand." Dick implored for forgiveness without offering an explanation.

"Then tell me, Dad." Chase wanted to understand his father's foray into unimaginable violence.

"It's not so simple."

Chase still held onto hope. Yes, his father was selfish, brash, obsessed with status and money, but Chase still had difficulty accepting the man was a killer. Perhaps he was being coerced into this sick scheme.

He took a deep breath. "Dad, come on. Let's you and me go

someplace where we can be alone and talk. Tell me what you're involved in." Chase's request was almost a plea. "I'm a lawyer. We can come up with a way to get you out. We'll talk to this special agent. It'll be okay."

"There's your mother's idealism showing," Dick scoffed.

Chase persisted. "Dad, there's a baby coming. A boy. How long have you wanted a grandson? We need to put this mess behind us and bring the baby into a happy, safe environment."

"Grandson?" A gleam entered Dick's eyes. "I want to be in my grandson's life."

Chase put a hand on each hip. "Not if you're a criminal," he said, his tone adamant. "You think I'm taking my son to see grandpa in the federal pen every third Sunday?"

Dick hung his head, his shoulders slumping. For a big man, well over six feet, he suddenly looked very small. "Chase, I wish it were that easy."

Chase despised the uselessness enveloping him. "I want to help."

Dick straightened. His old confidence, defiance, and insolence returned. "I covered for you. When you forced me to tell my partners you had thrown Ron and Lou off the boat." His face twisted and his voice hardened. "I covered for you when I said Laura was pregnant and you married her. I insisted you deserved the right to have your child."

"Dad . . ."

"I don't want your help," Dick snapped. "I don't want you caught up. The less you know, the better."

"I *am* caught up. Whoever the hell these partners are, they tried to kill my wife," Chase spat, frustration nearly choking him. His father just wasn't getting it.

"She wasn't your wife at the time."

"Small point," Chase said with a huff. "What are you doing, Dad? Scamming the customers? Jacking prices? You and Oliver Daniels? What the hell are you doing?"

Dick ignored the inquiries, facing his son head-on. "My partners want Laura. I maintained we could count on you. Promised you would keep her from those agents, but that's only stalling. I was very convincing. Said she's so taken with you, she can be led like the proverbial lamb to slaughter. Once the baby's born, you need to face the inevitable."

The inevitable? At the inkling of more harm to his wife, Chase's consideration for his father disintegrated. "I don't know whether you're sick . . . or just plain nuts."

Dick's eyes held his son's glare. "I can protect her until the baby's born. Afterward, all bets are off. Don't get too attached to Laura."

Dick's words punched Chase in the gut. *"Don't get attached?"* It took all his willpower to control his rage. "She's my wife, damn it!"

"You got your mother's bleeding heart." His expression warped into a sneer. "You married Laura and got her pregnant because you knew I would protect my grandchild. You're a fool, and we both may end up being sorry."

Chase wasn't sure if anger or fear rushed through him. "You know what I'm sorry for," he said, his manner deliberate. "I'm sorry that when I found Laura bound, beaten, terrorized, I didn't take her to the police. Have them haul your ass in."

"The choice was between my life, your life, or Laura's. Her well-being didn't even enter into the equation." He looked Chase squarely in the eye. "But now she carries my grandchild."

"You have your cell phone?" Chase asked. This conversation disgusted him.

"Yes. Why?"

"Call yourself a cab and leave. Or I will call the police and, unlike Aunt Lonnie, I don't mind causing a scene. Or care how much I tell them."

"Chase, when you were a little boy, nothing held your interest for long." Dick frowned as if apathetic to these memories. "You got all excited over some new toy or game for perhaps ten minutes and then moved on. You were constantly searching for a new amusement."

Chase listened.

"You wanted to be a lawyer," Dick said. "I advised you to go corporate. Make money since you enjoyed spending it so much. No, you wanted to help the little people, the disadvantaged. That lasted perhaps fifteen minutes, and you asked me for something at the warehouse. But nothing to interfere with your drinking, gambling, and whoring. You have no idea what it's like to have a real job."

"Does your homily have a point?"

Dick continued. "You have this wife with a baby coming, a good time playing husband and father. Eventually, they'll bore you, too. You'll ask me for help in disassociating yourself, and to find you a new diversion. And I will, because you're my son. I only pray when the time comes, we're alive and not in jail."

Chase was untouched by his father's monologue. "I guess I do have my mother's idealism. I believed we could solve the fix you're in, and be a family. Do you want to call that cab?" he asked. "Or should I?"

Dick brushed by his son and walked out the front door. Chase moved to the living room's picture window. His father stood on the porch and talked into his cell phone. Where Chase had been concerned, Dick never encouraged any trait or behavior that wasn't his own. He had discouraged any quality, ambition, or temperament he hadn't wanted in a son, especially when it came to Chase's moral being.

Chase had spent his life floundering, searching and hoping for direction and a reason. The drinking, gambling, and whoring were diversions that temporarily took away the emptiness, and at times, his worthlessness.

He continued staring out the window. After ten minutes, the cab arrived and Chase looked on as the yellow sedan took his father away.

Terror cruised through him, smelling the scent like a rabbit running from a fox. Chase was frightened. For his wife and baby.

For himself. Even for his father.

"Chase."

He turned to see Laura standing in the doorway, hugging herself. Her hands brushing up and down her arms in an effort to warm herself, not from cold, but from fear. She took a step toward him, and he ran to her, enveloping her in his arms in two quick steps.

"It's okay, honey."

"How did he find us, Chase?" she asked, a slight quiver in her voice. "What does he want?"

She pressed closer to him, so close that he actually felt her heart's rapid beating.

"It took him a while, but he remembered how when I was a kid and angry at him, I ran to Aunt Lonnie." He pressed a kiss to her forehead.

"Chase, I'm frightened. I hate feeling frightened."

Added to his own fears, Chase hated feeling helpless. So he lied. Just like he had lied to the men on the boat. Again, this tale was a . . . good . . . lie, one for her benefit . . . or perhaps this time for his.

"Don't be, honey," he said. "Dad wanted to tell me that you were safe."

Chapter Twenty-one

Now, in her sixth month, Laura's baby kicked and stretched, a lively, spirited little fellow. With an ear pressed to his wife's belly, Chase continued having his one-way conversations with his son. Often, he insisted he heard the baby sneeze, hiccup, or snore. He fretted if he thought Laura wasn't getting enough rest. He was always ready to accompany her on her daily walks. One day, while the couple browsed in a bookstore, she found him skimming a book on what parents should look for in a good preschool. Although they hadn't discussed their feelings for each other, his actions proved to Laura his love and commitment to their child.

It was a Friday evening in mid-September. Lonnie had traveled to Baltimore to attend a friend's daughter's wedding. She was due back Sunday afternoon. After a quick seafood casserole, Laura sat at the table, sipping decaf tea, while Chase loaded the dishwasher.

"When we first arrived in Sea Tower, we looked at some house brochures," he said. "Since then, we haven't talked about where you want to live after the baby comes. Aunt Lonnie loves the idea of us staying with her. She's dropped enough hints." He placed her empty mug in the dishwasher.

"She's excited about the baby," Laura said with a huge grin. "Little ones have that effect." Her heart leaped. *He had said us? As in Laura, Baby Donovan, and Chase?*

He took Laura's hand, eased her up from the straight-back chair, and led her into the living room.

"I love my aunt, but trust me, you don't want her hovering." He helped Laura get comfortable on the sofa, tucking a small throw pillow behind her back. "How's that?"

"Fine, thanks." She loved the way he cared for her. "I don't want to keep imposing on Aunt Lonnie. I like Sea Tower. I can sell my condo in Philly and set up house here. Quiet, peaceful, Sea Tower is the perfect place for a child."

He sat on the ottoman, facing her. "You don't need to sell your condo."

"I can't afford a house and the condo's upkeep."

"Rent out the condo. I'll lease a house in Sea Tower. You'll live in it. If you like it, I'll buy it."

"Chase." She wasn't comfortable with him buying her a house. "I can't have you buying me a house."

"The house is for my son, and you go with him. You two are a package deal," he said with a grin.

His sly, impish smile, especially the twinkle in his blue eyes, curled her toes.

"Where will you live?" Recently, Laura had had her fantasies. The three of them living together in Sea Tower as a family was her favorite.

"In my son's house. If he approves. I'll bring the idea up to him after he's born."

Her fantasy come true. "Ask him now." She enjoyed Chase's one-way conversations with his son, topics ranging from sports to politics to the weather. His warm breath would tickle her belly, and his comical expressions amused her.

Chase paused. "Remember when you were in the hospital, the first conversation I had with him?"

"Umm-hum."

"He forgave me for my disgusting words at your condo. When I said that I didn't care about you." Gently, Chase caressed her left hand, twirling her gold wedding band between his thumb and index finger. "This is one smart kid we're having. He knew I didn't mean any of what I said. He told me I was in love with his mother."

Tears stung Laura's eyes, and she dissolved at the tenderness etched in his features. "Chase . . ."

He gripped her hand, as if afraid she might leave. "I love you,

Laura. I love you so damn much. Sometimes I feel like you're aware, and other times I decide it's only me pretending you love me."

Her free hand reached up, running her fingers through his brown, wavy hair. "Oh, Chase," she whispered. She had hoped so long for this moment, often resolving the utterance would never happen. When she did imagine the scene, it was dramatic and soap-opera-like.

But the reality moment was short, simple and sweet—like the ceremony making her his wife.

"Our first night together, when I said I was thinking," he said softly. "I was thinking I was falling in love with you." He paused before a mischievous smile widened on his handsome face. "Do you think a gorgeous, introverted, smart, unassuming bookkeeper could love a former spoiled, overindulged, self-absorbed playboy?"

"You're a bit confused there, pal. In case you didn't notice, I'm not exactly introverted." She kissed him quickly. "And you are not self-absorbed." She kissed him again. "I love you, Chase Donovan."

He smiled at her. "This is from the bottom of my heart. You, me, our son, us together, it doesn't get any better." He kissed her lips before resting his forehead against hers. "We'll make this work, Laura. Please say you want us to be a family."

His mouth covered hers, all warm and moist, devouring her with an overpowering passion. Her arms slid around his neck and she kissed him back. She clung to him as if he were a life preserver pulling her upstream.

Laura drew away. "We'll be a happy family, Chase."

They sat, kissing, whispering, soaking in their love. Then, excited over their own home, they browsed through the real estate brochures. Months outdated, more recent ones were needed. Nevertheless, they pored through pages, picking out neighborhoods, house styles, and discussing their preferences.

"This is a pretty house." Laura surveyed the room. "I like the fireplace in the kitchen. Aunt Lonnie said her father bought the house as the family vacation home."

"Yeah. When he passed away, he left the house my father and I live in to my mother," Chase said. "Aunt Lonnie got this one. With both her parents gone, her sister married, Aunt Lonnie hung around Philly for a few years, then moved here permanently."

He sighed, then continued. "I think the real reason Aunt Lonnie left Philly was she couldn't stand seeing my mother married to my father." He hesitated. Laura waited for him to speak, clutching his hand.

"Aunt Lonnie feels my father beat my mother." He was quiet, shaking off a memory before going on. "I never saw any marks on Mom. Not that it means much. But I did hear her cry. A lot."

Laura held his hand tighter. "Oh, Chase," she whispered.

"Even if his abuse wasn't physical, I'm sure my mother got plenty of emotional cruelty from him."

Although Chase was a grown man, he still lived in his childhood home. He joked that the house was so big, he and his father went weeks without bumping into each other. Eventually, while they waited out the rainstorm on *Madre*, he confided to Laura that if he moved out, he felt as if he were leaving his mother alone with his father.

That sentiment, she knew, stemmed from the depths of his heart and was part of what made her love him.

"Chase, why didn't Aunt Lonnie marry?" Laura asked. "I never wanted to embarrass her by asking, but I'm curious. She's a great lady."

"Aunt Lonnie was engaged. Doug was a soldier and killed in Vietnam." He paused for a moment remembering. "She said he was the love of her life, the best, and no one could replace him. She wasn't going to try."

Chase got up and took two steps toward the varnished-stained desk. "There's a scrapbook with some pictures." He opened three drawers before he found the book. "Here we go."

He sat down next to Laura, their feet propped on the ottoman. Chase's arm automatically swung around her shoulders, and she nestled against him.

The first picture was a black-and-white snapshot of two dark-haired little girls in bathing suits, one about four years old, the other about six. Chase pointed to the older girl. "That's Aunt Lonnie." His index finger moved to the other child. "That's my mother."

"Chase, you look exactly like your mother."

He snickered. "Much to my father's chagrin. Of course, he would rather that I resembled him."

A page flip revealed a similar picture, but this one in color. Michelle Donovan, as a child, stared back. Full head of mixed dark and light brown wavy hair, big sapphire blue eyes, long, lean nose. Chase would never allow Dick Donovan to forget his late wife.

"Your mother was beautiful," Laura murmured.

"Yeah, she was." He stared a few long moments. He flipped the page. "That's my grandmother and grandfather."

The picture appeared to be a Christmas card photo, in color. A toothily grinning family dressed in their Sunday best, sitting on a sofa surrounded by a mass of holly. Mother, father, and the two girls who were perhaps ten and twelve.

"Or as Aunt Lonnie refers to your grandfather, the dummy who convinced your mother to marry your father," Laura said.

"That can get her on a pulpit." Chase frowned. "Aunt Lonnie feels strongly my father married my mother for the business. I hope she didn't bore you with her stories."

"No, I don't find Aunt Lonnie boring at all." Laura truly enjoyed the women's breakfast chats. "She filled me in on the family history. She talks about her days as a teacher, and funny 'whatever happened to' stories of her students."

They looked at several more pictures of a teenaged Lonnie with Chase's mother before they came across a young, twenty-something woman, with waist-length dark hair wearing jeans and a white tank top. With her was a soldier, around the same age, in U.S. Army fatigues. Smiling, wrapped in each other's arms, were a beaming Lonnie and Doug, her soldier/fiancé.

"Chase, she's positively radiant. I've seen Aunt Lonnie smile, but never like that."

He studied the picture. "Yeah, it's as if these days, she only goes through the motions."

"You can tell looking at this picture. They were so much in love," Laura noted with a touch of melancholy.

"While I was growing up, Aunt Lonnie talked about Doug all the time. Almost as if he hadn't been killed. She doesn't anymore."

Chase flicked through several more pictures with Lonnie and Doug before stopping at a bridal party. The bride dressed in layers of white chiffon, three bridesmaids in pink satin and lace, and a groom with his three groomsmen wearing black tuxes.

"Mom and Dad's wedding," he said, eyes glued to the group. "I'm sure there was lots of arm twisting to get Aunt Lonnie to be Mom's maid of honor."

"She loved her sister more than she hated your father." Laura looked at the photo more closely. "It's uncanny how much you resemble your mother. You both have the same beautiful blue eyes. I love your eyes."

"Me, too. They help me see," he quipped.

Laura's elbow poked him playfully. For a man who claimed he was self-absorbed, Chase had difficulty accepting a compliment.

He turned the page. "This is the happy group at some momentous anniversary bash," he said. "The twenty-fifth, I'm pretty sure. It wasn't long after this party my mother started feeling sick." He turned back to the original wedding party, then over to the anniversary photo, comparing and contrasting. "Same people twenty-five years apart."

"Chase, Oliver Daniels was your father's best man."

Chase stared at the pudgy man. "Oh, yeah. I forgot."

"And these other two men?" she inquired curiously.

His index finger pointed to a tall, lanky man next to Daniels. "This one is Chuck Hunter." His finger moved to the man next to Hunter. "This is Alan Blair. If you're up on your politics, Blair's some fancy federal judge."

She studied the picture. There was something familiar about the two men with Dick Donovan and Oliver Daniels. The mass of silver hair on one man, the tall, stick-like figure of the other.

"I've seen these men," she muttered.

"In the newspaper, sure. Blair presides over a lot of drug cases. Chuck Hunter. Well, he's far from an upstanding citizen. He was convicted of embezzling from his company some years ago. Drug charges, too, but they were dropped on a technicality. He's probably still serving time."

Laura stared at the photo. She was totally convinced. "Chase, Chuck Hunter isn't serving time anymore. I've seen all these men, together, with your father at the warehouse."

"My father hasn't seen Blair or Hunter in years. Since my mother's funeral," Chase said. "If Blair knows what's good for him, he'll stay far away from Chuck Hunter. An embezzler slash drug trafficker hobnobbing with a judge, old Alan can kiss the federal bench goodbye. You're mistaken, honey."

Laura was adamant. "No, Chase. I saw your father with these three men. About a month before Saunders came calling."

He looked at her seriously. "Tell me what you saw."

She paused, gathering her thoughts. "Those warehouse guys never remember to send the packing slips up with the receipts. I need both for the invoices. One day, it was pretty late. Rachel had left so it was after five, and—" she stopped to recall more.

"It was a Thursday, and I was taking a vacation day on Friday for Kate's wedding rehearsal dinner," she said quickly. Laura had been her friend's maid of honor.

"I wanted to print checks and leave them for you to sign," she told Chase.

He nodded his head, acknowledging. One of his few, but major, responsibilities was to sign account payable disbursement checks. If he were in the office while Laura printed checks, she passed them over for his signature. But if he wasn't around, she left a note letting him know checks were locked in the safe, awaiting his signature.

Chase was attentive. "So you went to the dock for packing slips. Go on."

"They were having an intense tête-à-tête behind some crates," she said. "Your father, Oliver Daniels and these two men. Your father saw me and asked if he could help me. I had my slips and went back into the office."

Chase was quiet. Laura, having learned her husband's habits well, knew an idea was shaping behind his intense blue eyes.

"Chase, please don't go back and confront your father," she pleaded. "He's leaving us alone. Remember what happened the last time you played super sleuth? You got arrested. We almost ended up hating each other. Please, Chase. Don't go."

He kissed her, long, deep, touching every emotion. "I'm staying with the two people I love most, my wife and my baby."

"Good. Because we want you in Sea Tower where we can keep our eyes on you."

"Don't worry." Glancing from her, he turned the page to a picture of a toddler. "Oh, look. Now, we're getting to the good pictures. Me."

A smiling, curly haired little boy, no more than two years old, in a pint-size red, white, and blue-striped basketball uniform and clasping a baseball-sized basketball, stared back at them. One glimpse at the adorable little face, and Laura tossed aside their deep discussion.

"How precious! Those blue eyes! This is what our baby will look like," she decided.

Her interest heightened, Laura focused on the pictures. One by one, the various stages of Chase's life up to his law school graduation passed before her. Absorbed in the snapshots and hearing her husband detail the events, all other thoughts flew out of her head.

At her first yawn, Chase carried Laura upstairs. He turned down her bed while she attended to bathroom needs and changed into her plum nightshirt. When she returned to the room, she crawled into bed. Chase fixed her pillows, and after she leaned against them, he tucked the sheet around her.

"Goodnight, honey." He gave her a gentle kiss.

She raised an eyebrow. "Going out?"

"No. I'm going across the hall to sleep."

Laura pursed her lips. "You're going across the hall? To sleep? Chase, am I not your wife? Didn't you tell me you loved me? Didn't I say I love you?"

He mused over her questions. "Yes, on all accounts."

A furrow in her forehead brought her brows together. "Then why aren't you sleeping with me?"

"The baby."

"What? He won't mind." She laughed. "He has to learn mommies and daddies sleep together."

"Laura, I love sleeping with you, lying next to you. You're the only woman I've ever been in love with, or said those words to. I'm trying not to be selfish," he said proudly. "Right now I don't think I could lie next to you and not make love to you. After all, you're *very* pregnant. You're abstaining."

Laura's jaw dropped. Where did he get the idea that because she was pregnant they couldn't make love?

He sat on the edge of the bed and took her hand between both of his. "I remember before I went back to Philadelphia. There you were all sexy and come hither, and such an intense—workout—wouldn't be good for the baby. I mean, I was happy you wanted to," he said quickly, a pink flush tinting his face. "I wasn't sure you'd want to—you know—once you were pregnant. Since we had reached our objective," he pointed out.

When she offered no response, his words rushed out. "Laura, I wanted you so bad. But we had to be mindful of the baby. You turned over, insulted, and went to sleep. I got drunk, downed almost an entire bottle of Aunt Lonnie's best Irish whiskey, and then came to bed and held you while you slept. It was tough, honey. Just holding you."

Laura didn't know whether to laugh, cry, or smack him. "Chase Donovan, you're such a dumbbell."

"I'm your husband," he replied without missing a beat. "Add some affection to your tone when you say that."

"Don't bring up your hesitations to me," she chided. "Being pregnant doesn't prevent me from—you know," she said, mocking his term for intimacy. "There's no harm to the baby or me. The last few weeks I'm pregnant, though, I can't say I'll be in the mood. I'll be as huge as this house and as irritable as hell."

Overwhelming affection rushed through Laura as she realized when she thought she had slept alone, thought perhaps she had dreamed him, Chase had been cradled beside her.

He gave her the impish grin that had turned her life upside down. "You're kidding? We won't hurt the baby?"

She slipped her hand from his and folded her arms across her chest, resting them on her chunky belly. "No."

He was silent for a moment. "Oh."

He got up from the bed, plopped down in a chair, and began untying his sneakers. "In that case." One sneaker fell to the floor, then the other. He pulled off his socks.

"What are you doing?" she asked.

He stood, yanking his blue T-shirt over his head, revealing his broad chest. "I'm about to make love to my wife." He continued undressing. "Lucky for us, Aunt Lonnie's away the entire weekend." His bare body slid beneath the sheet, nestling beside Laura. "We have a lot to make up. A lot to get in before you're as big as this house."

Laughing, Laura slid her arms around his neck as he pushed her back into the mattress. Her lips parted under his kiss. She loved the way his mouth, always warm moved over hers, his tongue gently probing. Laura offered assistance as he lifted the nightshirt. The garment dropped to the floor.

"Chase Donovan, you're a dumbbell," she whispered sweetly.

"Now, wife, *that* has the right touch of affection."

Chase let a hand roam over her bare, very pregnant form, slowly worshiping the round, smooth belly. His hand glided up to caress her breasts. While he re-familiarized himself with the body he had denied himself so long, Laura cuddled against him. Her eyes closed as she soaked up his gentle caresses. Chase's touch, so tender and soothing, simply had a way of exciting her and making everything else completely fade away.

His hand stroked her cheek, and Laura opened her eyes.

"I'm glad you suggested I marry you," she murmured.

"I'm glad you agreed. I love you, Laura Donovan."

Hearing him say her name as a married woman excited her as much as his touch.

"I love you, too. So much, Chase."

His hand stopped stroking her cheek and cupped her chin, bringing her mouth to meet his. Tongues, lips, every sense came into play as his kiss electrified her. His hand cupped her breast, pregnancy making it rounder, firmer, and fuller than the last time they had made love. Chase fondled first one, then the other, her nipples tweaked into hard, erect peaks. His mouth, now nibbling her neck and shoulder, thrilled her beyond words, shaking her senses to their core. She felt him pressed, hard and swollen against her thigh.

Laura panted, urgent to release months of pent-up passion. She quickly wriggled over on her side, her back pressed against his chest. He tasted her available shoulder.

"Is this okay?" she asked. Lying on their sides was the most comfortable way to receive him at this stage of pregnancy.

"Any way is okay as long as I'm with you," he said huskily and went back to enjoying his light bites on her shoulder.

Laura sighed at his tingling touch. His lips and teeth excited her. His hand reached down between her thighs.

"Can I touch you here, honey?" His hushed tone a tender caution, as if afraid he might harm her, the baby, or perhaps just bring back bad memories.

Laura entwined her fingers with his, placing his hand at her crest. She glanced over her shoulder and smiled. "You can touch me anywhere you like. You're my husband."

Chase chuckled softly, and his lips returned to her shoulder. His hand slid between her thighs, pressing, caressing, arousing. His gentle style stirred living flames that burned her very being. She closed her eyes, melting with the magnificent sensations his spell produced. Laura was woozy, as if she'd consumed a quart of his Irish whiskey. If she didn't have him soon, feel him embedded inside her, moving, stirring, she was certain of fainting.

When his hand moved to her hip, Laura raised her leg, bending it at the knee. Cupping her hip, Chase pulled her to him, sinking himself easily into her velvety warmth. His arm encircling her head, he stroked her hair while leisurely easing himself in and out of her. He drove and pushed ever so slowly, yet not too deeply, as if they had all the time in the world. Laura moved easily with him, the pressure immersed within her brought about the most fantastic, spine-tingling sensations.

She pressed back hard against the burning heat of his yearning. Her breath coming in little pants, Laura moaned his name, devouring his rhythmic heaving, her muscles clenching him tight inside her, as his eager thrusts brought her a sequence of untamed, overpowering spasms that sent her spinning, spiraling, whirling away.

As she cried out her own erotic finale, Laura clawed the sheet as the ripples overtook her. Chase gasped, moving strongly yet carefully. His mouth closed over the tender skin of her neck as his final thrust shuddered through him, and he jerked with his ecstasy before pulling her close and slumping against her.

Dizzy, lightheaded, out of sorts, or any other word used that meant floating into oblivion was how Laura described her state of mind. When his breathing had slowed, Chase rolled over on his back, tugging Laura with him. She happily squirmed around, settling herself as close to her husband as physically possible with her expanding belly between them. She loved curling against his long, muscular body; their damp, bare skin touching. His arm always wrapped around her, her head resting on his shoulder.

Laura was the most content she had ever been in her life.

Chapter Twenty-two

Steering Lonnie's Toyota into the parking lot, Chase pulled into the first vacant spot he came upon. Over the weekend, when he hadn't been looking at houses with his wife or making love to her, he had been silently pondering the old photo album.

Finally on Monday, while Laura napped at the house, he placed the telephone call from *Madre*. Rattling off the details, Chase's emotions had been a massive combination of apprehension, hostility, and relief.

After returning to Sea Tower back in July, Chase had twice brought up hiring a private detective to investigate Dick Donovan and Oliver Daniels. Laura had opposed vehemently. She didn't want to talk about what happened with a stranger. Chase respected her wishes. Then Dick Donovan showed up at Aunt Lonnie's door. Followed by the photo album.

So much for husband and wife talking. Chase had lied to his wife. The first time, when he had told her Dick assured him Laura was safe. Chase hadn't known what else to say to her, and had feared another panic attack. He thought it a harmless fib that he would deal with later. His father's visit got shoved in the background as the couple excitedly prepared for their baby, and discovered each other again.

Friday night and the photo album brought out the memory Chase had suspected she suppressed. This morning he heard himself sprouting lie number two. He had nearly choked on the words as they left his mouth. He told Laura he needed a part for the boat. So anxious to get out the door, he had almost neglected to kiss her goodbye.

Now, he stepped through the double glass doors and into the

wood paneled and linoleum eatery. Several patrons sat at the counter with coffee and newspapers. An elderly couple sat in a booth, conversing over salads.

Chase scanned for Ned. His friend sat in a booth, facing the front door. He spotted Chase and waved. Two other men sat in the booth, their backs to the door. As Ned had promised over the phone, he hadn't wasted any time in setting up this meeting.

Ned moved toward the wall, and Chase slid in next to him. The waitress quickly appeared at the table. Chase ordered a black coffee.

Once the woman left, Special Agent Ross Saunders introduced the man sitting next to him. Jake Morgan was a detective with the Philadelphia Police Department. Several years older than Chase, Morgan had brown hair, gray streaks combed through. He sported a full matching beard. He wasn't dressed in a police uniform or a dark suit as Saunders was, but casually in jeans and a navy cloth bomber jacket.

"Detective Morgan works as Philly PD's special liaison with the FBI. He assists us with cases that start as local, but end up being federal," Saunders explained.

Chase and Morgan, who faced each other across the table, shook hands.

The waitress, a petite brunette in her early twenties dressed in a pink uniform with the nameplate, *Lily*, arrived with an empty white mug. She placed it in front of Chase. Pouring from the pot she carried, Lily inquired if anyone cared for a refill. Each of the other men accepted. She obliged, reminding them to call her if they needed anything.

Chase took a swig, then spoke. "Let's get one thing clear, Saunders," he began, his voice bitter. "I don't like you. I don't like the way you do business. You held me on a charge that could've been cleared up in less time than a roulette wheel spin."

Saunders, unfazed, stirred cream in his coffee. "You pulled a gun on two federal agents. We were looking for a woman who had been observed, by an agent, on your boat," he said. "It appeared to the agent you attempted to throw the woman overboard. That she may have screamed."

"The woman is my wife," Chase said. "I picked up my wife to carry her down to our bed. She wasn't screaming, Saunders. She was laughing. I wasn't tossing her anywhere. I was playing with her." He arched an eyebrow cynically. "Don't you ever play with your wife?"

"I'm not married," the agent answered.

"Well, you better learn how to play, if you ever want to be." Chase shook his head. "You thought Laura was my hostage?" He added a caustic laugh. "We were docked. She was on deck reading a magazine. She had a cell phone. *One I gave her.* I don't know whether I'm a lousy kidnapper or you and your Baltimore counterparts are inept FBI agents."

"Chase," Ned warned.

Chase didn't care who he offended, especially not Saunders. "You used Laura. Dragging her out of the diner, frightening her. You wanted the jackasses you're after to know you were watching them," he said tersely. "Then you screwed with her head, trying to convince her I was in shit up to my eyeballs. That I married her to save my ass."

"You have to admit, Donovan, a sudden marriage appeared awfully suspicious," Saunders countered. "I didn't take advantage of Laura. I presented her with evidence."

"Give me a break." Chase snickered. "How dumb do you think I am?"

"You two are still married, seem to be on track." The agent put the coffee mug to his lips. "No harm, no foul." He took a swallow.

"That's true," Chase said. "Laura and I are married, happy, and expecting a baby. Laura and the baby are the reasons you and I are meeting today. So let's stop the 'who's on first,' and each put our cards on the table. I want my wife and baby safe."

Saunders was quiet, giving the impression he was contemplating. Chase considered the pause a dramatic affect.

"Okay, Donovan," the agent finally said. "Let's get down to business. To show you what a nice guy I am, I'll open."

"Good enough," Chase said, his animosity not wavering.

"I better start," Morgan said. "Give you two a chance to go to your respective sidelines for a time-out."

Chase was silent, glaring at Saunders.

"Before my promotion, I worked undercover," Morgan began. "I was assigned a low-level bookmaker named Zippo Leon."

"What's low level?" Chase asked.

"Zippo was a wanna-be who wasn't gonna be," Morgan said. "He liked to think he was in with the big boys, but he couldn't get the time of day from them. Zippo had his fingers in a lot of petty stuff, but all we got him for was a small-time numbers operation. He took a plea."

"How much time he get?" Ned inquired.

"Seven years," Morgan replied. "It didn't take him long to bitch he wanted out. Less than a year into his gig, he called me with a tip. In exchange, of course, my federal contacts were to reduce his sentence."

"Why you?" Chase asked.

"Undercover, I was his gopher. While working the case, I met my wife, Kristina." Morgan smiled. "Zippo thinks Kristina, him, and me are buddies."

"He sounds like an interesting character," Chase observed.

"Colorful would be a better word," Morgan said. "He sold beer and soft drinks to major restaurants, legally and illegally, in Pennsylvania, New Jersey, and Delaware."

Morgan paused, drinking from his mug before he continued. "Anyway, Zippo gives me some restaurant owner who had approached him about a drug deal. The drugs came from South America. Shipped to a produce warehouse. A warehouse client picked up the drugs along with his regular legit orders."

Saunders continued. "The guy sets up in various parking lots, deals his produce out of the back of his truck, and the drugs out of the front."

"What was the connection between the restaurant owner and Zippo?" Chase asked.

"The restaurant owner wanted Zippo's trucks for delivering drugs," Morgan said. "Zippo wasn't interested. He was content with what he was doing."

"Why didn't Zippo bargain with this information at his original arrest?" Ned asked.

"I can count off Zippo's undesirable traits," Morgan replied. "One thing I did find laudable was his loyalty. He was no snitch. Prison, undoubtedly, changed his perspective."

Saunders picked up the story. "Detective Morgan came to us, but by the time we got people in place, the restaurant proprietor had died. Heart attack. Restaurant closed." He mentioned the restaurant and proprietor's name. Neither rang a bell with Chase.

The agent continued. "Everything might have stopped there if not that in the restaurant's parking lot, our people observed the white truck exactly as Zippo Leon had told Detective Morgan."

"The guy in the white truck?" Chase asked even though he knew the answer.

"Oliver Daniels," Saunders said. "We observed customers buying more than apples and oranges. Certain individuals came up to the truck, Daniels took a bag from beneath the front seat and the deal went down."

"Why didn't you raid the truck? Confiscate the drugs and arrest him?" Chase asked.

Morgan interjected. "We want more."

Saunders picked up a white sugar packet from the tray on the table. "Since we established the drugs came in through a Food Mall warehouse, our next step was to find out where Daniels bought his produce."

"My father's warehouse," Chase said.

"Your warehouse, too," Saunders reminded him.

"My name's on everything my father owns or leases," Chase

admitted. "Half of which, if you asked, I couldn't tell you. I never paid attention."

"We staked out the warehouse, Chase," Morgan said. "But couldn't get a handle on specifically what Daniels was buying, how often, or where it came from. We were looking for a pattern, and that's why we brought in Laura Roberts. Who better to ask than the person who keeps track of purchases?"

"Her name is Laura Donovan," Chase corrected.

"Sorry." Morgan gave a half grin. "Laura Donovan."

"Is that your only interest in Laura? The invoices? At any time was she a suspect?" Ned asked.

Chase shot his friend a cutting glance.

Ned disregarded the warning. "I'm an attorney, Chase. I'm *your* attorney, and I want this out there."

"Everybody's a suspect until I prove otherwise," Saunders said. "I asked Laura a few questions regarding invoices. She confirmed merchandise arrived from South America. She recalled some of Daniels' purchases. I let her go. It was all harmless."

Chase's animosity wasn't waning. "How magnanimous."

Saunders stare was bold. "Later, we had more questions. Only you conveniently had a car whisk her away, married her, and sailed off yonder on your boat."

Chase hadn't had anyone whisk Laura away. Saunders' word, *harmless*, when referring to taking Laura to headquarters stuck in Chase's gut.

"How did you discover Laura and I docked in Beach Bay?" Chase asked. "You had her under surveillance?"

"Not exactly Laura. We had people watching the warehouse," Morgan said.

Saunders reported on Laura's comings and goings at the warehouse the day after he had questioned her. Surveillance agents had observed her getting into a car, close to six in the evening with a box Dick Donovan had handed her. Those agents, interested in its contents, hadn't been authorized to leave the warehouse. They called for backup agents to grab Laura and the box when she reached her condo. She never arrived.

"We didn't know what happened to her." Saunders turned to Ned. "To answer your question, Counselor, we didn't know if we had a suspect in Laura, a victim, a witness, or what?"

"Our interest in Laura piqued only when we saw her with the box," Morgan said.

Chase felt his blood pressure rising. "Your intimidation, Saunders, raised my father's antennas. The box contained her personal belongings. Simple woman's crap she kept in her desk, like her makeup case and toothbrush. Let me tell you what involving Laura in your bullshit cost her."

Leaving nothing out, his righteous anger in full force, Chase detailed the scene on his boat. Morgan's compassion was immediate. To Chase's surprise, the generally detached Saunders seemed sensitive to Laura's ordeal.

"I didn't know what I was dealing with." Chase hesitated, needing to go on, but hating to remember. "I was afraid those guys were returning with back up. I concentrated on convincing Laura she was safe with me. She was so scared. I wanted to get out of Magic Lake."

Morgan agreed the boat was a smart choice rather than the car. *Madre* was more difficult to follow. "Why didn't you call the police? Take her to a hospital?" the detective asked.

Chase explained Laura's refusal.

Shaking his head, Morgan exhaled deeply. "My years on the street, I saw too many sexual assault victims. Often a victim's negative response to police or medical treatment is her denial the assault happened," he explained. "She just wants the whole thing to go away."

Chase clung to Morgan's words. Wanting the whole thing to go away, the detective had used Laura's exact words.

"When she didn't show up at her condo, we passed the word to our field offices. Person of interest with information," Saunders said.

"How did you find us in Beach Bay?" Chase asked.

Saunders explained a surveillance photo of Laura walking into the warehouse had been circulated. "Funny thing about your wife," he said, his tone easy. "She's one fine looking woman and people remember her. An agent with the Baltimore office was looking to buy a boat at the marina where you docked."

"Why didn't your agent identify himself and approach us? Instead of hiding in the shadows like a stalker?" Chase asked.

"When he called in, there was a discussion about getting a warrant for your boat. The real life system moves much slower than a one hour TV show." Saunders sat back in the booth. "Our agent saw your boat leave, and there wasn't much we could do."

"All wasn't lost," Morgan added. "We had enough to get a sign-off to tap your father's office phone. Daniels, wise bastard, uses a cell phone. Those can't be tapped."

He wasn't sharing that he and Laura had already been intimate, but Chase revealed their decision to marry.

"It took me a while to admit it, but I know my father and Oliver Daniels are involved in God only knows what." Chase drained his mug. "I just had to shield Laura. No matter who my father's working with, he'll protect his grandchild. Funny how things work out. Laura and I love each other, and we're excited about our baby boy. He's due in about eight weeks."

"Chase, do you still have the evidence? The knife? Laura's clothes?" Morgan asked.

Chase nodded, explaining how he bagged everything per police procedure. He signaled the waitress. "Laura and I don't talk about it, but the more time that passes, I want those bastards to pay." He gave Morgan the abductors' names.

The waitress arrived carrying a freshly brewed pot of coffee. Conversation stopped until each man had a new cup of the hot, steaming liquid.

"Those names you mentioned haven't showed up in the investigation. That doesn't mean they're total innocents," Morgan said.

"It's unlikely Daniels recruited two novices to commit murder," Saunders agreed.

Chase moved the conversation to Dick Donovan's visit. "After the baby's born, they're going after Laura," he said.

"So I'm hearing you suspect illegal drugs are being shipped to the Donovan warehouse," Ned, ever the attorney, summarized. "This Daniels character picks up the merchandise with his legit produce order. Then sells the drugs from his truck like peaches, two pounds for a dollar."

Saunders nodded, and the group was silent, concentrating on their coffee.

"I was always convinced Laura saw something that freaked my father and Daniels," Chase said. He exhaled a deep breath, and told the men of his aunt's old photo album.

"Alan Blair, the judge," Ned gasped.

"Hunter's no novice to drugs," Morgan said. "If not for a search warrant error and his megabucks attorney, his ass would still be in jail. Leech lawyers." He turned to Ned sheepishly. "No offense, counselor."

Ned's reply was a civil smile.

Morgan pointed out the evidence still needed.

"That about it, Saunders?" Morgan turned to the agent, seeking confirmation. Saunders stared forward, his expression blank. "Saunders, you listening to me?"

The agent spoke directly to Chase. "Because you father had handed Laura that box she carried, I wanted whatever was in it. I went to a judge for a warrant to search her condo, and he laughed me out of his chambers," Saunders said. "Granted, the warrant was ambiguous, but I've gotten them approved for less. The judge who shot me down was Alan Blair."

*

Laura sat at the kitchen table, staring absentmindedly into mint tea that had grown cold twenty minutes ago. It was Tuesday evening, Lonnie's book club night. Chase had gone to Annapolis early that morning. He had missed dinner, calling and insisting the women have their meal without him. He claimed difficulty finding a compressor for *Madre*.

His wife didn't believe him.

She washed out the teacup, then shuffled up the stairs. Her heaving belly now a hindrance, slowing her movements more each day. She was anxious for the baby's arrival for many reasons. Most notably there was more joy in holding him in her arms, than his weight pressing on her lower back.

Having changed into a new blue terry nightshirt, Laura was brushing her teeth when she heard Chase walk through the front door.

"Laura, honey," he called.

"Upstairs." After a quick rinse to her toothbrush, she shuffled down the hall. "Did you have dinner?" She watched him climb the steps. When he reached the top, she walked into their bedroom.

"I passed a drive-by and got a burger," he said, joining her in the bedroom.

"Not exactly dinner."

"It'll do. You look good." He eyed her with playful glee. "How about a hug and a kiss for dessert?"

Chase's arms were around her, his hands moving over her back. She kissed him quickly.

"What took you so long?" she asked.

His lips brushed her cheek, then he disentangled himself from her. "I called you, honey. I had to try several places before I found the right size compressor," he said, his eyes not meeting hers.

She lifted an eyebrow skeptically. "Where's this new compressor?"

He turned his back, shrugging off his denim jacket. "I wasn't bringing it into the house. I dropped it off at the boat."

He hung his jacket in the closet. Laura pursed her lips. Chase never hung his clothes. He always tossed them over the chair, even when they had been on the boat, and Laura hung the garments. She didn't mind. His negligence with his clothes was one of those annoying husband traits a wife grew accustomed to.

Hanging his jacket allowed him to keep his back to her.

"Chase, look at me. Where were you? Tell me this instant." Her words were sharper than she intended, but she piloted on irritation and fear.

He turned, a hand on each hip. "What's with the tone?"

"What's with the lie?"

"Who's lying? I got a new compressor," he insisted. "If you don't believe me, get dressed and I'll take you to see it."

"Where did you go for this compressor? China?"

He turned away, his eyes clearly eluding hers. "What's with the third degree? Your hormones out of whack today?"

"My hormones are fine." Her wary eyes ran over him. They weren't going to have much of a marriage if he refused to be truthful with her. "I hate that you're lying to me."

He sighed, and turned back in her direction although his eyes remained preoccupied with the hardwood floors. "Laura, I'm . . . tired." Exhaustion was clear in his voice; his demeanor aimed at pacifying her. "Let's go to bed." He paused, then added, "We'll talk in the morning."

He was keeping something important from her. "I don't want to go to bed."

She barked, and Chase bit. "Look, I didn't have the greatest day and can't deal with your meltdown tonight!" he shouted. "Go have a fit somewhere else."

His words spiked her anger. "You broke your promise," she screeched. "You promised me you wouldn't go to Philadelphia and confront your father. That's where you were today. Now you're lying. You're always lying to me."

Chase's eyes narrowed. "Hey, hey, hey, what's with the accusations? I wasn't in Philadelphia."

"Where were you?"

He inhaled, then exhaled deeply. "Laura, let it go."

"If I'm wrong, tell me. Where were you today?" Her chin came up, demanding an answer.

"We're not having a conversation while you're in this temper." His fingers raked his wavy hair. "I wasn't looking forward to the discussion to begin with. It'll wait until morning."

Laura thought her heart would break. If not in Philadelphia, where had he been all day? Perhaps he had decided the marriage wasn't working out. "You're preparing to divorce. You're leaving me after the baby's born. You don't want to be with us, after all," she concluded.

"Me? Divorce? Where the hell did this come from?" His eyes widened. "You're the one who said you wanted a divorce," he reminded her. "On the boat." He repeated her words verbatim.

Laura fought back tears. "Because I knew eventually you'd want to go back to your playboy ways." Water pooled in the corners of her eyes. "You backed out of being a husband and father once. You can just as easily do it again."

"Where the hell are these asinine ideas coming from?" he growled, then paused and took an inaudible breath. "Laura, I wasn't in Philadelphia. I don't want a divorce." Chase said nothing for a moment. "Because you're pregnant, I'll ignore what's running through your head and spitting out of your mouth." His gaze moved over her. "I love you. I love you so much, that where I went today was for you."

"For me?"

"Yes." He scowled, his mouth tight. "I thought we could get a good night's sleep and talk in the morning, but it doesn't seem like you intend to let up."

"No, I don't. Talk about what?"

"I went to Baltimore to meet with Ned, Special Agent Saunders and a detective from Philadelphia."

A swarm of bees fluttered in her gut, and the stinging sensation had nothing to do with the baby. "For God's sake, why?"

With a frustrated sigh, his words rushed out. "Because when I told you my father assured me you were safe, that wasn't true. These people he's involved with are only waiting until after the baby's born."

"My God." Laura's legs weakened and she grabbed the top of the headboard for support. She wasn't sure what frightened her more, Dick Donovan's threats or her husband's lies.

"Honey, I didn't want Dad's visit to bring on another panic attack. Assuring you that you were safe was the only thing I could think of to say at the time."

"And meeting with Saunders?"

With weary but clear-cut precision, Chase relayed the significance of the meeting she had witnessed at the warehouse, his phone call to Ned and meeting with Saunders and Morgan in the diner.

"I planned on telling you everything in the morning, Laura. I swear." His arms wide, he held out open palms appealing to her to believe him.

Laura had listened, hanging onto his every word, not knowing if she was frightened for him, or fuming mad at him. Chase, who all these months insisted the FBI and Special Agent Saunders weren't to be trusted, was now in bed with them.

She expressed these sentiments. "I don't want you involved." Her request was a command.

He spoke his words slowly. "What did you say?"

"I don't want you involved," she repeated. "Stay out of it. Grabbing criminals is Saunders' job, not yours."

"My job, Laura, is to protect my wife and child." The blue of his eyes was darkly bitter. "We're not living our lives waiting, wondering when these buffoons will show up and finish what they started on *Madre*."

"Suppose these buffoons realize what you're up to. You're in danger and you leave the baby and me unprotected anyway," she pointed out bitterly, tilting her chin upwards. "You're to stay in Sea Tower and let Saunders do what the government pays him to do. Catch bad guys."

"Laura, this isn't open for discussion," he said, his tone deceptively calm. "I wouldn't be the man I want to be if I ignored the fact that someone's out to harm my wife."

"Oh, you just like playing the hero," she taunted. She was terrified. *Why wouldn't he listen to reason?* "It really feeds your ego to save the poor damsel in distress," she went on. "It gives you a kick."

He stared at her, mouth slightly ajar, as if she had slapped him. "I can't believe what I'm hearing."

She softened her features and tone, trying a different, gentle approach. "Chase, all I'm asking is that you stay here, with us, where we're all safe," she said. "One day you're angry with your father, and the next day you aren't. If you go along with Saunders, how will you feel on the days you aren't angry with him? Will you be able to live with yourself? With me?"

"My father brought this chaos on himself."

Laura stood immobile as the situation's depth sunk in. "Chase, did you ever consider that everything you've done these past months, including marrying me, was to defy and annoy your father?"

The color drained from his face. "Everything I've done was to first help a human being, then keep safe the woman I love."

"If you love me, you'll stay with me." The haughtiness in her tone covered her fear. "Tell Saunders to go find another lackey, or you'll find yourself another wife."

Turning her back to him, she stared at the wall and waited for the answer she wanted.

"I don't like ultimatums, Laura."

Maliciousness wasn't motivating her attitude, but angst and helplessness. Swallowing the bitter nausea rising in her throat, Laura feared losing her husband one way or another. "We all have to make choices. I'm giving you one." She turned and faced him.

The silence hung heavy in the air.

"Goodnight, Laura," he said and strode out of the room.

"Go ahead and leave. Walk away," she called after him. "That's what you do when things get tough."

Chapter Twenty-three

Laura lay in bed, sniffling back the latest round of tears. A quiet Baby Donovan rested inside her. She was convinced he had felt his parent's tension earlier, and had concluded tonight wasn't the night to disturb Mommy with his baby aerobics.

"Mommy and Daddy had a bad argument." Her hand passed over her belly. "Grownups do that sometimes. Our words had nothing to do with you. Your daddy and I love you, Baby Donovan."

Chase getting mixed up in his father's schemes was so painful her tears refused to stop. Every time she decided she had no more left, a fresh batch started. She understood why Chase wanted to get involved; she regretted he felt he had to.

She shuddered, recalling the awful, hurtful barbs she had thrown. Where did they come from? Her tears launched another free-for-all gush.

Chase had lied to her. Although he'd had this foolish notion that his actions were for her best, he had still lied. But her reaction hadn't been any better. Insinuating he had only helped her to stoke his ego. Accusing him, taunting him, insisting that he prove he loved her.

Although Chase's actions were shameful, her words to him were deplorable. First, after Saunders had put irrational thoughts in her head, unfounded ideas she had actually considered. Then, because Chase hadn't been honest with her. Her reaction was based on fear, consistently motivating her severe responses. Only, Laura couldn't figure out what she was afraid of.

While she and Chase shared an intense passion and need for each other, Laura realized they still had a lot to learn about one another. On the boat, they had shared some childhood memories. While Laura's had been of two affectionate parents, particularly with each other, Chase recalled a father who was critical and a mother who had been ridiculed, maybe even physically abused. Michelle Donovan cried behind closed doors, overheard by a son who felt powerless to help her. One thing Laura now realized about her husband—he despised feeling powerless.

Between her dread, and knowing she had hurt the man she loved; the man who loved her . . . Laura's nose and throat burned from crying. The man, who no matter how illogical his thinking, felt he had to risk his life for them to have a life. She recalled her panic that day on the boat as he ran after the man who had been watching them. She shuddered, feeling the panic once again, the terror burning through her like acid, fearing she would never see Chase again.

Misguided though her husband may be, Laura knew in her heart whatever Chase did was for her and the baby. She had nearly lost him once before. She feared she might lose him again, forever.

She waited for the recent stream to stop, then slid out of bed. He hadn't left the house, but instead had gone into the spare bedroom he had used when first returning to Sea Tower. When they were finding their way back to each other, he had said. The thought made her smile. With a hand massaging her stiff lower back, she padded across the hall. Without even a light knock, she opened the door. A slight creak announced her visit.

Chase lay on his side, unmoving, his back to the door. The dark quilted bedcover was drawn, covering him to the waist. The small lamplight on the end table bathed his form with a yellow glow. She admired his smooth bare back. The mere sight of him— he didn't even have to do or say anything—caused her heart to flutter and a warmth race through her.

Stepping into the room, Laura would let him sleep. She slipped into bed. Pressing her head against his shoulder, her arm glided around his waist. Her round, full belly brushed his back. He was wearing his boxer shorts, and she grinned at an image of his taut buttocks, hard stomach, and muscular thighs. When Chase woke up in the morning and found her in bed, he would know she was sorry. She loved him. No matter how badly they disagreed over current circumstances, he had her support. She was his wife.

"I'm a married man," he said, his firm voice startling her. "If you're not my wife, you better leave this bed."

Her small grin widened. "This *is* your wife," she teased back. "Your one and only."

"The only one I want."

Laura closed her eyes. His tone so tender, she fought back tears of a different kind.

"You're the only husband I want," she whispered.

"Good. Because you're stuck with me." He brought the hand slung leisurely around his waist to his lips, and kissed her opened palm. "Did you bring the baby?"

"Yes. We're a package deal, remember?" She laughed.

"Best package I ever received."

The tenderness in his voice stroked her heart. "Baby Donovan and I were lonely across the hall." And she couldn't sleep with harsh words wedged between Chase and herself.

"I was lonely, too, honey," he said softly. "You stole my plan. I was waiting for you to fall asleep and sneak into bed with you."

"Let's make a pact," she suggested. "Since we'll be married for years and years, this probably won't be our last argument," she said with regret. "Let's promise no matter how bad the disagreement and how angry we are, we'll always sleep together. No one uses another bedroom."

He rolled over, gathering her in his arms and cradling her. "We fall asleep like this, holding one another."

She kissed him lightly. "I like that."

His tender eyes met hers. "I love you, Laura."

"I love you, too. I'm sorry for those awful things I said," she whispered, her heart still aching. "I don't know where those words came from. Panic, fear. I opened my mouth, the words fell out, and I couldn't take them back."

"Been there, done that." He recalled his vile remarks at the condo. "I drove to Atlantic City trying to understand why I said what I did. I certainly didn't mean it. And, the lying, honey. About my father's visit. I was trying to spare you some anxiety. And seeing Saunders; I didn't want to say anything until I had spoken to him and knew what we were dealing with."

"We have both done hurtful things. Me, listening to Saunders in Philly, refusing to hear what you had to say. And you not being honest with me about your father and meeting with Saunders. But all is forgiven for the both of us?"

"You bet." His head dipped, and his lips met hers.

The tension left her body. Chase's arms around her, holding her close, comforted her. They were silent for a while, soaking up the calm they gave to each other.

"Chase, what did you do while we were apart those months? After you left the condo?" They had never actually discussed that short period in their lives. It had been too painful, and she had always assumed she was better off not knowing.

"I was in Atlantic City. I drank. Gambled. Tried to forget I loved you," he said. "Too proud to call and say 'I miss my beautiful wife.' Too afraid you'd tell me to go to hell."

Laura grunted. "Beautiful wife? Look at me. I'm a shrew who resembles a whale in the Atlantic."

"Oh, no, you're not," he said, his tone insistent. "No one insults my wife. Not even my wife. Agreed?"

She smiled. "Agreed."

"Honey, you're as beautiful today, if not more, than the day we were introduced at the warehouse. I remember that day like it was this morning. I was in awe."

"Get out of here." She laughed. He loved teasing her. "We hardly said 'hello.'"

"You were standing at the copier."

Laura rummaged through her memory. "Yes. I was." She was amazed he remembered.

"It was spring. Beginning of May," he went on. "A clear, sunny day. You wore a green blouse that matched your eyes."

Yes, it had been spring, May sixth, when Laura had started working for Dick Donovan. The emerald silk blouse she had purchased online still hung in the condo's bedroom closet.

"I walked in the office," Chase continued. "Holding a cup of coffee from the diner, because Rachel makes lousy coffee."

Laura thought back. She had been at the photocopier. He remembered exactly and, yes, Rachel did make lousy coffee.

"My father introduced us." He stroked her hair, affection in each touch. "You smiled real fast and went back to your copying."

"You were so handsome. I didn't want to stare."

"I stared." He chuckled. "I took one look at your gorgeous face, framed by all that golden hair, and I reminded myself of my no-fraternizing rule. I couldn't believe we had such a hot number for a bookkeeper, and I had to keep my hands off."

"Not anymore," she whispered.

His hand cupped a full breast, covering the swelled softness and caressing the quivering peak. She would never be able to get enough of his touch.

"I had lots of reasons for wanting to marry you. Besides loving you and wanting to protect you."

"Lots?"

"Sure. You make better coffee than Rachel," he joked.

Laura laughed with him.

"After the first time being with you on *Madre*, I liked making love to you," he said simply. "I wasn't chancing your actions were an impulse, and one night was all I was getting. I had to marry you."

"If this is true confession time, I'm next."

"Nah, you're coming up with something to return a polite sentiment," he scoffed.

"No, no. This is true," she insisted. "Many times, at the office, I would watch you play on the computer."

He feigned insult. "I wasn't playing. I was working."

"You were online, reading *ESPN* or *CNN*."

"Oh. I didn't know you were aware," he said sheepishly.

"Anyway, I watched you—and wished you fraternized."

"You did?" He laughed. "Well, well. What they say about those quiet gals is true."

Chase's mouth touched hers, and Laura knew she was always meant to be his. Why Jack hadn't worked out, why no other man had held her interest. Because she had been sitting next to Chase Donovan nearly every day, watching him intently, her instincts telling her there was a special man behind the jokes, charm and those blue eyes, and he was the man she wanted.

He took a deep breath. "Honey, you understand why I need to be part of Saunders' operation, don't you?"

"No," Laura said plainly. "But that doesn't mean I won't support you. You're my husband. I love you. You do whatever you need to do. I'll always be here for you. Just promise me no more holding back. No more thinking keeping stuff from me is for my own good. I want to know everything."

"I promise. This husband stuff is new to me," he said with a quiet laugh before his lips brushed her temple. He turned serious. "Everything will work out. You have to trust me."

"I do." It was Dick Donovan, his cronies, and even Saunders she didn't trust.

"Chase, I think I lash out because I'm afraid we're too good to be true. We're so happy, and I'm just waiting for Fate to say 'gotcha.'" She paused. "Maybe it's my wacky hormones."

He chuckled. "Well, you just tell Fate, and your wacky hormones, that we're the real deal."

She tilted her head upward for a kiss. Chase closed his mouth over hers, his tongue slipping inside and touching hers. Laura concluded, when they were old, completely gray, and sitting on porch rocking chairs, his kisses would still leave her weak.

"Laura, I have to tell you." He pulled her closer. "When I found you on the boat, I was wrong for not taking you to a hospital, not notifying the police."

"I didn't want to go. You respected my wishes."

"You needed help in dealing with what had happened, and I didn't help you very much." He told her of his conversation with Lonnie in the condo hallway. "My common sense told me I needed to take you to professionals, but I didn't. I wasn't acting in your best interest."

"Chase, it wasn't you. It was me." She wasn't letting him shoulder all the blame. "I was ashamed."

"Ashamed? You didn't do anything to be ashamed of."

"I was foolish. I knew your father was into something shady. I shouldn't have gotten into the car with Ron."

"Honey, Ron was someone you knew," he said. "What happened wasn't your fault."

"Then it wasn't your fault you had a boat for them to take me to." She had suspected these months that his guilt over the use of his boat ate a hole right through him.

Reaching up, Laura stoked his stubbled cheek. "There was nothing wrong with refusing to accept your father would attempt murder. Who wants to believe horrible things about their father? If nothing's my fault, it's not yours, either."

They were silent for some time, lost in their own thoughts while secure in their embrace.

"When is this jamboree with Saunders?" she asked.

"I'll know tomorrow. He needs to run the deal past his supervisor. Soon, though."

Chase, she knew, couldn't concentrate on what lay ahead if he worried about her. "It won't be like the last time you went away. I know you're coming back." The need for positive thinking. She was amazingly proud of holding back her tears. "When you get home, Baby Donovan and I will be waiting."

Chapter Twenty-four

It was nearly the dinner hour when Chase arrived in Philadelphia. He parked the olive-colored rented Honda sedan alongside the parking meter, switched off the ignition, and took a few minutes to catch his breath. The past forty-eight hours raced before him.

Saunders and Morgan had been uncomfortable with Lonnie and Laura remaining in Sea Tower. If his father knew where Laura was, so did the others involved. Once the players were aware Chase was back in Philadelphia, Saunders insisted the women were easy targets.

Arrangements were made to move the women to a secret location and guarded by agents. The location so secret, Chase hadn't been told where Saunders had placed the women. When he had insisted on knowing where his wife and aunt were being taken, Saunders maintained the confidentiality was for the woman's protection. At a little past eight that morning, two Baltimore agents had showed up at Lonnie's front door.

One of the agents had introduced himself as Carl Newrome. Laura recognized him immediately as the man she had observed watching *Madre* in Beach Bay. She gently chastised Newrome for having frightened her that day, and the agent sheepishly apologized.

Chase, his heart heavy, had stood on to the porch watching the brown sedan cruise down the street. Shortly after, in the Honda, he had started his drive to Philadelphia, the federal building, and a briefing with Saunders' investigation team.

Jake Morgan was on Saunders' squad. The detective had relieved Chase of his personal cell phone and given him a government-issued replacement to keep in his hip pocket. Chase also wore on his belt a listening device resembling a cell phone. The gadget enabled Saunders and company to monitor Chase's conversations.

They heard Chase; he was unable to hear them.

Now, as the Philadelphia sky dimmed to a gray twilight, it was show time. Chase glanced at his watch and satisfied with the time, he stepped from the car. The air was muggier than it had been in Sea Tower, but he wore his denim jacket with his listening device safely hidden.

He slid the payment card in the parking meter. While parked at a rest stop on the I-95, Chase had made the cell phone call as Saunders instructed. Chase had convinced Dick Donovan that they needed to meet for a badly needed drink. Dick had been aloof, but agreed to meet with him.

The dark, bawdy, *Cockeyed Bumblebee*, in the city's Olde City section, seldom had a weeknight crowd. One long bar and a series of tight booths against the wall, it was a spot where people actually did stop for a quick drink.

Chase stepped inside, jolted by the saxophone blaring from the jukebox. The waitress, flaxen-haired, tiny, wearing a white cotton T-shirt that read in black script *Trish can do it for you*, approached Chase while his eyes adjusted to the muted light. He saw his father and waved the woman away.

Dick sat in the back booth. Sipping his usual Scotch, he wore his dark Armani suit of the day. Chase thought of Laura. Despite her animosity toward her father-in-law, she had always been complimentary about his stylish suits.

"Hey, Dad," Chase said with a nod. He slid into the booth facing his father.

"Chase," Dick said curtly. "I was surprised at your call."

"No, you weren't." Chase and his father had never dealt with preliminaries. They always got to the point promptly. "You've been waiting, counting the minutes to gloat."

Trish stood at the table. Chase ordered an Irish whiskey; his father another scotch.

Dick waited until the woman was back at the bar. "How's your wife?"

Chase shifted uncomfortably, giving the appearance they were broaching an unpleasant topic. His answer was quick, his tone bothersome. "Pregnant."

Dick didn't attempt to hide his contented smile. *Good,* Chase mused, *he thinks I'm unhappy and here to chow down some crow.*

"How long before the baby is due?"

Chase shrugged. "A few more weeks."

"Laura's healthy? The baby?"

"She's eating anything that isn't nailed down," Chase replied dispassionately. *Not true.* Laura was very conscious of Dr. Silver's recommendations on eating well during the last trimester. Gone were the ice cream sundaes, replaced by a constant craving for Red Delicious apples.

"Baby's okay, I guess," Chase added. "I tune her out when she talks." He said a silent, thankful prayer that his wife and baby were enormously healthy.

The waitress arrived. Chase grabbed his glass and gulped.

"And how are you?" Dick asked coolly.

"I've been better." Chase swallowed the rest of the whiskey, savoring the sweet taste.

There was a long silence.

"If I'm wrong, feel free to correct me. I'm getting the impression your life isn't the Norman Rockwell painting I saw during my visit," Dick said with a pompous chin tilt.

Chase cleared his throat. "Look, don't get me wrong." He exhaled a deep breath and leaned in closer. "I want the baby and Laura to get through the delivery okay, but the woman's getting on my nerves."

"Who?"

"Who?" Chase signaled the waitress, lifting his empty glass for another drink. "Laura. My wife. She's on me about my drinking. Can't enjoy a good Irish whiskey without her nagging."

"Laura a nag? She hardly talks," Dick said casually.

His father played it cool. Chase had figured as much.

"You haven't lived with her. She can talk. Nonstop. Her whining voice grates on my nerves," Chase mumbled the deceit.

There was a long pause. "Dad." Chase ran his fingers through his hair, and put on his best hangdog grin. "You were right." His eyes lowered in a humble gaze. "I mean in the beginning, I enjoyed it. Being Laura's hero. Gratitude got me great sex. I was pissing you off. It was fun."

Dick sat patiently, waiting like a priest in a darkened confessional for the next declaration of sin.

The waitress arrived with her tray. Chase grabbed his glass, took a mouthful, and swallowed hard.

"She tells me how a husband and father should behave," Chase said. "Reminding me I didn't have the best example. She eats up the money. She wants twenty-five thousand dollars to hold a spot at some fancy preschool. The kid isn't even born yet."

Chase had shown Laura an Internet article on the school's two-year wait list. The absurdity had them laughing for an hour. At this moment, Chase ached to hear Laura's animated laugh.

"I want out." Chase snickered. "I want my life back."

Dick sat back and studied his son.

"Chase, what do you want from me?"

"Help me out of this marriage. I'll stay with her until after the baby's born, but that's it. It'll cost me, though. She knows how to go through the cash," Chase repeated, aware of how fondly Dick related to money. "Besides bugging me about the preschool, I withdrew fifty thousand yesterday to put down on a house."

Chase kept his eyes downcast, focused on his glass like a remorseful little boy. Saunders' plan called for Chase to crawl with his tail between his legs, hat in hand, and beg to be let back into the fold, the usual humiliating drill. To go along with the set-up, the agent had Chase withdraw the money from the account held in both Chase's name and his father's. The money was transferred into a special, dummy account used by Saunders for undercover purposes.

"What does your precious Aunt Lonnie say?" Dick's tone displayed his distaste for his late wife's sister. "I'm sure you confided your problems to her."

"She said pregnancy does strange things to women. Plays with their hormones. Laura will be fine after the baby's born. Only Aunt Lonnie doesn't know how Laura and I came together," he lied. "I haven't a clue what Laura's like *not* pregnant. She could be worse."

Dick raised an eyebrow. "Chase, I'm at a loss," he said, his tone victorious. "This is an extreme U-turn. You pleaded with me to be a family. Laura, the baby, you, and me."

"I was naïve," he said, as if ashamed.

"Unless I'm there guiding you, you generally are."

Chase choked back his indignation and remained on track. "I'm happy to give her whatever she wants and adios," he continued. "We're not even having sex anymore." He pursed his lips. "She's either too tired, or too uncomfortable. Besides, a protruding stomach is not sexy. She watches me like a hawk. I can't even go get laid somewhere else."

Chase managed not to wince. Insulting Laura was like having a tooth pulled without novocaine.

"Where does she think you are?"

"I told her I needed a part for the boat," Chase replied. "A part I could only get in Magic Lake."

Dick swallowed some Scotch. He let the silence be long and painful, his features half exasperated, half sorrowful. Finally, he let out a sigh.

"Chase, sometimes you're too much your mother's son. I tried like hell to deter those noble qualities, but apparently I wasn't successful," Dick said. "You took one look at Laura in a distasteful predicament, you felt sorry, and she had you eating out of her hands." He added crudely, "or some other body part."

"Everything seemed like a good idea at the time." Chase ignored the ill-mannered comment, keeping his temper in check.

Distasteful predicament? Is that what his father called a woman being assaulted?

Dick continued. "Clerking in the public defender's office, where you met every inappropriate lowlife ever created, seemed like a good idea, also."

Chase shrugged uneasily.

"I told you from the beginning not to get involved with Laura, let it be, and you didn't listen."

"I'm sorry, Dad," Chase said timidly.

"First of all, when you make a woman your wife, you need to show her who's in charge, even if you have to smack her around to get your point across." With a smug tilt of his lips, Dick sat back. "Take it from me, women have to be taught who's the boss."

By some miracle, every splinter of control within Chase remained fixed. His eyes studied his whiskey, and his only reaction was his heart sinking to the pit of his stomach. Dick had confirmed what Lonnie had always insisted. The man had hit Michelle Donovan.

"Can you help me, Dad?" Chase muttered.

"Do what?"

Chase lifted his eyes. "Give me the money to send Laura on her way."

Dick's attention sharpened. "What about the baby?"

"You can go visit on my day. I'm not leaving the blackjack table to change a dirty diaper. Besides, you're the one who wanted a grandson." Tossing his head back, Chase finished his drink. "I'm not cut out for fatherhood. Do you know where the hell I have to go next week? Two freaking Saturdays?"

"No."

"La-something classes." Chase laughed. "I have to waste two Saturdays while Laura learns to breathe." He sucked in a deep, disgusted breath and exhaled. *Another lie.* Chase was honestly looking forward to Lamaze classes. *He* had made their reservation.

"I have nothing against the woman," he said. "I'm past wanting to spend my life with her, or split two a.m. feedings." He bit the inside of his cheek, restraining his zeal. Changing, feeding, holding, rocking this baby and others he and his wife had talked of having, before growing old together excited Chase beyond words.

"I'm telling you. No amount of sex, good or otherwise, is worth this crap."

"What will it take to get rid of her?"

Chase put his elbow on the table and leaned his chin on a closed fist. "She sees I'm unhappy. Besides a healthy chunk of actual change, she wants a quarter of the warehouse. If she doesn't get it, she's going to the authorities about the party you tossed on my boat, and something else she said she saw."

Dick's solid frame went rigid. "What did she see?"

"Beats me." Chase frowned as if the inquiry was a nuisance and not solving his problem. "She's hedgy. I figure she's full of hot air," he said with casual ease. "Don't worry. When she started her threats, I tossed the evidence, knife, her dress and whatever else." *Not true.* Chase, with Laura's permission, had given Saunders the secured bags. "With no physical evidence, who will believe her almost a year after the fact?"

"Chase . . . " Dick's tone was guarded.

Chase went on. "What's left is what she claims she saw." He straightened his body, stretching out imaginary kinks. "Like I said, she's full of it. There was nothing to see, Laura doesn't know diddly, and that's why those FBI people let her go."

Dick was quiet. Chase, in keeping with his role, paid his empty glass more mind than his father.

"Chase, to give Laura any part of the business involves accountants and lawyers," Dick said warily.

Chase considered. "I am obligated to provide for my kid."

"I'll ask you again. Are you sure the child is yours?"

"Pretty sure," Chase said, sounding defeated. "We can do a paternity test once the baby's born. I looked into it. To do one before isn't good for the baby." He explained what was involved, Internet information supplied for this meeting.

"We can put a small percentage in trust," Chase suggested. "Laura's paws get nowhere near it."

"That still involves people examining the business."

"A bean counter. So what?"

Dick was direct. "Chase, I can't have anyone scrutinizing the business. Do you understand?"

"Why not?"

Dick didn't answer.

Chase pursed his lips. "Dad, I'm not in the mood." He waited for a response. When none came, Chase's scowl deepened. "Tell me those agents aren't still buzzing around."

Dick took a long gulp from his glass.

"Ah, damn it, Dad," Chase shouted.

"Keep your voice down," Dick warned.

"Well, it figures. Because you got yourself involved in some stupid shit, I'm stuck with a wife."

"Don't blame your troubles on me, young man. If you're stuck with a wife, it's because you followed your childish, rebellious streak," Dick said hotly.

Chase took a few minutes, pretending discomfort from the dressing-down.

Chase let out a mournful moan. "Damn. I can't believe I'm in this mess."

Dick was quiet for a few minutes, then spoke. "Chase, what does Laura claim she saw?"

"You and Oliver Daniels. Some other guys. Hovering, whispering. Claims her FBI friends will be interested. I tuned her out."

"Chase," Dick muttered. "Chase, you can be so gullible."

"What?" He paused. "All this time I thought Laura was blowing smoke. Aggravating me." Raising an eyebrow, Chase added, "you telling me, she wasn't?"

There was a long silence. "We need to talk," Dick said.

"Will it help me out?" Chase knew Dick expected his son to only be thinking of his own quandary.

Dick spoke as if he hadn't heard Chase. "Oliver came to me. A one-time favor that didn't turn out to be one-time."

"Is this the place to talk, Dad?"

Dick's eyes shifted around. Their spot was secluded. "We're fine. Only keep your voice down."

"What's going on?"

Again, another silence on Dick's part, and Chase waited.

"For years I knew Oliver was involved with illegal drugs," Dick said, his voice barely above a whisper.

"How many years? What kind?" Chase asked, as if only slightly interested.

"Many years. Cocaine." More silence, then Dick went on. "He's my friend. A good friend. Several times the warehouse was almost down the crapper, like when Artie moved into the next store. Oliver kept us afloat."

Chase silently recalled when Artie Colina bought the vacant warehouse next to the Donovans. The business had been a fish market and was great for the Donovans' produce business. But Colina turned it into another produce market, selling his goods at much lower prices. After a year, Dick bought out Colina and merged the two warehouses.

"I didn't know we were in trouble," Chase said, his disbelief sincere. "When you bought Artie's warehouse, I only noticed more money coming in."

"I never involved you in business problems. You were in school. Your mother had recently died. The business was my responsibility." Dick frowned. "I worried, though. Thought I might have to pull you from that pricey, fancy university, and send you to a state college. I wasn't about to do that."

Chase said nothing. Of course, a state college wasn't adequate for Dick Donovan's son.

"So what happened?"

"Oliver did more than loan me money. He made sure Artie sold. Oliver knows people. If you get my drift."

Chase got the drift very well. Coercion, bullying—Daniels was good at intimidation—he forced Artie to sell. "Was that the only time you borrowed from Daniels?" Chase asked.

"No, many times. Never any questions or hesitation, and we're not just talking the business, Chase," Dick said with a difficult sigh. "Certain times it was me. I don't have your flare at the blackjack table. As I get older, it costs more for a pretty little trophy holding my arm and spreading her legs."

The warehouse, Dick's status within the trade, the businessman's association, having a gorgeous—and lately, much younger—woman, his envied lifestyle, motivated the man.

"I tried to get money the legit way, borrow from the bank," Dick said. "Turned down every time. Assets over-extended. You and I spend more than the warehouse makes."

Chase decided another round of drinks, this time a double for each, was needed and signaled the waitress. Juke box jazz hummed, the men not resuming their conversation until after the fresh glasses were delivered.

"Dad, why didn't you tell me?"

"Chase, you didn't even notice the accounts dwindling. You handle money worse than I do," Dick said with a light laugh.

Chase realized this father's actions were partially due to Chase's spending. He had never cared where money came from, as long as it was there.

His private account from his gambling winnings had remained untouched over the years. Chase hadn't tapped it until these last few months with Laura, to pay for their excursion down the Atlantic, to secure their wedding, to reimburse his aunt for their expenses.

Had his father approached Chase, the money would have

been available.

"I wish you'd told me, Dad," Chase said gently.

"Maybe if we were more like those TV fathers and sons." Dick smiled. "When you were growing up, I remember you always watching *Bonanza* reruns."

"I liked the horses."

Dick arched an eyebrow. "Oh, was that it? I thought you wished I was more like Ben Cartwright to your Little Joe."

"You're up to your eyeballs in debt. Can't get a second mortgage." The house in the Philadelphia suburbs was worth nearly two million dollars. "What happened?"

"All the money Oliver had loaned me over the years didn't come through his legit businesses, but from the drugs." Dick took a mouthful from his glass, swallowed hard, and went on. "He had used couriers, traveling by plane, exchanging the drugs and money. Only after nine-eleven, the security got tighter, searches weren't so random anymore, and the damn customs dogs got nosier. Oliver was looking for a new route."

"I see." Chase had stepped on a tightrope with his method of eliciting details. He envisioned Saunders holding his breath and turning blue, afraid Chase would make a mistake.

"Oliver came up with a plan," Dick said. "He would special order fruit. Packed with the fruit would be the drugs. Everything would be shipped to the warehouse, picked up by Oliver, and I would receive a share of the profits."

"Dad! Drugs? How many times did you lecture me? Since grammar school?" Chase regarded the one sincere, nurturing fatherly act Dick had fostered.

"I know, Chase. I'm not so lacking in a paternal nature. Plus, with you having a baby, I've stopped to consider someone peddling that shit to my grandson."

The older man let out a low breath, almost as if disgusted with himself. "The money was damn good, Chase. When Oliver came to me again, I couldn't say no. It became a regular thing."

"Oh, Dad," Chase muttered.

Maybe it was Chase's own guilt that he had spent money as foolishly and rapidly as his father. Maybe it was compassion for a man who had been seduced, and couldn't refuse the lure of easy money. Maybe it was hearing Dick Donovan refer to a grandson in such an adoring tone. Whatever it was that started a rip through Chase's soul, he knew he had to help his father. The *how* appeared an entirely different story.

"Laura. She hadn't a clue what she had observed," Dick said. "She was roaming the loading dock for packing slips. Had I known she was working late," his voice drifted off. "She saw my partners. They will go to any lengths not to be identified."

Legalities dictated the information come freely. Chase, choosing to nurse this drink, felt as if he sat on Laura's knitting basket with both needles sticking upwards.

"I sanctioned Laura's fate. I had no choice." His voice was reserved. "I was in deep. My partners were unbendable. The bawdy intentions before they got rid of her, a bonus to those doing the job."

Chase managed not to suffocate on the only words legally permitted. "Dad, I don't know what to say."

"Did Laura tell you specifics with the FBI?"

Chase gave the response Saunders had dictated. "They asked about invoicing procedures. She had no idea why they asked, but the FBI snooping scared her. That's why she resigned."

"When she resigned, my partners panicked," Dick said. "I insisted Laura was no threat. I was out-voted."

Silence hung heavy. Dick stared into his glass. Chase considered his father as he contemplated the frenzy called his life.

He needed Dick to name those partners. That was the evidence needed to convict those bastards, protect his wife, and aid his father.

Dick's slumped shoulders and defeated expression made Chase physically ill. Either by the detriment of his dirty deeds, or the torment of admitting them to his son, sitting across from Chase was a severely broken man.

"Dad, we've hashed enough problems for one night. You okay driving home?"

Dick nodded. "You heading back to Sea Tower?"

"No. I told Laura I'd have to wait for the boat's compressor to come in," he lied. "I need a night away. I'm staying at a hotel. I didn't think I was welcomed at the house." At the house, he wasn't able to converse freely with Saunders.

Chase forced his best cheerful voice. "We'll meet for breakfast," he said. "How's that sound? After a good night's sleep, we'll talk and find a way out of both our hell holes."

Chapter Twenty-five

When Chase arrived at Rita's Diner the following morning, he found his father sitting in a booth nursing his coffee. Upon seeing his son, Dick's apprehensive stare broke into a huge grin, almost as if he feared Chase had changed his mind.

For Chase, entering the diner had an eerie feeling. This was where it all began. He blinked quickly, escaping the vision of Laura perched on the stool, her green eyes wide and confused as Saunders beleaguered her.

Chase smiled. "Morning, Dad."

The bacon and egg breakfast started on a pleasant note. At times over the years, the two Donovans had shared diner breakfasts, easily discussing the few mutual interests they had, horse racing, basketball, football, Dick's golf handicap and Chase's skill at the gaming tables.

The conflict between Dick and Chase Donovan arose when the father refused to accept his son's decisions, arguing against or ridiculing them—and Chase.

"Chase, under different circumstances you, Laura, the baby, and me as Grandpa, may have been welcome," Dick reflected after the waitress had poured fresh coffee.

"Yeah, maybe. Laura turned me on initially, but the reality is I don't love her. I don't want to be a husband, or a father." Harmony wasn't Saunders' plan.

"You don't have to love your wife, any wife." After a long pause, Dick tilted closer to his son. "Yours, on the other hand, is a subject requiring further discussion."

Chase eased back. "Dad, don't worry. If you don't have the money, I'll get it somewhere. While she's in the hospital with the baby, I can get to Atlantic City. Win some at the tables."

Dick was direct. "Your financial dilemma isn't the issue." He glanced around, then looked his son straight in the eye. "My partners insist on their original plan. Laura has to go."

Chase arched an eyebrow and faked ignorance. "Go? Go where?"

"Nothing's changed since the boat."

Chase pursed his lips, mustering up just the right amount of protest. "We're not heading back down that road, are we? I don't want to stay with the woman, but she is my son's mother. Besides, without Laura, who's raising this kid?" He snickered. "You can bet your ass, not me."

"Chase, listen. You didn't listen to me before and look at the mess you've created." Dick gulped his coffee. "Two of my partners *cannot* take the chance on being identified. What did Laura tell you she saw?"

Chase was casual. "She saw you and Daniels with two other guys."

"Who did she say she saw?" Dick repeated.

Chase lifted his mug. "She wouldn't tell me. She got all coy and shut up. Like I said, she's full of it. I'm calling her bluff." He swallowed his coffee.

"No!" Dick said sharply. "We can't do that." He looked around, ensuring no one stood within eavesdropping distance. With an index finger, he beckoned Chase closer.

Chase wore his best inquisitive expression. "What?"

"My partners, besides Oliver, are Alan Blair and Chuck Hunter."

Bingo, Saunders. The roller coaster spiraled in the pit of Chase's stomach. Cocking his head as if feigning unfamiliarity, his eyes widened on cue. "Dad, doesn't Alan Blair sit on the federal bench?"

His father nodded. "Worked his way up from traffic court."

Chase's features became pensive. "Blair and Hunter?" He paused, giving the impression he searched for recollection. Actually, he was weighing his words carefully. "Didn't I meet them at your twenty-fifth anniversary party?" Chase asked, of course, knowing the answer.

"We've been friends from childhood," Dick replied proudly. "Alan had the hots bad for Lonnie at my wedding, but she couldn't be bothered. She was extremely obnoxious. It figures that aunt of yours ended up a spinster."

Hearing that Lonnie loathed Alan Blair nearly made Chase laugh. Undoubtedly, she had gotten a whiff of the man's character flaws from the get-go. Lonnie had her great love, a brave soldier. Blair, federal judge or not, wasn't fit to lick the deceased man's army boots.

"We all make our choices," Chase muttered, his comment having various subtle meanings.

"True." Dick lifted his mug as if in a toast to his son.

"I don't care what Laura saw, or who's afraid, or who's got problems," Chase said. "I've got my own."

"Chase, you have to understand. Alan was brought in as insurance. If we ever got in a fix, he'd make it go away."

"Fix?"

"If Oliver or I ever got caught with a cocaine shipment. But now that Laura saw us all together . . . ," Dick added.

Guilt crawled through Chase as he considered the listening device attached to his belt. His father confided in him. He trusted his son, and what was Chase intending to do? The regret left Chase quickly when he remembered those he loved in Sea Tower.

"Whose idea was Laura's boat outing?"

"Oliver and Chuck. Alan had squared a few things for Chuck. Out of friendship, of course."

"Of course," Chase said. Like a technicality on a search warrant that got an arrest tossed.

"Anyone who may recall they once were acquainted, Chuck and Alan give the appearance of having severed their ties," Dick said. "If anyone ever found out a personal connection between them still exists . . . well, Chase, you can figure out the rest."

Chase nodded. He certainly could.

"I doubted Laura recalled seeing us on her first visit with the agents," Dick said. "I'm sure she was nervous. But if the agents persisted, my partners feared she would remember. Laura's resignation as my bookkeeper wouldn't stop the questions."

Chase said nothing. Too numb, too shocked, too sick by what he was hearing.

"Oliver suggested Ron Caldwell," Dick went on. "Laura knew Ron and would accept the ride. Ron and the other man, Lou Kent, moonlight as Oliver's couriers. He had complete faith in them. Laura, so sweet and unsuspecting, did exactly what was expected by accepting my offer of a ride and walked right into the trap."

Chase bit his tongue to hold back the acid retort.

"Inviting you to dinner was to keep you from the boat," Dick continued. "When I got your voicemail declining, I prayed you were shacked up with some overpriced whore."

Again, Chase didn't speak. Dick had prayed his son was with a hooker, a bizarre, let alone sacrilegious, prayer. On the other hand, one of Chase's prayers was just answered. Ron and Lou, their names, on tape for what they had done to Laura.

"Oliver had a fit when he heard the stunt you pulled, arriving on the boat, running his men off," Dick said with an ironic grin. "It took a fifth of my most expensive bourbon and a romp with Rachel to calm him down."

"Rachel?" Chase nearly choked on the woman's name. "Your secretary? With Oliver Daniels?"

Dick nodded. "You may ignore her, but most men welcome her invitations. Rachel likes her lays rich, and she doesn't give a hoot about the age difference. Frankly, my boy, I can tell you first hand, you don't know what you're missing."

Oliver Daniels and Rachel. His father *and* Rachel. Chase's digested breakfast revolted.

"Nothing surprises me anymore." Despite the grave situation

he was in, Chase suppressed a laugh. In all the years Rachel had worked for his father, she always referred to Dick as *Mr. Donovan*. He wondered if his father was *Mr. Donovan* while the pair engaged in a sex romp.

"I was able to cover for you good," Dick said. "I told Oliver you dated Laura a few times, gave her a tumble."

Chase said nothing.

"It was harder to convince Chuck to wait while Laura went through her pregnancy," Dick went on. "But I convinced all parties you could keep her mouth shut. I used the boat excursion and hiding Laura in Sea Tower, away from those agents, as evidence of your loyalty."

Chase sighed. "Dad, this is crazy. We'll pay off Laura. She'll go away."

Dick became agitated. "Suppose she decides the amount we give her isn't enough," he insisted. "She'll hang her federal friends over our heads. She'll threaten to take the baby, your son, my grandson. Her threats will be a constant. Besides, Chase, we don't have money to waste on her."

"I said I'll get it."

Dick continued. "Think of us as a family, Chase. The three of us, the Donovan men."

Dread filled Chase at the prospect of not having Laura in his life. "After the baby's born, we'll discuss my sham of a marriage," he said in keeping with Saunders' program.

"We'll take care of it now," Dick demanded, his gray eyes hard like steel. "You'll listen to me. You'll do what I say. You'll let me fix this mess you've gotten us into."

Chase hid his smirk well. This was the father he had anticipated.

Dick's cell phone chimed, and he excused himself. Chase recognized the caller as Rachel. Considering what he had learned this morning, he wondered if the call was business or pleasure.

"Chase, I need to get to the warehouse," Dick said, returning the phone to his inside jacket pocket. "Rachel set up a meeting with a new customer. Apparently, I'm late."

Chase laughed, a tactic to return a cordial note to the conversation. "Dad, how did you get Rachel to keep your trysts quiet? She's got the mouth that roars."

"Her mouth is good for other things, too," Dick said with a wink, and slid from the booth. "She's too fond of keeping her job to blab." He reached inside his jacket pocket.

Chase held up his hand. "My treat, Dad."

"Rachel aside, we're not done talking."

Chase nodded. "I can only stay another day before Laura gets suspicious."

"I understand," Dick said. "We don't want her suspecting you're cheating. Next she'll hire a private detective. Get a lawyer who will really take you for a ride." A whimsical look passed over his features. "See how inconvenient divorces are."

Chase replied with a frown.

"Why don't we have dinner tonight?" Dick proposed.

"Sounds good."

Dick smiled. "I'll call you later with the details. We'll make a real night of it."

Chase gave his father the hotel where he was staying, and the cell phone number Saunders had given him. "I got this phone without telling Laura," he repeated the cover tale. "I left the other on the bureau. On purpose. I don't need her calling me for every little baby kick."

Chase watched his father leave the diner. He silently bemoaned last night's restlessness without Laura and their hyperactive baby, the latter who generally woke his parents at two in the morning while he practiced his field goal kicking.

*

In the small hotel room, Saunders, Morgan, and Chase sat at

the square table by the floor-to-ceiling window eating Philly cheesesteak sandwiches and discussing their progress so far.

Morgan swallowed from his water bottle. "First off, we don't know how the money's exchanged. And we need to find out how the stuff's getting in."

"If the airports are out, it's coming by boat," Chase said.

"How's that work?" Morgan asked.

"The fruit arrives on a ship and gets unloaded at the waterfront," Chase said. "Customs inspects, but not every little nook and cranny. They may even be paying someone off. You'll need to check that."

Morgan nodded his head, acknowledging, and Chase went on.

"Even without someone on the inside, if the coke bags are small and sandwiched among the fruit, they would be difficult to detect." He turned to Saunders. "You guys are so worried about undesirables busting the airports, start paying more attention to the seaports."

Saunders nodded, filing the comment before returning to the current discussion. "We have to find out who their contact is in South America."

"It's either the supplier or the shipping firm. I might be able to get that information tonight." Chase took a generous bite of his sandwich.

"You've done great so far, Chase," Morgan said.

Saunders agreed. "That was good stuff on Caldwell and Kent. They're not walking from anything. What about this Rachel broad? She in on what's going down?"

At Morgan's more raunchy interpretation of the secretary's role, the small group laughed. Chase munched on his fries as he gave a verbal dossier on Rachel.

"If you told me she banged the warehouse guys, I'd agree." Chase laughed. "Oliver Daniels? My father? Incredible."

The cell phone on the nightstand rang, interrupting their amusement. Chase excused himself. He sat on the bed's edge and flipped the top.

His father sounded in good humor. He had ordered a car, legit and not from Leisure Limo.

"The Donovan men deserve a guys' night out," Dick insisted. "I mean big time. Dinner and gambling in Atlantic City. I'm looking to pick up some skill at the blackjack table before we grab a couple of girls."

Chase controlled his wince. Girls? Hookers? He hoped Saunders had some notes in his manual on getting out of *that* situation. There was no way Chase was cheating on his wife. "Dad, sounds like a night," he said as if there were no place else he'd rather be. "I have the best luck at *The Nile*."

"That's where we'll go. Meet me at the warehouse around six," Dick suggested.

Chase ended the call and briefed the two men.

"I don't like it," Morgan said immediately.

"What don't you like?" Chase asked. Everything seemed casual enough.

"All of it," Morgan replied. "The warehouse. Driving in a car, Leisure or otherwise, to Atlantic City. Why can't you take the Honda?"

Chase sipped from his soda can through a straw. A Honda wasn't Dick Donovan's style.

"We got time to get a team in the hotel," Saunders said.

"Suppose they don't go to *The Nile*," Morgan said.

"We'll follow the car," Saunders countered.

"I don't like it," Morgan repeated. "How do you feel, Chase?"

"I didn't give the invitation much thought until I looked at your gloom and doom expression." Chase said matter-of-factly. He paused. "My father won't hurt me if that's your concern. If anything, I'll be brow-beaten into giving up Laura."

"Chase, I'm not saying it's your father who would set you up," Morgan said. "We've seen how gullible and loyal he is to these people. You and your father could be walking into a trap where you'll both end up on a slab."

Saunders considered before agreeing with Morgan. "They believe Laura's in Sea Tower. Remember what Daniels and Hunter planned for her, Chase. What's to stop them from killing you and your father? Then going after her. No waiting for the baby to be born."

Chapter Twenty-six

Morgan and Saunders, in a black van with two other special agents, followed the yellow cab carrying Chase to the warehouse at a safe distance. Daylight savings time had come and gone. Tonight's sky was in full twinkle with a shadowed half-moon hanging over the area.

Earlier, Chase had given Saunders duplicated keys to the Food Mall's front gate, the Donovan warehouse, and Dick's office. Now putting his own key in the lock, Chase pulled open the gate and stepped inside.

He wore his jeans, and a blue button-down shirt. His denim jacket protected against the autumn night breeze and kept the transmitter hooked to his belt looking discreet. He also had a companion; his revolver tucked in the back of his pants. Chase had argued against it. But he was entering a dangerous situation and held a permit, Saunders had reminded him. The special agent ordered Chase to carry the weapon.

He walked up the loading dock stairs, stepping into the faintly lit warehouse. The silence and scarcity of people wasn't unusual. What was unusual to Chase was the clear sound of his heart pounding wildly. He had ignored the tension all day, but at this moment, his gut screamed loudly, and his day-long unease revolved into full-blown fear.

The outer office was empty. Rachel flew out the door at five. Laura's replacement appeared to have acquired that same skill. Laura . . . the love of Chase's life. Saunders had arranged a phone call to her before leaving the hotel. Apprehension, due to Morgan's irksome reservations over tonight's meeting, had overwhelmed Chase. He had feared that the call might be the last time he heard Laura's voice. She had been ecstatic to talk with Chase. And how well he knew the woman he loved. When she prattled on about knitting Baby Donovan a blanket, how nice the motel was, Aunt Lonnie was catching up on her reading, and that Special Agent Newrome made the best pancakes, Chase knew her nonstop talking was her way of hiding her own anxieties.

Dick's office door was closed. He heard muffled voices. One voice, his father on the telephone, wasn't odd. Two voices chatting together, when Chase expected his father to be alone, was peculiar. Pressing an ear to the door, he listened, attempting to gather pieces of conversation and the owner of the other voice. He was unsuccessful at both.

"Someone's in the office with my father," he whispered, cluing in those in the nearby van.

Chase knocked.

"Chase? Come on in," Dick called.

Irish whiskey, sweet smelling and expensive, hit Chase as he opened the door. Dick sat leisurely behind his desk, holding a nearly empty glass. Dressed in the same suit as the morning, his jacket was draped over the back of the chair and his gently shaded gray tie was loose at the knot. A half-filled Irish whiskey bottle was on the desk.

"Chase, my apologies for starting without you," Dick said. "Let me pour you a drink."

Since when did his father apologize? Let alone for a trivial detail as having a drink without him.

Chase then noticed the man lying on the leather sofa; short, stout, and completely bald. Dressed in his customary greasy denim overalls, it was Oliver Daniels. His smooth head rested on one arm of the sofa, his sneaker-clad feet were propped on the other. His arm dangled to the floor, a full glass in his hand.

"Chase, you remember Oliver?" Dick handed Chase his drink. "You haven't seen one another in a while."

"How you doing?" Chase asked with a mannerly nod. He put

the glass to his lips, prepared to take his usual gulp, then stopped. This scene bothered him, as did the drink.

Dick scrutinized his son. "Chase, you're hesitant to accept a drink from your own father?" he asked with a laugh.

The corners of Chase's mouth curved in a grin. "We have a packed night ahead. I should nurse this one." He eased himself into the chair across from the desk.

Daniels had yet to acknowledge Chase's presence.

Dick turned to his friend. "My son has spent the last few months in a bad family oriented sitcom." He laughed. "It'll take him a while to join the real world." Dick returned his attention to Chase. "I invited Oliver to have a drink with us."

"You know, Chase, you gave me some shit to handle." Daniels let out a laugh that was a little more than a grunt. "I got two boys real pissed off at you. Your daddy and me promised them a good ride on that little filly."

At least Daniels got down to business quickly. Chase put the words together for a noncommittal response, but didn't get the chance to offer one.

"The filly he's talking about is Laura," Dick said to Chase. "Ron Caldwell and Lou Kent had never killed anyone before."

"We needed to give them an incentive. A good hump job always works for me." Daniels laughed, a loud, snorty sound, and gulped his drink. "Laura looks like she gives a first-rate jaunt, too. Slim, sleek, maybe a bit wiry. You had her, Chase. She any good?"

Chase maintained a stoic expression despite the fury festering. Daniels' impudence toward Laura ate at Chase, leaving him unable to reply without sarcasm. His rescue came from a surprising source. His father.

"Oliver's referring to the evening Ron and Lou abducted Laura, then took her to your boat to rape and kill her," Dick said. "Neither man was happy with the foiled plot."

Oliver grunted. "Or your measly hundred dollars."

The elder Donovan went on. "When Ron and Lou returned to the warehouse and told me what you had done, saved Laura and ran them off the boat, I called Oliver. He pitched a fit, and I didn't have any answers for him at the time. It wasn't until you confided in me Laura was pregnant. I told Oliver you had been desperate to save your unborn child."

Chase kept his facial expression blank, his cool intact, and his mouth shut.

Daniels concentrated on his drink, looking lovingly at the glass, either not hearing or not comprehending Dick's words.

"Isn't that correct, Oliver?" Dick addressed his friend. Daniels perked up and Dick repeated his words.

"Oh, yeah. Your daddy insisted you had a right to your baby. Lucky for her." Daniels snickered. "You knocking up that broad bought her some time before turning her into shark food."

Chase had a vision of a limp, bound Laura being tossed over *Madre's* side. He choked back the nausea clotting in his throat.

"Oliver, explain to Chase why Laura needs to be dealt with in such an extreme manner," Dick said. "My son and I are often not on the same page."

Daniels grumbled, followed by a loud groan as he sat up on the sofa. He stretched his legs out before him and finished his drink before speaking.

"See, Chase, your daddy, me and a couple of buddies are as tight as can be. We'd do anything for each other. When we were kids, we cut our third fingers and pressed them together. Saw it in some movie." Daniels looked at Dick, perplexed. "You remember the name of that movie?"

"No," Dick replied.

The man shrugged. "It'll come to me."

Dick approached, and Daniels held out his glass. The elder Donovan filled it to the brim. Dick returned the near-empty bottle to the desk, then perched himself on the edge.

Daniels hiccupped. "See, we're so tight, I don't have to tell your daddy I want a refill. He knows."

With the man seated in an upright position, Chase got a good look. Daniels' pudgy nose was apple red. His small brown eyes were glazed. Sweat poured from his forehead.

Oliver Daniels was drunk.

"Oliver, you're supposed to convince Chase to see our situation," Dick said. "I told you. You can trust my son."

Chase noted his father was stone, cold sober. The entire whiskey bottle had practically been consumed, a smidgen remained. The glasses were juice size and not shot glasses, as Dick generally used. It didn't take a rocket scientist to conclude who had consumed the most liquor.

"Any son of yours, Dick, is a son of mine," Daniels said firmly and gulped from his glass.

A revolting thought, Chase mused.

"Chase, we got this nice, little business going," Daniels began, his voice intact despite his inebriation. "We can't gamble with your wife screwing it up."

Chase, prepared to say he intended to divorce and send Laura away, opened his mouth. Before the words came out, Dick glared at him. He shook his head, silencing his son.

Chase snapped his lips tight. The scene was totally weird.

"It goes like this, Chase. Chuck Hunter gets the drugs. Your father accepts the drugs. I distribute the drugs. Alan Blair saves our asses if need be." Daniels took another swig. "Old friends are the best friends," he concluded, raising his glass and draining it.

Dick offered another refill. Daniels' glass was filled. The bottle was empty.

"You're not giving Chase the whole picture, Oliver." Dick moved around behind the desk, not taking his seat, but remaining standing. "If you want to convince Chase why Laura needs to be eliminated, connect the dots."

Daniels let out a frustrated sigh, then a belch. "A bunch of years ago, me and Chuck started this operation with his buddy in South America—Argentina, Columbia, Bolivia, Venezuela—one of those places. Guy runs some fancy vacation resort. When I think of South America, I see a jungle," he pondered aloud. "Who the hell goes to the jungle for vacation?" Guzzling his drink, Daniels turned to Dick. "What the hell is that guy's name?"

"Whose name?" Dick asked.

Daniels smirked. "Chuck's friend. Black haired guy."

Dick shook his head. Chase looked at his father. The older man knew exactly of whom Oliver Daniels spoke, but wanted Daniels to offer the name.

Daniels thought for a minute. "Balls, it'll come to me."

Chase made mental notes, sure Saunders and Morgan were getting an earful.

Daniels continued. "We had a good thing. Send a guy down with the money, he'd get a little R&R, and we'd get our drugs."

"Tell Chase about the drugs," Dick suggested.

"Cocaine. People love snorting that shit. Gives me a nosebleed. The money, shit, it's unbelievable." Daniels nodded his head as if he was a wise old lecturing scholar, and raised his glass to Chase before gulping.

"Everything was good," Daniels said. "Everybody did their jobs and got their piece. Couriers, airport folks, and we had Alan. Who better to have as your best buddy than a hotshot judge who knew the ins and outs? If anybody got caught, he'd find a way to fix it. Just like he did for Chuck."

"Help Chase understand that," Dick said.

An anxious, suspicious feeling crawled through Chase.

Daniels swallowed more from his glass. "When the dicks were watching Chuck some years back, the warrant read *search a black sedan*." Daniels laughed, a gurgling sound. "But Chuck's car was like a navy, some kind of shitty dark blue, and Alan got the warrant tossed."

How convenient. Chase couldn't help but purse his lips. It wasn't as if the arresting law was talking yellow from green. A respectable, more efficient, ethical judge possessed the brains and morals to work around the mechanical error. He wondered if there had been others Alan Blair had immorally and illegally accommodated over the years.

Daniels rambled on about automobiles, sizes and colors. Chase hadn't a clue as to the gist but concentrated on the man. Daniels followed up with a monologue on gasoline prices.

Dick let out a low sigh. "Oliver, how did we start receiving the merchandise through my warehouse?" Daniels, either from whiskey or plain lack of focus, needed Dick to put him back on course.

"Nine-eleven," Daniels answered incredibly. "Security's tighter. Our airport guys got scared and pulled out. So, we had Chuck's friend—" He stopped speaking. "Louie. Louie Reynaldi!" He was proud at recalling the name.

"What about Louie?" Dick asked, calm and in control.

Chase eyed his father. His peculiar feeling grew more intense. Dick was giving his son the exact information needed. When Daniels started speaking again, Chase returned his attention to the man.

"We had Louie go in the fruit business. Lemons, apples, the shit depends on the season. He got an office and alleluia, we're still in business!" he shouted as if having a religious experience. He laughed again. "LR, Inc. is the company name."

Chase froze. He had noticed those crates in the warehouse. They had looked like any other crates from any other supplier. No one ever would have suspected there had been cocaine in those crates.

Daniels continued. "The fruit business turned out to be a nice side job for Louie. The drugs get packed so good, all you see and smell are the ballsy lemons. The drugs come here, get loaded on my truck, and I do business out of my front seat in all my parking lots."

"Tell Chase who your customers are, the ones who purchase from the front of the truck, so that he can see what an elite clientele we have," Dick said.

Numbness inched through Chase as Daniels rattled off his drug customers. He wasn't hearing a word. Saunders was getting it all. Chase was stunned by his own suspicions. Dick had filled Daniels with whiskey and wheedled the man into talking.

Chase's federal associates had everything they needed to start rounding up suspects. Dick Donovan had turned out to be Special Agent Saunders' mole.

Turning directly to his father, as if they were the only two men in the room, Chase stared at him, unsure of the older man's actions or the reason behind them.

"Dad?"

"You deserve to be happy, Chase," Dick said softly. "With your wife and child. I wasn't the best husband or father. You can be both."

Chase stuck to the script. "I'm divorcing Laura after the baby's born."

"Chase, didn't you hear? There'll be no divorce," Daniels said and belched again. "That wife of yours saw us. She knows where my stuff comes from. Once the baby's born, she's a goner. Besides, you and her aren't getting along, your father tells me. Why do you care what happens to her?" He drawled a speech on the ramifications should Laura recall LR, Inc. invoices, or blab about seeing Alan Blair and Chuck Hunter together.

"No harm will come to Laura Donovan," Dick said adamantly. "She's my daughter-in-law, my son's wife, my grandson's mother."

"Yo, wait a minute. Hold everything, Dick." Daniels labored and staggered until finally he handled standing. "You told me if I explained everything to Chase, he'd understand. Maybe even want in on the deal. Of which, I promised to get the others to agree," he offered proudly. "Don't forget, we're talking another partner." He banged his empty glass on the desk. "Splitting the profits an extra way."

"My son wants nothing to do with illegal drug trafficking. He loves his wife and will do whatever he has to do to protect her." Dick faced Chase, his demeanor inflexible. "Whatever you have to do," he repeated to his son.

Chase was paralyzed, making an attempt but failing to slide off the chair. His father knew. He knew what had brought his son back to Philadelphia. He knew full well Chase's agenda, and who had set it.

"No, no, no!" Daniels shouted. "Chase is one of us, and that bitch is dead once the kid pops out."

Chase put his untouched glass down on the desk and managed to stand on his own shaky legs. "We should leave now, Dad," he said, somehow finding the words and a level smile. "Can't be late for our dinner reservations."

Dick voice was low, partly sorrowful. "We're not having dinner tonight, son. There are some law men waiting for me. Perhaps you and I will have dinner some other time."

Father and son simply stared at each other, and the lump in Chase's throat nearly suffocated him. "Dad . . . "

"I'd rather you leave before those men arrive," Dick said.

Chase shuddered. His first phone call would be to Ned. In exchange for the details Saunders had gotten, there had to be a deal for Chase's father.

"What men?" Daniels interrupted, not comprehending the true meaning of his invitation to a simple, cordial drink. "We're going out to dinner? Dick, you didn't say anything about a dinner party."

Dick spoke to Chase as if no one else listened.

"Give me a little credit, Chase, for being skeptical in the *Cockeyed BumbleBee*. You and your wife are very much in love," Dick said. He spoke with what Chase thought was fondness.

"*Cockeyed BumbleBee*," Oliver interjected, his facial features askew. "They serve dinner? Since when? It was always drinks and munchies."

"I saw how much you and Laura mean to each other that day in Sea Tower." Dick gazed at Chase as if his son was the only person in the world worth any attention. "When you carried her from the car. You kissed her. She put her head on your shoulder. The way your eyes followed her into the kitchen. You have your mother's eyes, Chase. They tell the world everything. One look into them, and I saw your feelings for Laura right down to your soul. You love her."

"Dad, I—" Chase had no idea what words to utter.

Dick's lips parted in a smile. "It's time for me to be the father you deserve."

Again, Oliver interrupted, focusing on Dick. "Who's in love? Dick, you said you got him to see things our way."

Dick continued to disregard the other man. "Chase, leave," he said, his tone pleading. "Now."

By now, Chase sensed Saunders was opening the gate. He would respect his father's pride and leave before the agent arrived to arrest the two older men.

Daniels, having turned fully lucid, pursed his lips. He didn't like being kept out of the conversation. "Someone tell me what the hell is going on!" He took a step toward Chase. "Your father told me you were looking to get rid of your wife. Any way you could. That she had gone through your money. You were damn broke, and you wanted out after she had the kid."

He snapped at Dick. "Who's in love? What the hell you trying to pull?" The reddened veins in Daniels' neck popped. "Your son knows everything. He's not just walking."

Dick stood tall. His cloudy eyes focused on his son.

Chase, ignoring Daniels, met his father's stare. After an exchange of glances, Chase turned toward the door. His heart was breaking.

"Hey, you wait a minute, you little prick!" Daniels grabbed Chase's forearm and spun him around. The older man's features warped in rage.

Chase swirled with a force that knocked the transmitter from its clip and to the floor. The three men stared at the device lying on the dark brown tiles. Chase's blood iced over in his veins. Gathering his wits, he jerked from Daniels' grip and hunkered down. As Chase's hand reached for the transmitter, Daniels stepped on it, smashing the device into tiny pieces.

Fear gripped Chase, but he managed a deep breath. He eased himself upright and looked Daniels squarely in the face. "Why did you smash my cell phone?"

"Cell phone." Daniels snickered, taking a few steps back. He put some distance between the three of them, but was smack in the middle of both Donovans. "That's no cell phone, sonny. I got a buddy doing time in the federal pen. An undercover cop, named Morgan, got some bimbo he was banging to get the goods on my buddy by wearing a wire that resembled a cell phone."

"You're crazy," Chase said evenly. "You telling me I'd incriminate my own father?"

Daniels eyed Chase shadily. "I don't know. Why's a young, strapping stud like you want to saddle yourself with a kid? I knocked up plenty of bitches over the years. They got a few bucks and the name of someone who'd get rid of it. If they refused, I'd beat the damn brat out of them."

Chase glared at Daniels. The man sickened him. "You're crazy," he repeated and turned toward the door.

When the shot rang out, Chase instinctively reached for his own gun. He flashed the weapon in front of him. His immediate glance was to his father. Dick stood, solid behind his desk, a silver polished pistol clasped in his hand, still pointed forward. Chase followed his father's gaze.

Oliver Daniels lay sprawled on his back, each arm outstretched wide alongside of him. Bright crimson blood flowed from the back of his head. Daniels' small-set eyes were open, magnifying themselves ten times over as they fixed on the ceiling, gaping at nothing. His right hand held a small caliber revolver, index finger still grazing the trigger.

Chase recognized death when he saw it, but he crouched down and lightly touched the man's neck.

The door flung open and men leaped into the room. Chase

jumped up, noticing only Saunders among the crew. Wearing a blue jacket and cap, yellow FBI printed boldly on the front, the agent had his service weapon positioned securely in front of him.

"FBI! Drop the guns!"

Chase, having learned from experience, dropped his gun immediately. He set his attention on his father.

Dick did not drop his, but rather aimed the weapon at Saunders. Before the agent had the chance to give the *drop it* command again, Dick's gun discharged. The shot hit the forearm of a similarly dressed agent standing to Saunders' right. Hit with the bullet, the man cried out, dropped his own revolver, and grabbed the wounded area.

Saunders' reflex was to fire. He didn't miss and Dick hurled backwards, a gaping whole sputtering red from his chest. With one leap, Chase flew over the desk, and caught his father in his arms. Together they sank to the floor.

"Hey, Dad, hold on," Chase's said, his voice breaking. *Why didn't he drop the weapon?* There was no logical reason to shoot. "You got a grandson to meet. Remember? Hold on."

But Dick Donovan was already dead.

Epilogue

Two days before Christmas, Chase stood in a sterile white hospital room. He smiled, peering out the window and watching a light evening snow fall on the Chesapeake shores. Snow always added to the holiday's serene magic. A few short hours ago, he officially became a father.

Spinning wheels clanged on linoleum, and Chase swirled his attention to the door. Laura lay completely still on the gurney as it rolled into the room. He stood aside as the nurse and two attendants transferred her to the hospital bed.

"We'll bring the baby in soon," the nurse said to Chase with a smile and left the room.

Chase gazed down at his wife. Slightly pale, her eyes were closed, her breathing faint, and a slight grin curled her lips.

"Laura," he called softly.

Her eyes blinked open. "Hi," she whispered.

Chase wrapped his fingers around hers. "You did great, honey."

She smiled. "I had a great coach."

Six hours of labor and Chase had been with her every step of the way, coaching her breathing and giving her ice chips. "We make a great team."

"We sure do. Did you call Aunt Lonnie?"

"It hasn't stopped snowing," he said, nodding toward the window. "I was afraid she'd drive too fast from Annapolis. I left a message on her voicemail. She'll discover her new nephew when she gets home." Since the couple had moved into their own home, Lonnie had been anxiously hovering over Laura on a daily basis. Convinced they had a few days before Baby Donovan's birth, Chase and Laura swayed Lonnie to attend her annual Christmas luncheon with her former colleagues.

Baby Donovan had his own ideas.

Laura's green eyes twinkled like the lights on the Christmas tree they had been decorating when her first contraction hit. "Chase, isn't he a beautiful baby?"

"Beautiful? That baby?" Chase frowned, unable to resist teasing her. "How could you tell? His face was all screwy. He came out with gunk on him."

As promised, the curly haired nurse entered the room wheeling a Plexiglas cart with Baby Donovan.

Chase pressed the button on the side of the bed, raising the top half and enabling Laura to sit up. She leaned forward, and Chase propped her pillows. The nurse gathered the blue-blanketed baby, and Laura anxiously reached for her child. The woman placed the tiny bundle in his mother's arms, then quietly left the room.

Perched on the edge of the bed, Chase's arm wrapped around Laura's shoulders. She nestled against him. They gazed down at the precious chubby-cheeked face, flushed and wrinkly, wide blue eyes staring back.

"Now, *that's* a great looking kid. He's got your gorgeous blond hair," Chase said fondly.

"And your beautiful blue eyes," Laura said happily.

"He needs a name," Chase said. "We can't keep calling him Baby Donovan." Despite all their debates, Chase refused to name their child, Richard Chase, the fourth.

"I always liked my father's name. Matthew."

"Matthew Donovan?" Chase tried the name. "Matthew Donovan. Matthew Donovan," he repeated and paused. "I like it."

Laura hesitated, before her eyes met Chase's. "For a middle name, I thought we'd give him Richard."

"Richard." Neither Chase's tone nor his face held any emotion, favorable or otherwise.

"In his own way, your father loved you, Chase," she said. "He kept me safe to have the baby. We can call the baby Matthew, or

Matt, but we should acknowledge your father. He was the baby's grandfather, too." Laura waited for a response. When Chase didn't offer one, she returned to cooing at her son.

Chase believed, given the circumstances, his father would have been touched. "Dad would like the baby's name."

"You have a name, sweetheart," she murmured to her son.

Pulling Laura closer, Chase focused on his baby cradled in her arms. "Matthew Richard Donovan, welcome."

About the Author

Angela Adams writes and reviews contemporary romances. Her work has appeared in *Romance at Heart, Oysters and Chocolate,* and *The Long and Short Reviews.* In December 2011, Whimsical Publications published an anthology, *Winter Wonders.* Angela's short story "Burgers and Hot Chocolate," was among the collection. She is a member of Romance Writers of America and the online chapter, From the Heart Romance Writers.

In the mood for more Crimson Romance? Check out *Date with the Devil* by Jessica Starre at *CrimsonRomance.com.*

www.ingramcontent.com/pod-product-compliance
Lightning Source LLC
Chambersburg PA
CBHW010634100726
47900CB00011B/2824